'I am Delgrade, queen

of Scythia.'

'Scythia?' he said dumbly, 'but . . .'

'Do not tell me it is gone and do not think me mad. I was once the wife of Partholon, who led his people to this land three thousand years after the Great Flood cleansed this world of all life!'

Frazer forced a laugh, but a slow, cold terror was gradually taking hold of him. 'But that would make you . . . thousands of years old.'

'Would it?' she said wistfully. 'I do not measure time as you do. But yes, I am old . . . and weary.'

Also by Michael Scott in Sphere Books:

IRISH FOLK AND FAIRY TALES Vol I

Irish Folk and Fairy Tales Volume II

MICHAEL SCOTT

SPHERE BOOKS LIMITED
30–32 Gray's Inn Road, London WC1X 8JL

First published in Great Britain by
Sphere Books Ltd 1983

TRADE
MARK

Set in Garamond

Printed and bound in Great Britain by
Cox & Wyman Ltd, Reading

For Derek and Jacqui whom I missed the first time around.
Willie and Maeve. Catherine, Sara-Jane for various reasons.
And Anna, for one very good reason.

CONTENTS

CHAPTER 1

THE DAWN

The dark bulk of the island suddenly appeared out of the mists, rising from the flat ocean like the back of some great sea creature. The shouted warnings came too late, and the longship shuddered and screamed as it ran up onto the beach. It tilted once, righted itself, and then tilted again, its port side almost touching the sands. A small olive-skinned man, clad in rough animal skins and worn leathers climbed slowly from the wrecked craft and walked shakily down the beach. The muscles in his legs bunched and knotted, and he had to resist the temptation to roll as he walked. It felt strange to be back on dry land again after being so long at sea.

He climbed the dunes and stood on the grassy crest, staring down into the shallow bowl of land that rolled away into the distance. There were three lakes situated at one end of the depression and he counted nine small, swiftly-flowing rivers, some feeding into the lakes and then flowing out into the sea. He breathed deeply, savouring the fresh moist air, redolent with the tang of salt and growth. He ran his thick, gnarled fingers through his long coarse hair, and felt the peace of the new land sink into him. The swarthy southerner nodded decisively and made his way back down onto the beach.

The dull sound of hammering broke the silence of the quiet land as the crew attempted to secure the longship to the beach with thick hempen ropes tied to stakes driven into the harder high ground.

'Well?' His son lifted the heavy mallet and looked up, squinting into the morning sunlight which haloed his father's head.

Partholon nodded. 'It is the Land.' He clapped his son on the shoulder, 'Let's tell them.'

Brechan pushed himself to his feet and brushed his hands against his woollen jerkin. He stood a head taller than his father and had his mother's pale eyes and light coloured hair. 'How far does the land extend?' he asked.

'Far enough. There are rivers and lakes and a broad fertile plain over the lips of that rise.'

'Mountains? Hills?' Brechan stopped and looked up and down the beach. 'Cliffs?'

'I have told you all that there is,' Partholon said quietly.

'That's all? There must be more; there has to be more. Father, there are twenty-four families aboard that ship – there is no room for them all. We must move on.'

Partholon smiled grimly. 'We will stay,' he snapped, and added, 'we have no choice.'

His son opened his mouth to protest, but the older man raised his hand, the smile slipping from his face. 'Watch!' he commanded.

He knelt on the rough beach and plunged his hands deep into the coarse sands. He closed his eyes and his brow furrowed in concentration, beads of sweat starting out just beneath his hairline.

Brechan sat back on his haunches and watched his father with concern. The old face suddenly relaxed and then assumed a stiff, mask-like appearance, and under the dark tan it grew pale. The thin lips peeled back from startlingly white teeth, and his eyes rolled in his head. Brechan could feel the tension growing, could sense the gathering power, felt its static ripple along his arms, flowing through his fingers, sparking from his hands. He knew his father had access to a Power, a raw elemental Power that had been created with this world, a power which he, even though he was but a generation removed from it, could sense only dimly, and grope for blindly.

Suddenly Partholon began to mutter in a liquid, flowing tongue, totally unlike the guttural language of his own race. And slowly, the grains of coarse sand about his hands began to twist and twirl, shaping themselves in strange and arcane patterns, spirals, ovals and complete circles.

Partholon's eyes snapped open. He regarded his son's fear and awe with amusement. 'You see; there is Power in this land, Power beyond measure. It was one of the last to be created and the gods spent themselves in its making. The magic is strong here.' He stood and smiled mirthlessly.

'We are now tied to the land, we are now a people of the land, and as we grow, so shall the land. The eternal sea will wash back, relinquishing the land to us so that each man might have space enough to expand.' He held out his hand and let the golden grains fall like liquid onto the beach. 'Is that enough for you?'

Brechan nodded. 'It is enough. I will tell the others.'

Partholon nodded, dismissing his son and then turned away and climbed the dunes again. He stood there, staring down into the green bowl. The sun had not long risen and the pastures gleamed in the warm golden light and the waters of the lakes and rivers flowed like metal. It was not the harsh burning sunlight of his own homeland, but a rarer, finer light; it would give life and heat without slaying, give light without searing. It was indeed a fine land.

The southerner took the first steps down onto the broad plain, his shadow dancing on the grass before him. A tiny cloud obscured the sun, abruptly chilling him. He shivered as icy fingers touched the base of his spine and for a single moment he felt the cold hand of Death touch his brow and he was suddenly reminded that this day was sacred to Bile, the God of Death: Beltaine.

That night, the shipwrecked crew of the longship and their passengers gathered in a huge tent of wood and hide on the edge of the plain. The atmosphere was light and bantering, but the laughter was forced and overloud and Partholon could almost taste the undercurrent of fear. Brechan and his brothers moved quietly through the crowd, filling goblets with the last of the stored wine, making some pretence at celebration.

Partholon sat at one end of the tent, well back from the

rushlights, in the shadows. His dark eyes darted about the crowd, noting the allegiances and cliques forming and re-forming; his agile mind singling out those likely to cause trouble. There were two, he knew, he had most cause to fear: Aeolas the sorcerer, a wild-eyed sun-worshipper from the Isle of Samothrace, and Mercan, the proud young general who had covered his retreat from the gutted remains of the palace. He sliced into a fruit with his knife, the rushlight dancing along the blade and abruptly, the Scythian saw the knife in his hand rising and falling, rising again, streaked with red, and the body of his father falling across his mother's . . .

He had been close; so close.

The crown of Scythia had been almost in his hands. And then it had blown away like wind-strewn ashes. The guard had remained loyal to Bescosmis, his brother, and had turned on the renegade prince and his forces.

Not many had survived the massacre that followed. The loyalists had pursued Partholon and his followers to the harbour where a score of ships waited as a last line of retreat. There the fighting had been fiercest and the waters of the Mid-Sea had run with red. And only two ships had sailed from the small harbour; and one of those had been lost between the Pillars of Hercules.

And now here he was, a murderer, and worse, guilty of both parricide and regicide, hated and feared by his men, mocked by his sons and loathed and despised by his wife. His generals were plotting against him and there was some talk amongst the families – especially the Tocket and Detchu – of returning to Scythia and throwing themselves on the mercy of the court.

But no, they would never do that, not while he still lived. He surged to his feet and moved out of the shadows, calling loudly for silence. When he had their attention, he began.

'My lords . . . ' he acknowledged them with a short nod, 'there are some decisions we must make now. This is a fine land, a young land, still steeped in the Elder Magic. It is admirably suited to our needs, but like all new things, it must be explored carefully, with every aspect considered . . . '

'But there is nothing here,' Aeolas the sorcerer interrupted. 'I have stood on the lip of the world and looked across the plain. You speak as if we are staying here, but save for a few rivers and lakes, there is nothing here.'

Partholon raised his hand, his dark eyes flashing dangerously. 'You are a mage, a sorcerer, surely you can feel the Power in this land?' he snapped. 'There is enough Power here to fashion whatever one needs; to bring forth mountains if one wishes, call up forests if that pleases one. What more do we want; what more do we need?' he demanded.

'We need room. There is hardly enough space here for us now; what will happen in a little while when there are sons to stake their claim to the family holdings?' The voice was smooth and slightly rasping, cultured and deadly.

Partholon rounded on the speaker. He was a young man, a head and more taller than the prince. His hair and carefully curled beard were golden, and the torchlight burnished them with crimson highlights. His eyes were large and innocent – the eyes of a child, and with all the capacity for the vicious cruelty of a child.

'Mercan,' Partholon said quietly, 'there is nowhere left to go. We have reached the edge of the world.'

The young general waved his hand at the sorcerer. 'Aeolas claims that there is land to the west ... '

'I have never heard of it,' the prince snapped.

'It is true,' the Samotharcian said quickly. 'Beyond the horizon there is a land the like of which you have never seen before. The gods created it for their own use, and then abandoned it in favour of their sport with mortal man and the Demon-Wars. But it is there,' he added.

'And how many days sailing is it?'

The sorcerer's voice faltered. 'I do not know lord, but it would be many moons.'

Partholon laughed in disbelief. 'Many moons! And where will we find a craft that will take us to this land of yours? You know the condition of our own ship. Even if we had the proper tools and equipment there is several moons repair work to be carried out on it. And we'll have to strip parts of the ship for timbers for a new hull, which will leave us with no storage space, no crew quarters. Where would we store the provisions for such a lengthy journey, where would we shelter at night?' He spat at Mercan's feet. 'Am I surrounded by fools? You!' He jabbed a finger in the general's face. 'If you wish to undertake this fool's errand, then go, and do not let us detain you. I release you from your service!'

The assembly went suddenly silent and the thin keening of the wind across the flat plain suddenly seemed magnified.

The young man smiled coldly, thin lips drawing back from mis-shapen teeth. 'But I do not release you from your debt, Partholon. You owe me your life. If my forces had not been there to carry you to safety, you would have been torn to pieces by the people. To slay one's father is a terrible crime, but to slay one's mother also so that there could be no further claimant to the throne is surely abominable.' The words were cold and precise, delivered with a malicious delight.

'And if I had taken the throne, general, you would have been one of the ones to gain the most. We both gambled, soldier – and we both lost.'

The tension between the two intensified. Mercan fingered his flame-edged dagger uneasily. The older man was unarmed, but there was a strange, gloating look in his hard dark eyes, almost ... almost as if he wished the general could try and kill him.

The assembly were silent, but Mercan recognised the bright glitter in their eyes; he had seen it far too often during his campaigns in the islands and on the mainland; it was the look of a mob expecting blood. He swallowed his anger and forced a smile to his lips. 'Come now,' he protested, holding out his hands to Partholon, 'surely we must not sully our first night in this new land with harsh words and recriminations. We have yet to see this land in the harsh light of noon – because I, for one, was too busy hauling everything off the ship today to see anything. Let us wait until the morrow – we can pass judgement then.'

The Scythian nodded gratefully and returned Mercan's

smile. 'The night is far gone and we have travelled long and hard; we are all overtired. Let us retire for the night, the morning will bring many things.'

There was a general murmur of assent, and then a voice asked from the back of the tent, 'What should we call this land?'

Partholon gazed into the last flickers of flame still clinging to one of the torches and when he spoke, his voice was soft and gentle. 'This land will have many names, some fine and fitting, some shameful – let us not name it yet, for the land is not truly ours ... ' He blinked as the flame flickered and died. 'One names a possession – we do not possess this land.'

'Yet!' Mercan added as Partholon turned to leave.

The following morning the Partholonians awoke to find their sentries slain and their damaged craft reduced to tinder wood. It seemed they were not alone on the island.

Delgrade stood by the entrance to the tent watching her husband making his way slowly down the beach towards the remains of their craft. Her long blonde hair was unbound and fell in gentle ripples down her flawless back. She was wearing a long gown that had been fashionable at court over a year ago. It was low cut and gossamer thin, and she could feel the chill wind bite through the thin material and caress her smooth skin with icy talons.

She felt eyes on her, a dull tingling at the base of her neck, and turning suddenly, she caught one of the slaves staring at her, his eyes eagerly probing through the gown. Delgrade read the lust in his eyes and moved slightly, allowing the gown to fall open, exposing more of her body to him. She waited a moment and then said softly, 'My husband will have you flayed alive for what you have done.'

The wide-eyed youth started, blood rushing to his face. 'I ... I ... ' he stammered.

'Do not attempt to lie to me,' Delgrade said softly. 'Come here.'

The princess examined the youth critically. He was not above middle height and of slight build. His hair was dark and shining and the first touches of a beard were upon his cheeks. She took one of his hands and ran her nails along the palm, making him twitch. It was hard and calloused, the nails short and broken, encrusted with grime. She dropped the hand in disgust.

'Who are you?' She caught and held his dark eyes with her direct gaze.

'I am Togha,' he stammered.

'And your tasks, slave?'

'On board the ship, I scrubbed the decks, cleaned ... whatever was needed. But now ... ' he shrugged, 'I have no assigned tasks.'

Delgrade looked past the slave, down onto the beach, where a small figure made his way slowly through the wreckage. A strange gleam came into her light eyes and a curious smile played about her lips. She turned back to the youth and stroked his thin face with her long, pointed nails. She relished the fear that started into his eyes, but she caught the sudden increase of the pulse in his throat, and felt his breathing quicken. 'I want you,' she whispered, 'to attend me as my servant ... '

Togha blushed and his voice trembled. 'My lady, I know nothing of such ... there are others ... you have slaves to attend you ... '

The princess caught his jaw in her hand and squeezed. Her eyes widened and there was a glint of madness in them. 'I have slaves to attend me,' she agreed, 'and you too will attend me. You will attend me in all things.' And her laughter hung on the still morning air like a curse.

Mercan stooped and lifted a jagged spar of wood from the sands and handed it to Partholon. 'Look at this. See how this wood has been shorn through as if struck by a blade, but this,' – he held up another piece of wood – 'has been shattered by a blow.'

Partholon examined the wood, his dark eyes troubled.

'There was no storm last night and the tide was not running high ... ' he reasoned.

'The ship was attacked,' Mercan stated flatly, 'and you said this island was uninhabited.'

'I know, I know,' the Scythian said coldly, 'but it seems I was wrong.'

'It was a costly mistake,' Mercan said, kicking sand over a dried bloodstain. 'Eight men dead and our craft destroyed. We are now trapped on this cursed isle, and speaking frankly Partholon, it is indefensible. There are no mountains, no forests, no caves ... '

The prince silenced him with a wave of his hand. 'You will have your mountains, rivers and streams,' he snapped. And then his voice changed and took on a curious note, one almost of fear. 'This is a magical land, but it has tasted blood too soon and I fear its history will be steeped in bloodshed.'

Mercan snapped a piece of wood in half and tossed it into the sea. 'I care little for your fears for the future. My fears are for now; and I fear you have brought us to our deaths,' he said quietly.

'Perhaps.'

The last rays of the setting sun burned across the plain, touching the small rounded hillocks with shadow, gilding the beach in ochre and bronze. A thin, cold breeze whistled in from the sea, dispersing the smoke rising from the fire built in a small circle of stones near the dunes. Four figures stood on the beach about the wildly flickering fire, their hands raised to the darkening skies.

Partholon glanced anxiously into the west. The light was almost gone and the incantation must end with the death of the day so that the forces of night might gather and work their will in the darkness. He watched Aeolas, supported by his fellow sorcerers, Fos the northerner and Faud, the stout magician from the land to the east of Scythia, lower his arms and prepare for the final incantation. The Samotharcian's face was lined with fatigue, his crazed eyes glazed, and he could barely stand upright. Fos and Faud stood beside him, lending him their support and strength, allowing him to draw from their reserves – but they too, were rapidly weakening.

Aeolas made one final effort, raising his hands and calling forth into the gathering night, but the strain was too much and he staggered back as if he had been struck and fell to the ground. Partholon grabbed him, pulling him upright. 'Finish it,' he hissed, his voice harsh and chill.

'I cannot,' the sorcerer gasped.

'Too late,' screamed Faud, and even as he spoke, the ravening elemental forces gathered.

Lightning flared from the evening sky, coming to earth on the beach, fusing the sands into solid globules of glass. The air stinking of ozone and raw power, trembled and vibrated, awaiting the unleashing of the destructive elements that would utterly annihilate the puny forces that had dared to tamper with it.

The prince caught the sorcerer's head in both his hard hands and twisted it savagely. His dark eyes, as hard as pebbles, bored into the Samotharcian's. Aeolas felt the abrupt transfer of strength flow from the prince into his own exhausted body. He saw Partholon's eyes widen and then suddenly shrink to tiny pinpoints, and then he felt the pain lance through his eyes, rip through his head and erupt from his mouth in a long agonised scream.

He rose jerkily to his feet, moving like one possessed. And with his new found strength, he found that the forces gathered about him were almost visible, almost tangible. Shadows gibbered at the corners of his vision and he could sense the raw chaos lurking beyond them.

He cried aloud the final incantation and heard it shout from his throat in a strange commanding voice, totally unlike his own. And from behind him, he heard Partholon cry aloud, 'Fathers, aid us.'

Thunder and lightning detonated all about them, encircling them in a wall of light and sound. Low clouds rolled swiftly in from the west and north. Icy blasts of wind whipped in across the suddenly turbulent seas, carrying sleet and snow and howling like the damned souls of Hades.

A driving rain hissed across the beach, extinguishing the small fire, washing away the blood of the sacrificed fowl.

And then the earth moved.

Partholon grabbed Faud and screamed into his ear, 'Take Fos, I'll carry Aeolas; we must begone, even now the sea rises.' And, half-carrying, half-dragging the semi-conscious magicians, Faud and Partholon staggered across the still smouldering and hardened sands.

Partholon and his followers kept to their tent that night. The prince had surrounded it with a magical ring, and although he had promised them it was completely safe, they still murmured prayers to their gods and huddled together in fear.

Beyond the circle, the elemental forces of Chaos and Night raged and worked their will upon the land. The seas about the island rose, swamping most of it, and then swiftly retreated, leaving vast tracts of steaming land uncovered. The earth buckled and heaved, throwing up formidable mountains that crumbled and formed and then re-formed. The earth shuddered and split with rivers which quickly vanished only to reappear as lakes, only to disappear into the bowels of the earth again. Valleys were carved out and cliffs formed; parts of the island were cut off and surrounded by the sea, forming other, smaller islands.

And through it all, in the tent ringed about by the magical circle, the Partholonians remained safe whilst the land rose and fell about them.

And generations later, the savage northern Vikings would discover the small, almost circular valley surrounded by the mountains on the east coast of the fresh green land they sought to conquer, and there they would build the city they would call Dubh Linn.

Partholon led Mercan along the beach the following morning. The general had been silent ever since he had stepped from the tent and seen the low mountains rising to the south where none had risen the day before.

The prince stopped and pointed out across the waves.

Mercan squinted into the heavy morning mist that still clung despite the height of the sun. He shaded his eyes, unsure of what he saw. And then he gasped. 'It is an island!'

Partholon nodded. 'It is an island,' he agreed. 'And there are islands all about the coast now. The land itself is three times bigger than it was yesterday. There are mountain ranges all along the eastern and south-western, the northern and north-eastern coasts. Overnight nine new rivers have sprung up and there are seven new lakes ... '

The general shrank back from Partholon. 'How do you know all this?' he asked quietly, but with a tremor in his voice.

But the prince just smiled. 'I know,' he said, 'I know.'

'What else do you know?' Mercan demanded, his fear turning to sudden anger.

Partholon laughed gently, his laughter only serving to infuriate the general. 'I know,' he said, 'that there is an island to the north of this, an island called Taure. And there is a crystal tower upon this island, and about the tower are curious dwellings of creatures neither beast nor man, but something caught in between; the obscene fruits of the union between a demon in man's form and a woman once of this world.'

'What are they?'

'I do not know. They are creatures, intelligent creatures of sorts,' Partholon said. 'However, I do know that their lord is called Cichal One-Foot.'

'Are they dangerous? Will they attack?' Mercan asked quietly, for this was something he could understand; the clash of weapons and the screams of the wounded and dying were tangible and real, they were something he could deal with.

'They are already spying on us – and have been since we first landed. They fear us now – the enchantment last night slew many of them and the remainder have fled northwards for the present. But soon their fear will turn to hate – and then they will attack.'

'And until then?'

'Until then this land is almost ours; we can only strive to

make it wholly ours, build our forts and roads and prepare for that not too distant day.' He turned and gestured inland. 'There is ample room for all of us now. You have your mountains and valleys, rivers and streams: make of them what you can.' Partholon turned away and walked slowly down the beach, wisps of fog parting before him and swirling in behind, until it seemed as if he were swiftly fading from this world.

Mercan watched the prince until he was lost in the mist and then turned and continued up the beach. What Partholon had told him was disturbing – almost frightening – but the general relished the icy tingle of fear. To conduct a defence . . . no, not a defence he decided, an attack! He would not sit back and allow the creatures in the crystal tower to come to him on their terms; he would attack them on his terms, in his time, with his weapons. But before he could do that he knew he would need a map of this new land.

Delgrade sank back into the large crystal bath, allowing the warm water to lap about her midriff, feeling it caress her thighs with smooth intimacy. She ran a long polished nail along the edge of the bath tracing the outline of a naked faun pursued by a horned and tailed creature with an enormous phallus. The bath was decorated with thousands of such carvings drawn from the already ancient mythology of her people. The bath itself had been taken by her husband in an expedition to the continent across the sea to the south of Scythia, where the dark-skinned ones came from. It was, he claimed, the largest piece of crystal in the world, and though it was not a diamond, it was very close to one. Partholon had found it on the dried up bed of what had once been a huge inland sea. It had once been a perfect sphere, and there had been broken pieces of glass scattered all about it, but now little more than half remained. Bringing it back to Scythia, he had ordered the foremost artisans of the day to carve and decorate it according to Delgrade's instructions. The subject, the style and even the placing and manner of the carvings he had left entirely in her hands and although he had not been pleased when he had seen the finished result, there was little he could do, for the glass was preternaturally hard and had blunted even the sharpest tools and implements.

Delgrade opened her startlingly blue eyes, a slight frown creasing her forehead. 'Togha,' she called, 'where are you?'

The flap of the large tent opened and the youth entered, struggling with a heavy bucket filled with steaming water. 'My lady, the water ... ' he began.

'This water cools,' she said softly, a seductive note honeying her sharp voice, 'add some more – and slowly,' she warned.

Togha knelt beside the crystal bath and, taking a silver bowl from beside it, began to add the steaming water slowly, keeping his eyes low and concentrating intently on his work.

'Togha,' Delgrade said softly, 'look at me.'

The slave raised his head and stared defiantly into her wide eyes.

'Do you desire me?' she asked him almost in a whisper.

Togha shook his head. 'No my lady, I do not desire you.' His voice trembled, but he held her gaze.

'But surely you have some feelings for me?' she persisted.

'I fear you,' he said simply.

Delgrade's eyes narrowed slightly. 'You have nothing to fear from me,' she said reasonably, 'surely you have ... other feelings for me?' She reached out and, taking his hand, placed it on her breast.

'What do you feel?' she murmured, her cold eyes sliding over his body.

The youth shivered suddenly, and then, almost unwillingly his rigid fingers relaxed and he cupped her breast.

'Join me,' Delgrade commanded.

Trembling violently, Togha pulled his jerkin over his shoulders and ripped the loin-cloth from about his body. Smiling triumphantly, Delgrade spread her arms and pulled the youth into the warm water beside her.

*

Partholon sat on a smooth lump of stone on the beach and watched the waves wash up thousands of tiny silver fish, leaving them stranded to die. Mercan stood by his side, a tightly rolled chart in his hand, seemingly absorbed in the relentless action of the tide and the death of the fish.

The prince pointed out across the beach and said softly, 'We are like those silver fish. We have been cast up on a strange beach, where we will flap briefly and then die. In the morning we will be swept away again.'

Mercan shrugged. 'Such is life. We know nothing and we have no control over what we do know. We are playthings at the will of the gods.'

Partholon agreed, and then he added, 'Perhaps one day we will have control over our own destinies.'

The general smiled down at him. 'Perhaps. But neither you nor I will see it.'

'Agreed.'

Partholon moved aside and made room for the general to sit beside him. In the month since they had landed on the strange island, their previous animosity had changed to something akin to friendship, but with each fearing and distrusting the other. However, they each in their own fashion respected each other.

'Well, what have your spies discovered?' Partholon asked, tossing a pebble out into the sea.

The general smiled. 'Is nothing secret from you?' He shrugged and continued. 'My spies are in effect, cartographers; they have been engaged in mapping this isle. And this,' he held up the chart, 'is the result of the past month's work.' He spread the animal skin out on the sand, using heavy stones to hold down the curling corners. With a twig he began to point out various features.

'The island is roughly oblong – and by the way,' he smiled wanly, 'one of my men, Kullarn, has coined a name for this land: *Inis Alga* . . . '

'*Noble Isle*,' Partholon mused, 'it's as good as any, I suppose.'

'It will do,' Mercan said and continued. 'There are mountain ranges all along the coasts; the highest in the south-and-west and the north-and-east. There are several lakes of respectable size, but the largest seems to be in the north – here. There are rivers everywhere, although none of any great size or width.' Mercan pointed with the twig to the west coast. 'There are islands here, but not many and it seems likely that they will in time return to the mainland as the sea retreats . . .'

'I think not,' Partholon interrupted, 'but continue.'

The general pointed north. 'There is something here – and I'm not sure what. My man did not return . . . '

'Where are we on this chart?' the prince asked.

Mercan pointed. 'Here. It has been named *Sen Mag*, the Old Plain.'

'Therefore, if whatever lurks in the north mounts an attack, they will have to march almost half the length of the country.'

The general nodded. 'That is so. But we must have further information. I propose to send a small force northwards to spy out these creatures and their defences. Perhaps it is feasible to attack them first and wipe them out completely.'

Partholon shook his head. 'We cannot afford to send any more men out. Our forces are sadly depleted as it is and we must consolidate our position. Let them come to us, let them exhaust themselves doing so.'

'But we don't even know what they look like, we don't even know what weapons they use. Remember our ship,' he gestured wildly down the beach to where a few spars still rose from the sands like the skeletal remains of a whale, 'remember how that was attacked and destroyed. You remember the damage – we need to know how that was caused. We need information!'

Partholon nodded and sighed wearily. 'You are right of course,' he said, 'but I cannot spare you any men.'

'Give me slaves then – anyone, and if you do not,' he warned, 'then I must go alone.'

'I will see what I can do.' He rose stiffly, shivering slightly in the damp chill. 'Walk back with me,' he suggested.

They had almost reached the prince's tent when they heard the soft cries and moans coming from within.

Partholon looked at Mercan in alarm, but the general waved him to silence and, slipping a knife from its sheath, crept to the tent. Silently, he slit the leather ties that held the flaps shut and eased them aside.

Togha looked up from the supine body of the princess as a blast of cold air dried the sweat on his body. He saw the shadow in the door and attempted to pull away from her, but Delgrade clasped her legs about his waist and held him all the tighter.

They lay on the rug-strewn floor before a small brazier burning spices and scented coals. The warm light bronzed their bodies, gilding the sweat on their skins, the flames dancing in their eyes. Delgrade, looking over Togha's tousled head, saw the stooped figure of her husband in the light and smiled secretly. She moaned loudly and dug her nails into the young slave's back, pulling him even closer to her. Togha struggled to free himself – and then he was torn from the princess's arms and tossed across the tent. Mercan advanced on him, a feral smile glinting in his hard eyes, his knife slowly weaving to and fro. Partholon stopped him with a word.

The prince stood over his wife looking down at her naked body still flushed with lust. He smiled contemptuously. 'So this is how you amuse yourself: with slaves.'

'He is more a man than you will ever be,' Delgrade taunted.

'It is a change from dogs and rams,' Partholon said, turning away.

Delgrade screamed and spat. '*Sumer*: kill!'

A huge hound leapt up from the corner where it had lain and launched itself across the tent at Partholon's throat. The Scythian threw up a hand and the hound's jaws closed on the bronze wristlet he wore. The prince's left hand scrabbled for the dagger in his belt, but his wife suddenly gripped his hand and sank her teeth into it. Partholon grunted in pain and the momentary distraction was enough for the heavy dog to bear him to the ground. Scalding saliva dripped onto his face as the massive jaws came closer to his throat.

Mercan turned back to help his prince, but Togha, his eyes wide in terror, leaped onto the warrior's back. The general brought his elbow back and up, driving it into the slave's midriff; he slid off onto the ground and doubled up gasping for breath – and the general's knee came up and caught him under the jaw. His teeth clicked shut and his eyes rolled in his head. Mercan pulled Delgrade off Partholon by the hair and tossed her almost casually to one side. He kicked the dog once, with brutal precision, beneath the ribs, and the beast fell back howling. Partholon struggled to his feet as the dog rolled to one side. And then the animal was on its feet again, its belly low to the ground, its gleaming fangs wet and dripping. Mercan took a step towards the dog, and then Delgrade threw herself upon him, her clawed fingers tearing at his eyes. Sumer leapt at Partholon, its jaws wide, its eyes wild.

The general swore and then struck the princess with the back of his hand, sending her sprawling. He threw his dagger underhand, but missed the dog by a fraction, and the knife buried itself in the tent pole. Delgrade went for the knife, snarling like an animal – Mercan's fist caught her on the point of the jaw, knocking her backwards onto her groaning slave.

Partholon stepped to one side and caught the dog in his hard hands. He held it tightly at neck and crotch and hefted it above his head. The beast choked and kicked – and then the prince brought it down onto his upraised knee. There was a loud snap, Sumer shuddered and twitched and then lay still, and the tent was silent save for the angry sobbing of Delgrade.

Mercan dug his dagger out of the tent pole and turned to Partholon. 'I heard rumours of your wife's harlot ways back in Scythia, and aboard ship there were certain whispers ... But now – here is the evidence of her infidelity; she has betrayed your trust and sullied your name. Let me slay her now.'

The prince shook his head wearily. 'No. Killing her would be too ... easy.' He glanced at the groaning youth. 'She has chosen her road, let her follow it now.' He looked back to his wife, his eyes hardening. 'You will be gone by morning – and take him also. If I find you still here when the sun rises I will kill you both.' He turned away and pushed through the torn flap.

Mercan paused before leaving. 'And I will ensure he kills you slowly,' he added.

The firelight ran liquid in the small round chamber. The crystal walls reflected back the light with blinding intensity and the very air seethed with the amber radiance.

Loat sat before the fire staring into the wavering flames, her brow furrowed in concentration, trying to absorb and make some sense of the strange shapes therein.

A shape moved behind her, casting long towering shadows on the crystal walls, and a hooked talon sank into the hard flesh of her shoulder. 'Tell me what you see,' Cichal One-Foot hissed.

'Quiet my son,' Loat murmured, wrapping her gnarled fingers about a long bone and poking the fire, sending sparks spiralling up towards the hard translucent ceiling.

The Lord of the Fomors hissed angrily and moved about the chamber. He stopped by one of the circular windows and peered out into the misty morn. His talons gripped the scarred edges of the window and his single, red-rimmed eye glared out across his domain. To the north, west and east there was nothing but sea, disappearing flat and grey into the distance. It was true that in the east, on a good day, it was possible to see the distant shoreline of a land, but today, with the weather closing in he could see nothing but grey cloud. But to the south . . . Aaah, that was a different matter. For there was a sweet land, a young land, a land ripe for the plucking.

And it would be his.

Cichal One-Foot ground his fist into the window-ledge. It would be his. He turned back to Loat, his mother. 'What do you see?' he demanded.

The old woman turned and smiled fondly at her son. Time had made her blind to his deformities: his single foot with its hooked talons, his barbed tail, the barrel chest and the long simian-like arms which glistened with armoured scales; the huge head, with neither nose nor ears, the long curved fangs and the huge slit-pupilled eye set in the centre of his massive ridged forehead.

He was the product of her youth, oh, so long ago, in a time when the gods themselves walked their newly created world, and dallied with their creations. And Man, the last of the gods' creations, found favour with their parents, and in time there came forth upon the new world creatures that were neither men nor god, but something of both. And in some the best of both god and man mingled to form what later generations would call the Tuatha De Danann, the People of the Goddess Danu; but in others, what was abhorrent to both the gods and men was brought forth from where it lurked deep within them both. And so the Fomors were birthed, abominations shunned by both men and beasts and despised by the gods.

Cichal was a Fomor, a single-footed, clawed, tailed, single-eyed monster, and Loat loved him.

'Mother; what do you see?' he demanded once again.

Loat smiled, her toothless gums drooling saliva onto her stained shawl. 'I see the new race gathering, preparing for war, preparing to attack, preparing to destroy you.' She giggled and then lapsed back into silence.

Cichal howled like a dog. 'Impossible!' He leaped past the woman and scattered the flaming sticks with a sweep of his tail. 'Impossible. They are puny, soft-skinned humans.'

Loat nodded. 'That may be so. But remember the magic they worked soon after their arrival to change the very land to suit themselves. You are a fool if you think they are weak and defenceless.' She stood and stared up at her son. 'And remember, I too am a human, and you can judge for yourself whether I am defenceless.'

Cichal stepped back and bowed. 'You are different, mother,' he protested. 'You are not human now,' and then he added quickly seeing the fury rising in her mild eyes, 'you are more than human, you have transcended all human bonds, you are godlike.'

The old woman simpered and smiled. 'It is true,' she acknowledged.

'What would you have me do?' he asked.

'Attack – and attack now; strike before their preparations are fully complete.'

The Fomor nodded thoughtfully. 'It will take a little time, but it will be done as you say.'

Mercan knelt over the beast he had just slain. He cursed, examining his blunted dagger: the creature's skin was as hard as stone and its blood like acid. He looked over his shoulder at the crystal tower rising in the distance and then back down to the creature.

It had attacked the general and his young servant as they lay in the long grass watching the activity about the base of the gleaming tower rising out of the grey sea. Before Mercan could draw his dagger, the beast had shorn young Fea in two with a single blow of its sickle-like tail. The general had thrown himself onto its back, the armour on his forearms and wrist scraping metallically as it brushed against the beast's scaled torso. He struck at its throat – but it was like striking stone, and his fingers and wrist tingled numbly. He retched with the vile odour of the beast. And then its tail came up and flicked him across the back, sending him crashing to the ground. The creature swung around and Mercan could almost hear its long talons click into place like a cat's. It opened its mouth and hissed like a snake, its yellow fangs gleaming with saliva. The general came slowly to his feet, knowing that if this creature even got close to him . . .

His left hand dug dirt from the soft earth and flung it in the beast's face and at the same time his right hand flicked out – and his dagger buried itself to the hilt in the creature's single eye. It screamed – a high-pitched cry that grated along the nerves and set the teeth on edge – and clawed at its ruined orb. Scalding juices ran down its snout, leaving long smouldering tracks in its skin, crisping the earth where it fell. The creature stumbled towards Mercan and then fell and lay twitching at his feet.

The general turned it over with his foot and, careful not to touch the reeking ichor that still gouted from the centre of its forehead, plucked the dagger out. The bronze blade was pitted and scored where the blood had eaten into it.

A curious shivering sound in the chill air brought him back to his senses. It was coming from the crystal tower, a hollow tolling that pulsed in time to the tower's sudden changes in colour. Now the tall cylinder pulsed red and blue in long ripples and the plain before the tower was swarming with hopping creatures.

Mercan wrapped the ruined body of his companion in his cloak and ran for his horse ...

'A demon,' Mercan stated flatly.

'A demon,' Partholon repeated. The prince bent and scooped up a handful of pebbles. He tossed one into the oncoming waves. 'You're sure?'

Mercan swore. 'By all the gods – of course I'm sure! It was closer to me than you are now. It sliced Fea in two ... well you've seen for yourself, and that was with its tail.'

Partholon walked down to the water's edge, gravel and wet sand crunching under his feet. 'Describe it,' he said quietly.

Mercan breathed deeply, calming his ragged nerves. 'A round head, no ears, no nose. A single eye set in the centre of its forehead surrounded by a ridge of bone. Its mouth a slit, its fangs enormous and pointed, and they seemed to lock into one another. Huge chest, long arms. Its skin was scaled like a serpent's. It had one leg and a claw like that of a hunting bird's, with talons to the front and one behind. It also had a long barbed tail. Demons,' he said quietly.

'They sound like cousins to the harpies,' Partholon said, throwing a fistful of stones into the water, watching the white flecks disturb the oily swells.

The general laughed. 'They make harpies look pretty.' He looked curiously at the prince. 'You do believe me?'

Partholon nodded and sighed. 'Oh, I believe you – I have no reason to doubt you.' He shivered suddenly and drew his heavy woollen cloak across his shoulders. 'Before she left Delgrade prophesied that I would be slain by a one-footed man . . . ' He shrugged and turned back up the beach. 'Come, I set our three magicians a task: to discover the identity of our enemies and also, one of your men brought in some bones in your absence . . . '

'Human bones?'

'Aye, human. I am curious to find out who landed on this isle before us, and I'm sure either Fos or Faud will be able to tell us.'

The small tent reeked of spices and herbs and the choking tang of sulphur cut at both throat and eyes. As Mercan and Partholon entered, sparks ran along the general's sword and wristlets and danced from the prince's headband.

The three magicians were seated in a circle about a large shallow bowl in which oil swirled lazily. Tiny coloured motes drifted across the surface leaving long traces in their wake and, now and then, the oil would crack and snap with flashes of blue fire. The tent seemed full of whispers, sibilant susurations that lurked just beyond audibility, and the general found the hair at the nape of his neck rising.

The prince sank slowly to the ground before the three magicians and stared intently into the bowl; Mercan knelt by his side.

Aeolas passed his hand over the surface of the bowl and the liquid ignited with a sudden hiss. It burned furiously for a few moments and the whispers rose to hissing screams that reminded the general of the creature's death cry. The Samotharcian looked up at the prince, his eyes sunken and red-rimmed.

'Well, what have you found?' Partholon demanded.

'What do you wish to know?' Aeolas asked gently, mockingly.

The prince's eyes darkened and then he bared his teeth in a smile. 'The time for such games is past. Tell me what you have discovered,' he grated.

'They are called the Fomors,' Faud said quietly, looking quickly at Aeolas and then back to the prince. The stout easterner leaned back on a pillow and continued. 'They are what we would call demons – the result of breeding between gods and men. They embody the worst of both. Each one differs slightly, but in the main, they are as you described them. They are commanded by the one called Cichal One-Foot, and he in turn is controlled by his mother, a human called Loat the Active – or she was in her youth anyway,' he added with a grin. 'She is the more dangerous of the two. Cichal wants nothing more than to destroy, but that is not for her, she wishes to rule. Slay her and ... ' he shrugged expressively.

'Can it be done by sorcery?'

'She is an accomplished sorceress. And although her arts differ from ours, she has the ability to protect herself from anything we might send against her.'

'And that is all?'

'On that, yes. On the other matter however ... ' Faud sat forward and picked up one of the gleaming white bones that one of Mercan's cartographers had found on a beach in the far south. In the dim light the bone, polished by the elements, resembled marble. 'It is the thigh bone of an Aegypthian woman from the Isle of Meroe in the Nile. She was named Banba Caesir, the daughter of Bith, and she fled her native land some three hundred years ago.'

'Where are her descendants?' Mercan asked.

'She left no descendants. There were fifty women and three men in the craft that wrecked itself on these placid shores – and internal strife and plague destroyed them all.'

'So, it's just the Fomors we're up against,' Partholon mused.

'You will never destroy them,' Fos, the pale northerner said quietly in his guttural accent. His ice-blue eyes bored into the prince's, and his gaze was curiously vacant as if he stared into another, different time. 'You may succeed in wiping out this colony of the demon-race, but you will never destroy them entirely. For their fate is inextricably entwined with man's; they are man's darker shadow, a reminder of what he might have been – or what he might yet become.' The small magician smiled grimly, showing rough filed teeth, and his cold eyes were hard and sharp.

'You are fighting a battle in an ancient war, a war without beginning, a war without end.' He leaned back into the shadows and the firelight ran off his face like water, lingering briefly at his glazed eyes. 'It is a war you can never hope to win.'

The Partholonians set about colonising the land, settling along the banks of the rivers which had sprung up when their prince and his magicians had worked that first great magic: the Buas, Bonna, Leio, Bearbh, Saimer, Sligo, Mudhour, Maudh and Liffee. They built their forts and towns on the shores of the lakes that had come forth with the rivers: Loch Cam, Measg, Direchaiodh, Laighline, Eochtra, Rughraidhe and Luan. They built roads and bridges, cleared forests and reclaimed more land from the sea with the aid of their magic. Their merchants began trading further and further afield, and in turn, traders from the southern lands and islands ventured north and west to Banba or Caesir, as some of the settlers now styled it, bringing with them the exotic fruits and spices, metals and cloths which they had been accustomed to in Scythia.

But in everything they did there was the threat of the demon Fomors hanging over their heads, but it was not until seven years after their landing that the first great battle was fought.

Of course, over the years scores of bloody skirmishes had been fought and occasionally a band of Fomors would raid an isolated farm or village, and in retaliation either Mercan, Creachar or Eaocha would ride north and fire one of the demon encampments. But in all that time the Fomorians had been merely testing the humans' weaknesses and strengths, probing and probing again, seeking a weakness, biding their time and readying themselves for the ultimate battle.

It had been a mild winter and now the days were beginning to stretch and the year had almost turned back into spring.

The snows thawed in the mountains and the streams ran with renewed vigour, washing down the mountain debris onto the plains. The Partholonians rejoiced and Aeolas offered sacrifices to his sun-god, welcoming his return and asking his favour in the coming year. The new season started well, bringing with it clear days and a warm southerly breeze that augured well for the growing season.

It also brought the Fomorians.

They poured down from the hills in droves, slowly cutting off and destroying the Partholonian strongholds by sheer force of numbers. They cared little for their own lives and launched themselves in wave after wave of suicidal attacks on the walls of the forts. In that long cool spring and on into the summer the Fomorians, using surprise and absolute ferocity in their attacks, beat back the humans. But as winter rolled in, and the forces of Night and Darkness grew stronger, Aeolas by his arcane arts, discovered one of the demons' strongholds in the mountains of the west. With the aid of Fos and Faud and under the direction of Partholon they called forth the wild elemental magic of the land and tumbled the mountains in upon the Fomors. None of them escaped the mountain's shifting; none that is, except Cichal One-Foot, his mother Loat and a small band of demons who had already departed for the crystal tower.

Following the defeat of the Fomorians, the Partholonians renewed their attempts to colonise the land, venturing further and further afield, settling in even the most desolate spots, and the original colony at Sen Mag grew smaller and smaller as the years passed and the people drifted away. Partholon remained, seemingly ageless, still as agile and alert as before, although those who knew him personally could see the years beginning to lean heavily upon him. He spent many hours on the beach, watching the eternal waves washing the pebbled shore, listening to the rattle and hiss as the waters foamed back and forward. Occasionally, when he had drunk a little too much, he would walk on the beach with Mercan – who had become almost his constant companion – and he would speak of his wife.

During the First Fomor War, the prince had sent out scouts to try and find Delgrade and bring her into the safety of Sen Mag – for somewhere, deep in his heart, he still loved her very deeply. But the scouts had returned with no news of the golden haired princess nor of her slave, and Partholon sorrowed, for he feared she had been taken by the demons.

Little was heard of the Fomor now. The odd report of a wandering demon was carried back to Sen Mag, but these were usually unsubstantiated and were generally ignored. The crystal tower on Taure Isle was unapproachable – an old spell of the demons' still held and anyone who approached too closely to its gleaming walls was seized with agonising cramps and blinding headaches; even Aeolas couldn't break through the barrier, for it was constructed of an alien magic fashioned by an alien mind.

The Partholonians prospered and grew ... and so did the land, for it was, as Partholon had promised, linked to the people. The Partholonians settled its four corners, and there were even some who moved north and lived in sight of the crystal tower, and it was from these that the first rumours of a Fomorian presence came. They saw lights in the tower and occasionally strange cloud formations would gather above it and jagged streaks of lightning would dance along the crystalline walls. And slowly, the vegetation which in past years had crept closer and closer to the tower, began to die.

The Final Battle with the Fomorians took place on the Plain of Ith on that day sacred to Bile, the God of Death – the same day the Partholonians had first come to Banba.

The demon hoard had been massing in the northern and western hills all through the winter, which this year had been unusually severe. As the winter slowly and reluctantly drifted into spring, a thick white wall of seething mist had gradually swept southwards from Taure Isle, and the Partholonians had fled before it. Those who remained, or spies sent north by Mercan, returned – if return they did –

with tales of creatures that were neither Fomor nor beasts, but something akin to both, moving within the shifting walls. A stench began to pervade the fresh countryside – the stench of offal and blood, of roasting meat and putrefaction. The rivers and lakes in the northern half of the country were rapidly befouled and a thick scum sat upon the water, and the rivers washed the foul slime into the coastal waters. Soon the beaches stank with rotting fish and sea birds struggled helplessly in the thick muck. It snowed often that winter, and the pure white snow was tinted with a thick grey effluence that clung and hardened when the snow melted, leaving a scabrous coating in its wake. The rainwater was tainted and ate like acid into metal and rotted wood, and even stone seemed scarred by its corrosive effect.

The Partholonians were forced to abandon their newly colonised lands and retreat to Sen Mag on the shores of the eastern sea and there await the coming of the Fomorians.

Mercan leaned across the polished table and pointed with the tip of his dagger to the curve of a river on the painted chart. 'And here Eaocha?'

The grey-haired commander shook his head. 'I lost a troop of men trying to hold that fort,' he said softly. 'The mist rolled in and we suddenly found ourselves fighting in semi-darkness. Even the torches were doused by it, and the stench was unbearable. We stood no chance . . .'

The general tapped the chart with the hilt of his dagger. 'So we only hold Sen Mag,' he mused.

'Aye, but for how long?' Creacher asked. He leaned across the table and pointed. 'My troops hold the four roads about Sen Mag, but we cannot keep those positions if we have to fight in darkness and a poisonous fog.' His fist crashed down on the table. 'We have to do something – we just can't sit here and let them come for us!'

'I'm open to suggestions,' Mercan said quietly.

'Well then, we attack them – before they attack us.'

'Tell me how,' Mercan said, 'and you can command this army in my place.' He straightened and slipped the dagger back into its sheath. 'If you think you can do a better job of it than I can then you are welcome – more than welcome to it.' He smiled thinly. 'Well?'

The commander's shoulders slumped. 'No-one is trying to dispute your position,' he said wearily. 'I don't know what we can do ...'

'This gets us nowhere,' a thin voice said from the shadows at the back of the tent. A chair creaked and then Partholon came forward into the light, the torch flames giving his face a yellowish cast. He looked around the assembled warriors seated at the table, and he recalled with vivid clarity the first time he had seen very much the same group gathered together. It had been that night so long ago, when they had first come to these foreign shores; they had all been distrustful then, fearing each other, hating him, but drawn together because they had backed the wrong side and lost. And now they were gathered together again, dependent on one another, bound by a common enemy and the fear of death.

'My friends,' he began, his voice betraying his age and weariness, 'we have grown old together in this land; we struggled to make it ours – and we will not let these foul demons take it from us! We defeated them once before – and we will do so again; but we were united then – and we must remain so. We cannot allow petty bickering to divide us. Now ...' His blunt fingers touched the thick parchment chart and swivelled it about. Those seated about the table gathered closer. Partholon pointed. 'We are here ...' His fingers moved north and west. 'The Fomor are here, camped on the Plain of Ith.'

'How do you know?' Mercan asked.

'Aeolas informed me,' the prince said quietly. 'The demons are still surrounded by the mist ...'

'Then we cannot attack them,' the general said.

'Let me finish!' Partholon snapped, his eyes blazing, and for a moment he seemed a younger man, the man who had led them out of defeat in Scythia and into a new beginning in Banba. 'Aeolas, Fos and Faud are, even now, calling upon their Art to conjure up a wind that will shred the fog; and to re-inforce the effects of the wind, the Samotharcian has sworn that his god will shine tomorrow. We must be prepared to attack them. The wind will whip away the fog and the sun will shrivel some of the demons of the night, but there will be others used to the light of day – although the pure white light of the sun will undoubtedly hurt them.'

'Who commands the Fomor now?' Creachar asked.

'Our old enemy: Cichal One-Foot.'

In the first slanting rays of the morning sunlight, the fog wall seemed both insubstantial and beautiful. The crimson rays writhed along the shifting surface and sparkled with myriad rainbow hues, occasionally glinting off metal as they touched the creatures within. Shadows moved within the fog safe behind the undulating wall, and the Plain of Ith echoed with shouts and cries, animal grunts and chilling laughter.

Partholon stood with Aeolas and Mercan on a low hill at the edge of the plain. Behind them, the huge Partholonian army was gathered, standing silently, awaiting the order to attack.

The prince looked into the east, to where the sun had already risen above the horizon, and then he nodded at the Samotharcian sorcerer.

Aeolas raised his hands and faced his god. Crimson sunlight burned across his face, turning his eyes to hard points of light. He opened his hands and greeted the new day with an invocation that was older than man. The air, which had been cold and damp, began to move as a slight breeze blew warmly across the plain from the east, and almost immediately the day began to grow warm.

Below the magician, Fos and Faud worked over their smoking braziers, calling forth the myriad wind elementals and sprites.

And the Fomor began to move. The huge unbroken fog banks rolled nearer and now creatures darted out from its protective cover and raced for the foothills, their long bounding gait sending them flying across the smooth ground. Mercan called up slingers and archers to the brow of the low hill, and their specially-treated slingshot and arrows took a terrible toll of the Fomor scouts.

And then the sun came up in a blast of sudden heat that seared the morning air. Parts of the fog wall instantly dispersed and left demons writhing on the churned ground as the sunlight touched them.

But the central core of the wall held.

And then the braziers of Fos and Faud erupted blue flames that died in a rush, leaving a thin tendril of blue smoke drifting slowly skywards – a tendril of smoke that was suddenly torn and shredded by a hot gust of wind that whipped in off the sea and howled across the flat plain. What remained of the fog wall dissolved before the hot wind exposing the Fomor cowering beneath the pitiless white-hot orb of the sun. Some fell, immediately crisping into charred lumps of hard flesh, whilst others wandered blindly, ichor leaking from their faces where the sun had seared their sight.

And whilst the confusion reigned the Partholonians attacked.

Lines of archers and slingers rose above the brow of the hills encircling the plain and sent wave after wave of arrows and slingshot into the massed ranks of the demons. The metal shot and arrow heads – dipped in a concoction brewed by the sorcerers – hissed as they flew through the air and ignited into a blinding white-hot point of heat. The flaming missiles tore through the thick hides of the demons leaving gaping wounds. Scores of small fires started and soon the stench of burning flesh drifted across the field. The flames were fanned by the breeze and entire sections of the hoard were cut off by the fire and destroyed by the Partholonians. Lines of footsoldiers advanced slowly down onto the plain, their long pikes extended before them, presenting a solid wall of pointed death. The Fomor attacked in suicidal waves, impaling themselves on the spear-points so that their companions might use their twitching bodies to climb over the spear wall and throw themselves into the midst of the spearmen.

But the spear wall held and advanced inexorably into the heart of the demon horde.

Cichal screamed and raged as he watched his army being broken by the remorseless Partholonians. He shook a fist defiantly at the sun and attempted to call upon his magic to enshroud it with clouds – but the Partholonian sorcerers had command of the wind elements and he couldn't wrest control of them from the humans – not now in the midst of battle. He glanced at the sun again – it had barely risen out of the sea, but was hotter than a noon day, and already his army had been destroyed. He screamed in rage as another hail of burning meteor-like missiles tore into his ranks leaving almost two-score smouldering dead and another score screaming in agony as the molten metal ate through their flesh. He shook with an icy fever and a red mist floated before his single eye. His only thought was to kill . . . and kill . . . and kill . . . He spun around as something touched his shoulder and his huge fist rose as he saw the hateful shape of a human beside him. His fist prepared to crush the fragile skull of the human . . . and then a chill voice spoke inside his head.

'Cichal!'

He staggered as if he had been struck and the single word wiped away his killing lust. 'Mother . . .'

Loat pulled her son back from the ranks and pointed up towards the foothills with a long-nailed hand. 'Look Cichal, look! There is your enemy, the small man; he is Partholon. Destroy him and you destroy the army's morale. And beside him is Mercan, commander of this rabble, destroy him and they will run about like a headless fowl.' She squeezed his scaled bicep. 'Destroy them my son. Destroy them.'

Cichal grunted and began to move back through the ranks, picking out individual demons, forming an attack force. With a decade of monstrosities by his side he broke away from the body of the horde and raced for the foothills, making for Partholon and Mercan. Some fell before they even reached the slopes and most of the others died as they fought their way up the low hill.

Partholon caught Aeolas and pushed him down behind him and then, dragging his sword free, he awaited the Demon-Lord. Cichal and a monster called Caoinh reached the brow of the hill. Caoinh leapt upon Mercan, hooked talons reaching for his heart. The general threw himself to one side and his sword sliced through the demon's chest, bringing it down. Mercan pulled his sword free as the demon fell and neatly decapitated it before it hit the ground.

Cichal attacked Partholon. One long bound took him up and over the prince, his barbed tail lashing out, almost tearing the Scythian's head from his shoulders. Partholon's sword licked out and caught the edge of its tail, opening a long shallow wound. The demon screamed as it landed, more in anger than pain, spun and launched another attack. The prince turned aside the flailing claws with the edge of his sword and pressed home his attack driving Cichal back down the slope. And then the demon's tail came up and around and struck him across the back of his head; he staggered and fell, black stars dancing before his eyes. Cichal shouted in triumph and leapt upon Partholon – and was spitted upon his upthrust sword! The demon's eye opened wide in astonishment and pain and then snapped shut in anger; and as it died, its long filthy talons plunged deeply into the prince's chest.

Mercan dragged the demon off Partholon and knelt by his friend's side. 'Lift me,' the prince whispered, 'let my men see me ...' he coughed blood and spat. 'And get this thing hoisted up on spears so the Fomor can see it,' he coughed again and Mercan held him while he shuddered.

The general lifted the wounded prince to his feet and half-carried him to the edge of the low hill so he could look down upon the battle. A loud cheer went up as the slim, stooped figure appeared at the crest of the hill bathed in the crimson morning sunlight – and only those closest to him could see that it was not just the slanting rays of the sun that ran crimson. Mercan raised his sword high and the morning sunlight coloured the stained metal a deeper hue.

And then the obscene corpse of Cichal was lifted high, its

mis-shapen limbs flopping ungainly, its head lolling to one side. The Fomorians moaned and almost immediately began to fall back, some even turning and fleeing across the battle scarred plain – only to be cut down by the archers. The remainder of the demon horde continued fighting, but their morale was broken and their defeat inevitable.

Loat stared in anguish at the corpse of her son dangling like the carcass of a beast from the Partholonian spears. She screamed aloud, her curse suddenly stilling the noise of battle, calling upon her demonic lord to aid her now and lend her his strength. A monstrous shadow appeared behind her left shoulder, but it was thin and misty and writhed in the pure light of the sun. Loat screamed as her familiar drifted back into its infernal region, leaving her alone and unprotected. But a shadow of its strength had touched her and, plucking a sword from a fallen Partholonian, she raced across the plain towards Partholon and the general.

Mercan lifted his sword and awaited the long-haired, wild-eyed woman. A spear flashed by her and a sling-shot burned the ground by her feet; a warrior stood before her, a battle-axe in his hands. He cut at her – missed, and fell back with his throat slit. And then she was climbing up the low hill, her rage and the demonic strength and madness urging her on.

'Kill her,' Partholon said wearily.

The general brought his arm back and threw his sword like a spear. The point struck her in the chest and exited through her back, close to her spine – but Loat merely staggered and continued running.

'The blood ... the blood ...' the prince whispered, his shaking fingers pointing to the thick ichor that had seared the ground where Cichal One-Foot had fallen. Mercan stooped and dipped the point of his dagger into the thick leprous-green blood, and as Loat came over the brow of the hill, plunged the dagger into her throat.

The effect was immediate. Her face collapsed in upon itself and then her body folded, caved inwards, large grey flakes breaking away, whirling away on the wind like ash.

The withered husk of the old, old woman dried up into a crumbling powder and was swept away.

The Final Battle was over; the Fomorians were defeated.

But the Partholonians did not survive their victory over the demon horde. Partholon lingered awhile, but his wound grew infected and despite the attentions of Aeolas, Fos and Faud, he died seven days later.

And where the prince was buried became a barren spot, and as the years passed, the circle of desolation spread about his grave, for the infection survived him. And it was from this spot that the plague spread.

Its growth was insidious and it took several years to manifest itself, but eventually it raged throughout the country, wiping out whole settlements in a matter of days. And so, what remained of the Partholonians returned to Sen Mag, the spot where they had first landed, close to where they had defeated the demons.

And so on that feast day sacred to Bile, the God of Death, the remnants of the Partholonians succumbed to the plague. And they died where they fell and it was left to time and the elements to cover their bodies and make a mound over it.

A little while later, when naught but bones and scraps of cloth and rusted metal remained, a shrouded and hooded creature came to the spot and laid a small posy of flowers on the low mound that marked Partholon's grave, and whispered a name over the field of death: '*Tamlecht Muintre Partholain*' – the Plague Grave of Partholon's People.

And Delgrade wept as she walked away.

CHAPTER 2

DERMOT AND GRANNIA

'And Fionn and the Knights of the Fianna came to Tara for the wedding feast in Maecadre's Halls ...'

The young golden-haired woman rounded on the poet sitting by her side. 'You mean this is my wedding celebration?' she hissed in amazement.

Dara nodded dumbly.

'No-one told me!' the maiden snapped, her sea-green eyes flashing angrily.

'But Grannia,' he protested, keeping his voice low, 'you agreed ... you consented to this match.'

'I did not!' she said loudly, and then lowered her voice as heads were raised and turned in her direction. She smiled in their direction and then turned back to the poet. 'When did I agree?'

Dara drank deeply, trying to calm the panic that was rising within him. His dark eyes darted over the assembled knights and warriors now eating and drinking their fill about the long wooden tables. If Grannia were to spurn Fionn now, then the commander of the Fianna would more than likely loose his warriors upon the company.

He breathed deeply. He must remain calm now; he must convince this silly woman that it was in her best interests – and Cormac's, her father – that she agree to wed Fionn.

'When Oisin, Fionn's son, came here to ask for your hand,' he began, 'you said that if Fionn was good enough to be considered as a son-in-law by your father, then he was good enough to be considered as a husband for you.'

Grannia's slim fingers closed about the stem of the goblet she was holding and her knuckles whitened. 'But look at him,' she whispered, glaring past the poet and across the table. 'He is older than my father; even his son is older than me!'

'He is a renowned warrior, a veteran of many a campaign, the hero of many a song and ballad,' Dara explained patiently.

'He is old,' Grannia said, 'I would rather marry my grandfather, Art, than marry him.'

'Princess,' Dara pleaded, 'do not spurn him. He has a violent temper, and he has not been reconciled with your father for many years. Your marriage will unite the Fianna with Cormac's army.'

'I will not wed such a creature,' she snapped at the poet. 'And now,' she added, 'I do not wish to discuss the matter further.'

'Princess . . .'

Grannia placed her hand on his arm and, still smiling sweetly, sank her long nails into the soft flesh. 'I have given you a command.'

She dismissed the subject and began to pick at the remains of her meal. Her gaze drifted down the long table, and her hard eyes softened. 'Tell me,' she said quietly, 'who is the young man sitting next to Oisin and the boy?'

'The boy is Oscar, Oisin's son,' Dara said, nursing his bruised arm. 'Sitting next to him is Dermot Mac Dyna . . . by all accounts one of the noblest of the Fianna.'

Grannia smiled shyly. 'He is indeed handsome.'

'He is said to have a love spot on the centre of his forehead, and no woman who looks upon him can ignore his charms. He is called the "Bright Faced," for his looks.'

'I have seen him before,' Grannia said dreamily. 'It was during that hurling match between Mac Lugh and the Fianna against Carbi of the Liffee and Tara. The Fianna were losing and the match had not long left to run when he,' she nodded at Dermot, 'snatched up a hurley, hooked the ball from one of the Liffee-men and scored; he scored twice more before the match ended . . .'

'Princess ...?' Dara ventured.

The young maiden rounded on him and her eyes were hard and cold, her sharp-featured face set in a smiling mask. 'You must have something more to do than just sit here,' she said meaningfully.

The poet nodded stiffly and, bowing slightly to the princess, quickly left the room, his agile mind already composing the lay he would sing of the Battle of Maecadre.

Grannia looked past Queen Aeta her mother, and down at Fionn again. In his bulky furs and polished armour, with long strands of silver-grey hair still clinging to his balding pate, and his scarred face, he looked like an old bear – a toothless old bear. But like all such creatures, she reminded herself, still capable of wounding and killing and quick to anger. If she were to refuse Fionn now, to insult him ...

She looked down the hall at the Fianna sitting at the tables. Most of them were huge men, made all the more so by their polished armour and gleaming leathers or furs. Most, if not all, still carried their weapons, having refused to leave them outside the great iron-studded doors, and she noticed that no matter how much they drank, their hands never strayed far from their sword or knife hilts. They were beasts ... gross beasts. Except Dermot. He was neither as tall nor as broad as some of the others, but he carried himself proudly and his shining silver armour and supple leathers only added to his dignity. His hair was long and thick, as black as night's darkest hour, matching the colour of his eyes. His almost boyishly smooth face was unscarred, his nose long and unbroken and his teeth perfectly white.

And he would be hers!

Grannia waited until the night was far advanced and many of the knights of the Fianna and her father's men lay in drunken slumber. Cormac and Fionn – although deep in their cups – were attempting to play chess, and her mother sat with her head back against the tall wooden chair, her eyes closed and her mouth half-open, snoring quietly. She signalled her maid and, when the olive-skinned young woman stood beside her, instructed her to go to her chambers and bring her the Drinking Cup.

It was a small vessel of beaten gold, the handles incised with flowing script and glyphs, with tiny semi-precious stones set about the rim; a common enough goblet in Banba at that time. The princess poured a single drop of red wine into the bottom of the cup and swirled it slowly about. She passed her left hand across the rim of the cup and touched each of the stones in turn, bringing them to sparkling life. And slowly the vessel began to fill of its own accord.

The princess handed the brimming goblet to her maid and then watched anxiously as it was passed to Fionn. His red-rimmed eyes looked up from the chessboard and caught her tense expression and he smiled and raised the cup in salute. He drained it in one swallow – or thought he did, but when he looked into the goblet there was still liquid within. Graciously he passed the goblet to Cormac. 'Drink with me. Share your daughter's bride-cup with her husband.'

Cormac nodded and drank deeply from the cup and then, nudging his wife into wakefulness, he passed it to her to finish off what should have been the dregs. But there was still wine left in the cup when she was finished. The queen passed the vessel back to her daughter who raised it to her lips and pretended to drink.

Minutes later Fionn, Cormac and Aeta were sound asleep.

Grannia rose and walked slowly down the length of the hall. Nearly all the knights were asleep, snoring in drunken slumber, some lying across the polished boards of the table whilst others grunted beneath the tables like the animals they so resembled.

Dermot rose as Grannia approached, and bowed. 'May I offer you my congratulations,' he said quietly.

'You may not. I will never marry that gross pig!' she said calmly.

Dermot looked up in amazement. *'Princess!'*

'I do not love him,' she continued in that same level tone. 'I love you!'

For a moment the words didn't register with Dermot, and when they did he imagined that the princess was drunk.

She reached over and ran her fingers down the side of his face. 'No,' she said, reading his thoughts, 'I'm neither drunk nor mad. I love you. Flee with me now,' she urged.

The young warrior drew back in alarm. 'You *are* mad,' he snapped.

Grannia smiled and Dermot shivered, for her smile was cold and pitiless. 'I am not mad,' she whispered, 'I love you.' She gripped the long hair on either side of his head and, pulling his face to her, kissed him savagely. 'And I will have you,' she swore.

'Princess!' He pulled away, his dark eyes darting about the great hall ... if anyone had seen. But everyone was asleep, except for three warriors sitting at the far end of the table playing chess.

'Can you swear on your oath that you do not desire me?' she asked quietly, spreading her arms wide. 'Does my body not inflame you?'

'Princess, you are the most beautiful woman I have ever seen. In other circumstances perhaps ... but you are to be the bride of Fionn, my commander. My first loyalty is to him . . .'

'Listen to me warrior,' she said coldly, 'no such loyalty binds me, I feel nothing for your commander – nothing that is, except disgust. But if you hold your honour so highly, then let me impose on it. Let me bind you. I now place you under a *gaesa* to follow and attend me to the end of your days; I do so in the name of the Dagda and Danu, the Father and Mother of All.' She stepped closer to Dermot and smiled up into his troubled eyes. 'You are bound to me,' she said triumphantly, and then her eyes darkened as they looked over his shoulder. 'What do you want?' she snapped.

Dermot turned. 'Oisin ...?'

Fionn's son nodded grimly. 'Do you realise what you have done?' he asked Grannia.

Grannia stood beside Dermot. 'I love him,' she said defiantly, 'I must have him.'

'But at what cost?' Oisin asked, his voice chill with anger. 'Your love will kill him.'

'Oisin, what shall I do? She has placed me under a *gaesa*.'

'For your honour's sake, you must go with her – there is little else you can do.' He sighed and shook his head. 'I will see what I can do with my father; I will explain what has happened,' he said, glaring at the princess. 'But I fear he will want your head, for this will shame him greatly.'

'Go now, before he wakes, and may the gods watch over and keep you.'

Grannia's maid was waiting for them beyond the huge doors, a bundle of clothes and a small parcel of food hidden beneath her cloak. The young woman kissed the princess briefly, smiled piteously at Dermot and then fled down the echoing hall in tears.

The princess led him down through the palace corridors and out into a small walled area at the back of the huge rambling fort. It was a tiny herb garden, and the chill night air was redolent with the scents of herbs and spices. Grannia led the way through the garden to a small postern gate. But a short length of bronze-bound wood barred the gate. Dermot laid his weapons on the soft earth and, with muscles straining and the cords standing out in his neck, he levered the heavy bar from its metal clasps.

Grannia pulled at the door, the metal strips screaming as they tore across the stone path, and then reached for Dermot's hand. 'Come ...'

He shook his head. 'No, not yet. Wait for me just beyond the wall. I want to bar this door from the inside and attempt to throw off pursuit.'

'But how will you get out?'

Dermot grinned. 'Oh, I will.'

The warrior closed the heavy door as quietly as possible and then struggled to lift the massive bar into place. It dropped into the thick clasps with a solid booming that echoed and re-echoed from the dripping walls. He walked back into the midst of the garden, carefully measuring off his distance from the wall. He then examined his two spears: the *Ga-Derg* and the *Ga-Buidhe*, the Red and Yellow Javelins. The former was too stiff and unyielding for his purpose, but the latter was light and flexible ...

Dermot strapped the *Ga-Derg* onto his back and then, with the *Ga-Buidhe* held in both hands, he ran straight for the wall. His booted feet crushed delicate herbs and trampled fragile night flowers, and the scents, sharp and strong, sweet and sickly, acrid and cloying rose into the quiet air. At the last possible moment, at the very base of the wall, he ground the butt of the spear into the soft earth and, clinging to the end, rode the recoil up and over the wall. He balanced momentarily on the top of the wall, pulled loose the spear and dropped down the far side, rolling to his feet beside Grannia.

He stood beside her and looked back at the rising mound of Tara. 'There is still time for you to return,' he said quietly, 'no-one would ever know.'

She shook her head.

And then he kissed her gently. 'I'm not sure I can live up to such a love – a love that compels you to throw away a life of ease and luxury for that of a fugitive.' He stared intently down into her wide sea-green eyes. 'For make no mistake princess, we have taken the first step on a long and dangerous road this night. Fionn is a good friend – but he is an implacable enemy. He will hunt us down like animals ... and we cannot hope to outrun him forever.'

'Well, when we die, let us die together,' Grannia said smiling.

Dermot grinned. 'I hope to put that day off for as long as possible.'

'They travelled far that night. Dermot stole a pair of horses and a chariot from Tara's stables and, sticking to the hard roads so as to leave no tracks, they made for Ath-Luan where they abandoned the chariot and continued on foot to the Wood of the Two Tents where, in the very centre of the wood, Dermot constructed a large hut of reeds and mud and surrounded it with a tall fence of freshly-hewn saplings. He left seven doors in the fence, explaining to Grannia that when Fionn came – and he undoubtedly would – he would be forced to divide his force up into seven different groups to guard each of the seven doors. And above each door he placed a woven circlet of alder and oak which threw the openings and everything within the circle into shadow, so

those standing without could not look in; and the circlets also prevented anyone from entering without his express command.'

'What do you mean you've lost their tracks?' Fionn demanded, throwing the reins of the chariot to his charioteer, and leaning out over the side.

Cuan, chief tracker of the Clann Navin, stood beside the chariot and pointed down towards the river. 'The chariot tracks are clear and distinct up to that point, but then they suddenly veer northwards. However, they are not so deeply indented as before which would seem to indicate that both Dermot and Grannia were not in it.'

Fionn leaned over until he was staring directly into Cuan's eyes. The early morning sun gave his face an almost mask-like appearance and his eyes were flat and uncompromising. 'Your analysis is brilliant . . . and now tell me in which direction they are headed.'

Cuan shrugged. 'It could be north or south . . .'

'Or east or west,' Fionn snapped. 'Are there tracks on the far side of the river?'

'Aed is checking now,' the tracker said quietly.

'Well then,' Fionn hissed, 'report back to me when you have something to report – and stop wasting my time!'

Oisin rode up beside his father. 'You were a little harsh on him,' he said, dismounting.

'I do not suffer fools gladly,' Fionn said almost absently, his head tilted slightly to one side, his eyes half-closed.

'We need the Clann Navin,' Oisin reminded him.

Fionn straightened suddenly and glared at his son. 'I am Fionn, son of Cumhal . . . I need no-one.'

'Without Clann Navin we will never find Dermot and Grannia,' Oisin said.

'They could be anywhere,' Oscar, Oisin's son said, riding up alongside his father and grandfather.

The grey-haired commander of the Fianna shook his head and pointed down towards the river. 'No, they are not anywhere; they are there in the Wood of the Two Tents.' He glanced back at Oisin. 'They are there.'

He tapped the charioteer on the shouder and pointed down towards the river bank where the Clann Navin still sought signs of the fleeing couple. The chariot lurched and the iron-shod wheels spun and sank into the soft earth before taking hold.

Oscar turned to his father as the swaying chariot began to slide down the muddy incline to the river. 'Are they there?'

Oisin shrugged. 'If my father says they are, then they are there; you know he has the Sight.'

'What can we do?'

Oisin pulled himself up into the saddle. 'We will have to try and warn Dermot,' he said quietly. He turned and looked back down the ranks of the marching knights. 'Find Kylte and Dering, and get Bran, your grandfather's dog. Meet me in yonder clump of trees.'

Dermot awoke suddenly. The morning sun was slanting in through the woven branches that served as a roof for the crude hut, bathing the interior in a gentle emerald light. He sat up wondering what had roused him, his hands reaching for his sword. He rose quietly, careful not to wake the still-sleeping princess, and went and stood by the door of the hut and listened. But there was no sound, and then he realised that the wood, which should have been alive with birdsong at this hour, was strangely silent.

And then he heard it.

It was the whine of a dog, and it came from beyond the fence that bounded the small clearing and the hut. He slipped a cloak about his shoulders and padded on naked feet over to the fence. He could hear the creature moving restlessly through the fallen leaves, could hear its soft breathing. He peered through the closely-woven branches, but he could only make out the vague shape of a large hunting dog.

The beast whined again.

Dermot frowned – the sound was familiar. He reached up and pulled off the circlet of alder and oak above the door and then stood with his sword held in readiness whilst the shadow which had darkened the doorway faded. The huge dog came to its feet, lunged towards the warrior – and rolled over, its tongue lolling.

Dermot fell to his knees beside the dog, laughing. 'Bran!' And suddenly he understood; Fionn was never far behind the dog, and he knew that Oisin or one of his few friends in the Fianna must have sent the dog as a warning. He nodded to himself, running his fingers through the animal's long coat. 'Go home Bran,' he whispered, 'go back to Oisin, let him know I understand.' The dog watched him, its ears twitching as Dermot spoke, and then it rose smoothly to its feet, turned and disappeared back into the wood, its russet coat blending perfectly with the autumnal foliage.

Some time later that morning Dermot and Grannia heard a distant voice shouting in the east. Dermot stood and listened. 'That was Fergor Loud-Voiced, Kylte's servant.'

'Why was he shouting?' Grannia asked.

'It was a warning,' Dermot said quietly, 'Fionn and the Fianna are nearby.'

'What are we going to do?'

'Do? We are going to do nothing ... there is nothing we can do.'

It was close to evening when the Clann Navin found the hut surrounded by the wicket fence in the centre of the wood. One of the trackers, Aed – called the Smaller – climbed a tree and looked down into the enclosure. Grannia, looking up caught the sudden flash of sunlight on metal. She smiled secretively. The princess rose slowly and walked over to Dermot and knelt by his side. She took his head in her hands and kissed him passionately, turning his face slightly so the hidden watcher could see clearly.

What would Fionn say to that?

Fionn's wrath – when he heard – was frightening to behold. He almost beheaded Aed on the spot as he gleefully recounted his tale – for there was no love lost between the Clann Navin and Dermot. The old warrior raged and swore retribution upon Dermot, and promised on his oath that he would not grant him a warrior's death.

And as the last light of day was fading, Fionn sent his knights into the wood with orders to surround the palisade – and wait.

That night, Dermot and Grannia lay on their bed of moss and grasses and watched the campfires dance and flicker through the gaps in the walls of the woven fence.

The morning broke sharp and chill and the sky was pale and metallic, full of the promise of approaching winter. Dermot rose before the dawn however, and busied himself honing his two swords, *Morallach,* the Great Fury and *Beagallach,* the Little Fury, and sharpening the points of his two spears, the Red and Yellow javelins.

He had strapped Morallach across his back with the hilt by his left shoulder and was slipping Beagallach into the sheath on his right thigh when a shadow blotted out the wan sun. He threw himself to one side and rolled to his feet, both swords in his hands, ready to launch himself at the intruder.

'Angus!' The swords dropped from his hands as he embraced his foster-father, Angus, the God of Love and Lord of the Birds.

The young-seeming man smiled fondly at his foster-son, and although he was older than Dermot by several thousand years, he looked like his younger brother. 'You have changed Dermot. There are lines about your eyes, your brow is furrowed, and is that grey I see in your hair?'

Dermot grinned. 'It is called ageing, father. Something you will never have to worry about.'

The god gestured to the fence. 'Might it not be worry also? And you have worries enough, have you not? If you wish to live to age a little more, I think you and the princess should come with me back to Brugh na Boine.'

Dermot shook his head slowly. 'Thank you, but I cannot go. Take Grannia and I'll join you later . . . perhaps in the Wood of the Two Swallows.'

'If you're still alive.'

'If I'm still alive,' Dermot agreed.

'Well, I am going nowhere,' Grannia said angrily, stepping from the hut.

Dermot rounded on her, his dark eyes flashing angrily. 'You will do as I say,' he snapped. He turned back to Angus. 'Take her!'

Grannia screamed as the god enveloped her within his feathered cloak and disappeared. Beyond the fence, the princess's scream drove Fionn into a fit of fury. 'He is abusing her!' He spat at his son. 'I told you he took her by force.'

'And I tell you he did not. She coerced him ...'

'Liar!' Fionn screamed. He drew his sword and waved it aloft. 'Take them,' he cried.

The Fianna surrounding the palisade divided up into seven groups, each company taking up position before the doors. The charm that Dermot had placed above the doors prevented them from entering; the woven branches were like iron, and their weapons rung hollowly and struck sparks as they attempted to cut their way through.

Dermot walked slowly around the enclosure, stopping by each door in turn, and before each his question was the same: 'Who stands without?'

'Oisin with Oscar and the Clann Bashure. You can come forth under our protection; Fionn dares not set the Fianna against itself.'

'I thank you Oisin, but I dare not.' He moved on to the next gate. This was guarded by Kylte Mac Ronan and his clan, and they too offered him protection. Conan of the Grey Rushes and the Clann Morna guarded the third gate; they were old friends of his, but still he refused their offers of protection. Cuan and a company of the Munster Fianna held the next gate, and Fionn, son of Glore of the Loud Voice with some of the Ulster Fianna held the gate after that, and again Dermot refused them.

The sixth gate was held by the Clann Navin, Fionn's trackers. Aed the Lesser, his twin Aed the Greater, Gonna the Wounder and Gathan of the Loud Voice with Cuan the Tracker stood in a semi-circle outside the darkened doorway, waiting for Dermot to step out.

'Who stands without?' he called.

'Friends of yours,' Cuan replied quietly.

The young warrior laughed. 'No friends of mine I'll wager; I recognise that voice. So the Clann Navin have found me at last. I am amazed at their abilities,' he said mockingly.

'Step outside and we'll wipe that laugh off your face,' Gonna growled.

'I would like to,' Dermot said, 'but I have promised myself only to leave by that gate held by Fionn.'

'Then you will never leave here alive,' the huge bear of a man said loudly.

Dermot moved to the last gate. 'Fionn?'

'I am here, come forth.' Fionn waved his men back, drew his sword and took up position directly in front of the gate. The early morning fell silent, and even the breeze dropped as if the very elements awaited the outcome of the confrontation between the aged commander and the young knight.

'Fionn, I have no quarrel with you,' Dermot called out, 'let me pass.'

'You have stolen my bride,' Fionn snarled. 'I will kill you.'

'I did not steal her – she came willingly. More than willingly. Fionn,' he pleaded, 'she does not love you, and she loves me enough to place a *gaesa* on me to go with her. Let her go.'

'I will never let her go,' Fionn said quietly' 'she is mine – whether she wants it or not.'

Dermot pulled the ward from above the door and tossed it at Fionn's feet, and then he stepped out to face his commander. Both his swords were sheathed and he held his two spears point upwards. Fionn saluted him briefly – and then lunged with his sword. Dermot turned the blow aside with the shaft of one of his spears and, as Fionn leaned into the blow, deftly hooked his feet from under him with the butt of his spear. He leaped over the fallen warrior and ran – straight for the massed knights.

Gonna the Wounder of the Clann Navin unslung his battle-axe and prepared to meet Dermot's charge, swinging the great double-bladed axe in wide sweeping strokes. Dermot stepped inside the arc of the swing and struck the giant on the side of the head with the shaft of his spear. Gonna groaned and his eyes rolled in his head. Without breaking stride, Dermot leaped over the fallen giant and vaulted over the heads of the advancing warriors into the trees. He ran lightly from branch to branch, knocking aside the spears that came too close with his short sword. The wood seemed to close in and envelope him within its leafy vastness. The wan morning sunlight, slanting in through the branches created shadows that danced and quivered with a semblance of life ... and suddenly Dermot was everywhere, every limb, every branch seemed to have assumed his shape, and the Fianna spent themselves chasing shadows and hacking at branches whilst Dermot made good his escape.

'What did you do to the trees?'

Angus smiled and spread his hands. 'A little magic ...'

'I didn't really need a little magic,' Dermot said quietly.

'I know that,' the god said, 'but who is to know what the outcome might have been if you had not had a little magic to aid you.'

'I don't need magic to defeat Fionn,' Dermot protested.

'Perhaps not,' Angus said, and then he added, 'What will you do now, where will you go?'

Dermot threw dirt over the last glowing embers in the fire and shrugged. 'There is nothing we can do – keep running, I suppose. Perhaps one day Fionn will find someone else, and Grannia will no longer be as important to him ...'

'Fionn will never forgive you,' the young god said quietly, 'and it's not that Grannia is that important to him; he had never met her until the wedding-feast. But what has infuriated him is that you have taken – yes, I know she oath-bound you – his bride. You have made him look a fool; he will never forget, nor forgive that. He will hunt you to the end of your days.'

'Well then, we run and keep on running ...' Dermot repeated.

Angus leaned back against the smooth bark of a tree-trunk and only his eyes were visible in the light, reflecting back the glittering stars. 'Then let me advise you: do not dwell near a tree having only one trunk; do not go into a cave with only one entrance, and do not land on an island with only one channel of approach.' He leaned forward, a rustle of silken cloth in the darkness. 'And do not eat your food where you have cooked it; do not sleep where you have eaten, and do not sleep in the same place twice.'

'You are advising me to keep moving?'

'Never stop.'

'It will be hard on Grannia,' Dermot said, looking over at the small figure wrapped in furs and curled in sleep beside the remains of the fire.

'It is a life she has chosen for herself. She loves you Dermot, and for that love she has renounced her family, her friends, her position and her honour. That same love will make her strong and enable her to endure the hardships'. The god paused and added quietly, 'I do not know if you love her, my son. But whatever you do, you must not betray her trust in you.'

The young man shook his head wearily. 'At first I hated her', he confessed, 'she trapped me, took me away from my friends, made me an outlaw with a price on my head. I hated her ... but it is hard to hate someone as lovely as Grannia for long. I don't think I love her ... but I do like her.'

Angus laughed quietly. 'Well, it's a start.'

'Dermot and Grannia travelled west at first light. They stopped briefly at the Rough Stream of the Champions and then continued onto the Grey Moor of Finnlia. It was in the grey wastes of the marshland that they came across the last of the Fomorians, Modhan, who had been birthed of a human woman who had had congress with one of the demons. He was almost human in every respect but for a single eye set in the centre of his forehead. He stood almost

twice as tall as Dermot and was proportionally muscled. But for all his huge size, he was gentle and unassuming, and shunned the company of men, preferring to keep to the lonely places where his great size and deformity would not attract attention.

He travelled part of the way with Dermot and Grannia and listened to their story, and when they came to the River Connagh in the south, he carried them both across on his broad shoulders – and thus was their friendship forged.

Modhan accompanied them south and west, across the River Behan and up into the hills where the giant used his great strength to enlarge an existing cave and fashion a crude dwelling place for them. And whilst the giant pounded the rock to powder with his massive fists and Grannia dragged away the dirt and grit on her cloak, Dermot hunted and fished.

And thus, in a single night, they broke nearly all Angus' warnings: not to sleep where they had eaten, not to eat where they had cooked their food, not to cook where they had caught it – and not to enter a cave with only one entrance.'

Dermot arose with the first grey light of dawn and found the giant sitting in the mouth of the cave, his broad back to the cold stone and his great studded mace lying across his knees. He was staring out into the west, watching the last remnants of night slip across the waves of the endless Western Ocean.

Dermot knelt by his side. 'What do you see?' he asked quietly.

Modhan pointed with his mace, like a monarch with a mighty sceptre surveying his kingdom. 'I sometimes pity you, son of Man, for even with your two eyes you do not truly see. Tell me what you see?'

'I see the ocean, I see the waves rising and falling ...'

'Aah, but you cannot see *beyond* ...' The giant turned to Dermot and the warrior was surprised to find his single eye glimmering with unshed tears. 'There is an empire beyond the horizon,' Modhan said, 'a vast land of richness and beauty; it is still young, but it will soon be great.'

'Why do you weep?'

'I see its destruction and downfall,' the giant whispered. 'I see men in strange garments coming from the west in mighty vessels bringing with them death and destruction. I see the invaders stripping the land bare of its precious metals and jewels; I see the small brown-skinned-men – and they are not unlike Picts – in chains, sick and dying with the diseases the invaders have carried with them. And I see the great stones of the huge stepped mounds – even the smallest dwarfing Tara – tumbling in smoke and fire.' The giant stood suddenly, towering over Dermot. 'I will sleep now, awaken me at noon.'

The warrior watched silently as the giant made his way into the back of the cave, where he lay down and began to snore almost immediately.

Dermot looked into the west, curiously disturbed by the giant's vision, and he wondered if Modhan had looked into their future, and knew what lay in store for Grannia and himself. And decided that he didn't want to know.

He stood and stretched, feeling the muscles in his back twinge and protest after a night spent on a damp rock floor. He leaned against the cool stone and stared down onto the beach that lay far below the cave – and stiffened suddenly. He knelt slowly, careful not to make any sudden movements that might draw attention, and then sprawled flat out in the mouth of the cave and peered over the ledge.

There was a small boat coming in to beach on the rocky shore, with tiny ant-like figures moving about, hauling the craft up the beach. Dermot squinted out across the waves, mirror-bright and blinding in the morning sunrise, and there, black against the waves were the three silhouettes of tall masted ships.

Dermot armed himself with his swords and spears and crept from the cave and stealthily approached the small group of heavily armed warriors moving restlessly on the beach. They were small swarthy men with jet-black hair and sallow skins. Their features were crude, with lowering brows and protruding jaws. There was something familiar about them ... but although he knew them – they were either Picts or Gauls – he couldn't put a name to this particular group. The warriors were dressed in different shades of green: emerald, olive and sea-green, but three stood apart, and these were clad in richer garments, although of the same colours, except that they wore high boots of black, white and grey fur.

And then Dermot knew them: they were the Sea Champions of the Iccian Sea, pirates and mercenaries, and were commanded by three brothers, Duncoss, Fionncoss and Threnncoss – Blackfoot, Whitefoot and Strongfoot.

He had no doubt that they were looking for him, for the brothers had occasionally been employed by Fionn in the past. Their price was high, but they had never been known to fail. And they controlled a most formidable weapon: the Hell Hounds, three great wolfhounds that were immune to fire and water, sword and spear.

Dermot shouldered his spears, rose from the tall grass atop the dune and walked across the beach to the warriors. He smiled pleasantly and saluted them, 'A good day to you.'

Duncross nodded politely.

'You are far from the road,' Dermot said innocently, 'are you lost?'

'We are not lost,' Duncoss said, slowly drawing closer to Dermot, whilst Fionncoss and Threnncoss began to edge around to either side.

'Can I help you,' he asked, edging backwards almost imperceptibly.

'Perhaps,' Threnncoss said, and while Dermot looked over at him, his two brothers edged closer.

'We are looking for someone,' Fionncoss said from Dermot's left.

'A warrior,' Threnncoss added from the right.

'Have you see anyone strange around here lately?' Duncoss asked.

Dermot leaned on his spears. 'Describe him.'

'Oh, surely you have heard of Dermot Mac Dyna?' Fionncoss asked.

'One of the greatest warriors in all Banba,' Dermot said, fighting hard to keep his face expressionless.

'We are looking for him,' Threnncoss said, coming closer.

'Have you seen him?' Fionncoss asked.

'What are you doing here?' Duncoss suddenly asked, closing on Dermot.

The point of Dermot's spear snapped up and rested against Duncoss' throat. 'You are crowding me,' he said coldly. 'Now why don't you two just move back, and perhaps then we can continue this conversation like civilised beings.'

Fionncoss' right hand edged slowly towards his knife. The point of the spear pressed deeper into Duncoss' throat, drawing blood, the cold metal seeming to burn. 'Tell your companion to leave the knife alone,' Dermot said, almost casually, never taking his eyes off the warrior standing before him. Duncoss turned his head – the spear point scored a long cut across his throat – and brusquely ordered his brother to drop the knife.

The three Sea Champions backed away slowly, Duncoss wiping the blood from the puncture and cut on his throat.

Dermot smiled. 'I know you, I know your reputation, but I do not think you can catch Dermot Mac Dyna. He is no ordinary warrior, he has never been defeated in battle or single combat.'

'He is a man,' Duncoss said grimly, 'and no man can stand against us.'

Dermot shrugged. 'That may be so; but let me show you a feat I saw Dermot Mac Dyna himself perform some time ago,' he suggested, 'and then perhaps you will see what you are up against.'

'Any feat he can perform,' Threnncoss said arrogantly, 'we can perform.'

'Let us see if that is so. First I need a tun of wine ...'

The barrel of wine was brought over from the ship, and more of the mercenaries gathered around to watch, until eventually nearly the full complement of the three ship's crews were present. Dermot lifted the barrel in both hands, tilted back his head and began to drink. And he didn't lower the barrel until it was empty.

Threnncoss laughed scornfully. 'That was no feat.'

'It wasn't meant to be,' the warrior said quietly, 'I only needed the empty barrel!' He turned and walked back up the beach. 'Stay here and watch,' he called back.

Dermot carried the barrel up the dunes and climbed up the side of the hill. When he reached the crest, he set it on its side and pushed it down. He raced after it, leapt onto the rolling barrel and rode it downwards to the beach without stumbling or losing his balance.

The mercenaries laughed and mocked, saying that it was nothing but a mere balancing trick, but the first to try it missed the barrel completely and slid down the cliff face, breaking both arms and his neck. The second broke both legs, the third cracked his skull, the fourth shattered his spine ...

Nearly fifty mercenaries tried to ride the barrel down the cliff – none succeeded. By nightfall, the base of the cliff looked as if a battle had been fought about it, and the stones were slick with blood. Dermot departed at sundown, promising to return with the dawn with some news of Dermot Mac Dyna.

The three Sea Captains were waiting for him on the beach the following morning. 'What news of Dermot?' Threnncoss demanded.

'He is said to be heading in this direction, and was seen just to the north of here practising his spear-standing.'

'What is his spear-standing?' Duncoss asked.

Dermot shrugged. 'I would find it difficult to describe ...'

Duncoss laughed harshly. 'Then show us.'

Dermot took one of his spears – the *Ga-Buidhe* – and set it point upwards in the soft sand. The razor-sharp point glittered in the early morning sunlight and the yellow wood of the shaft glowed a deep bronze. Dermot stepped back a few paces, ran at the spear, somersaulted – and landed feet first on the point. He then somersaulted off and landed beside the three Sea Champions.

Duncoss shook his head doubtfully. 'It looks simple – it is, after all, only a matter of balance ...'

The first mercenary to try and copy the feat mis-timed his

jump and spitted himself upon the spear, the second actually landed on the spear point – and the point passed up through his foot and impaled him through the groin, the third lost a leg, the fourth his head ...

Again, nearly fifty of the mercenaries died or were severly wounded attempting to copy the feat, and by mid-afternoon the golden sands and polished stones about the spear were thick with the reeking gore of the mercenaries.

On the morning of the third day, Dermot again reported that he had heard nothing of the Mac Dyna, except that he was approaching the area, and once again he offered to show them one of the feats he had seen the warrior perform.

He took his sword Morallach – Great Fury – and set it between two forked sticks set upright into the sand. The sword was almost chest high off the ground, with the glittering edge pointing upwards, so sharp that it was almost invisible. Dermot leaped up onto the edge of the blade and quickly walked from hilt to point and back again. From his position atop the sword hilt he grinned down at Duncoss, 'Again, it's nothing more than a matter of balance.'

The first mercenary to try the feat fell before he reached the blade and, putting out both hands to save himself, lost them. The second landed on the edge of the blade – and lost both legs, the third slipped and lost his manhood, the fourth landed on the sword, tripped and fell forward – neatly severing himself into two halves ...

By noon the blade was so covered with blood and gore that it was almost invisible, and the Sea Champions were counting the cost of fifty dead and severely wounded men.

'And Dermot Mac Dyna can do all this?' Fionncoss asked in amazement.

'And more,' Dermot said quietly.

Threnncoss looked over at his brother. 'If even his simple feats are beyond us – what then of the man himself? Will we be able to take him?'

'He will run from us,' Duncoss said confidently.

'I don't think so,' Dermot said in amusement, 'I have heard that he is looking for you.'

'For us?'

'For the three Sea Champions of the Iccian Sea,' Dermot agreed. 'He should be here on the morrow!'

What remained of the mercenaries and pirates were waiting on the blood-encrusted beach the following morning when Dermot arrived. The sun had barely cleared the horizon and the beach was still shadowed, whilst above, the last remnants of the night still lingered as the tiny points of starlight faded before the coming of the day.

'What news of Dermot?' Threnncoss asked.

'He comes.'

'When?' Duncoss demanded.

'Now!' Dermot cried, drawing both swords and cutting down the mercenaries nearest to him. For a moment confusion reigned and in that short time he managed to slay many of them. In the heat of battle a curious change overtook the warrior; it was almost a beserker rage – but without the beserker's callous disregard for his own safety. He threw himself into the midst of the milling warriors, using both swords with equal proficiency, and pushed them back, using their own numbers against them. He could attack at will, but they were restrained and hampered by their companions. His attack lasted barely a hundred heart-beats before the terrified men broke and ran, leaving him alone on the bloody beach with the butchered remains of the green-clad warriors ... and the three Sea Champions.

They circled about him warily, keeping their distance, jabbing with spear and sword and then leaping back out of range again. Dermot easily parried the blows, turning slowly to face each of the brothers in turn, until it seemed as if he suddenly wearied of the game and dropped his swords to the sands. Threnncoss shouted and jabbed with his barbed spear. Dermot side-stepped the blow and caught the spear behind the head and yanked it – and the warrior – forward. He fell sprawling at Dermot's feet and the knight, still holding the spear, reversed it and struck him across the back of the head. Duncoss, seeing his brother fall, came in fast and low – and the shaft of the spear caught him across the side of the head, sending him reeling backwards. Fionncoss pulled a long throwing knife from his belt and flung it at Dermot. He shifted his head slightly, his hand snapped up and caught the knife as it flew by, reversed it, and flipped it back towards the mercenary. The leather and bone handle struck him full between the eyes, bringing him slowly to his knees, the look of absolute amazement frozen onto his broad face even as his eyes rolled in his head.

Dermot gathered the three senseless warriors into a circle and fettered them with chains of wood and iron he had fashioned the previous night; frail-seeming things, but blessed with the old magic, and unbreakable.

Dermot was half way up the cliff when he met Modhan and Grannia on their way down, having heard the noise of battle and fearing for his life.

'And so they fled the Cave on the Cliff. They travelled on to Slieve Lougher but were overtaken by the three dogs of the defeated champions: the Hell Hounds.'

They heard the baying of the hounds from afar, echoing over the hills and marshes, growing louder and wilder, with the unmistakable howling of bloodlust in their cries. The giant lifted Grannia in his strong arms and together, he and Dermot raced across the fields fleeing the hounds.

About mid-morning however, it became apparent that they would have to stop and fight, and it would be far better to do so in a place of their own choosing rather than be overtaken by the dogs on open ground. They marched on until they reached a barren, rocky incline which rose sharply and was broken only by a narrow defile, barely wide enough for three men to pass abreast. In this spot, only one, or at most two of the dogs could approach together.

Modhan lifted the princess and set her on the pinnacle of

a tall pillar of stone called Dobar's Stone that rose like an accusing finger into the darkening skies. Then he and Dermot retreated down the defile to await the dogs.

They appeared suddenly, breaking out from the cover of the trees and racing across the field towards the human and Fomor. They were huge beasts, standing almost fifteen hands high and with heads larger than any horses'. As they ran their coats rattled and sang metallically, and their paws struck sparks from the stones. Their eyes were wide and slit-pupilled like a cat's, and burned with an unholy intelligence. One of the beasts pulled away from the others and, although he was almost twenty paces from the warrior, leaped for his throat.

Dermot threw himself to the hard ground and rammed the *Ga-Buidhe* into the cleft in the rocks with the point tilted upwards. The huge dog came down onto the spear point, its massive jaws snapping the shaft, swallowing the bronze head and jagged lump of wood: it coughed and choked; blood-flecked foam spattered the front of Dermot's jerkin. The dog howled – the piteous cry shut off suddenly and the heavy carcass fell on him, pinning him to the ground ...

Modhan stepped forward and kicked the second dog as it raced for the fallen warrior, sending it rolling back down the rocky defile into the grassy glen. His gnarled hand slipped inside his rough woollen jerkin and pulled out a small black pouch. He carefully undid the drawstring ... and a tiny green and gold lizard scuttled out onto the palm of his hand. And he threw it into the face of the third animal.

The Hell Hound snapped and swallowed the lizard, never faltering as it raced towards the giant. Suddenly it stopped and howled. It stood twitching, its massive head thrashing from side to side, snapping at itself. It rolled over and its iron shod paws began to tear at its skin, striking sparks from the heavy fur. The animal screamed and screamed again, its cries almost human. The giant raised his mace ... and the second dog leaped across the body of the fallen dog and threw itself at the giant's throat, its long yellow fangs glistening with acid saliva. Modhan realised that, with both arms raised and both hands clutching the mace above his head, his throat was exposed ...

The beast's jaws clicked shut barely a blade's thickness away from his throat. Dermot stood, still holding the snapping dog's hind legs in both hands and swung it against the stone walls again and again, pulping its head.

Meanwhile, the third hound now lay still, and only the occasional rippling of its legs or stomach muscles indicated that it still lived. A thin red smear appeared on its throat. It grew and spread, and then its whole throat folded back like some obscene flower opening, and the tiny green and gold lizard crawled out, its hard eyes glittering blackly. Modhan carefullv lifted the creature from the hound's carcass and thoroughly cleaned it with a corner of his jerkin, urged it back into the black pouch and tucked it back into his inner pocket.

Dermot and Modhan had defeated the invincible Hell Hounds.

And on the beach where Dermot had left them bound and fettered, the three Sea Champions of the Iccian Sea slumped in exhaustion and drifted into that long final sleep ...

'And so Dermot and Grannia wandered the length and breadth of Banba pursued by Fionn and his warriors. Many were their adventures in the woods and hills, the fields and dales of the Green Land.

Modhan, his term of service to the two lovers now completed, left them at the Wood of the Two Swallow Trees, and they continued north to the Forest of Doros where they settled in the shade of the magic quicken tree guarded by the giant Shavran the Surly, kin to Modhan. And Dermot made a pact with the giant to protect the tree and its fruit from all thieves.

And so the years passed. But Dermot and Grannia aged not, for the fruit of the quicken tree was blessed and sacred to the De Danann, who had left it behind when they retreated to the secret and lonely places. There were others like them in the silent groves in the Isle of the Ever Young, and the quicken tree garnered something of their magic and power.

Many tried to steal the fruit of the tree – but none succeeded, for none could prevail against Dermot, and the heads of those he had slain hung like grisly fruit from the branches of the trees in the Forest of Doros.

But in time, Grannia longed for the older, more mature fruit – of which it was said that man could be made immortal. But Shavran refused to share it with the lovers, he quarrelled with Dermot, and in a battle that lasted a day and a night, the knight slew him.

As time passed, Angus interceded with Fionn and Cormac begging forgiveness for Dermot and his wife – for they had been wed in the midst of the forest by the god. Reluctantly, both king and captain agreed.

And so Dermot and Grannia returned in triumph to Kesh Corran where they lived in peace and happiness for many years.'

Grannia sat in the streaming sunlight brushing back her golden hair with a small ornate comb of elk's horn. 'I'm lonely,' she said plaintively.

Dermot looked up in surprise. 'Lonely?' He stood and dropped the knife he had been sharpening onto the polished wooden table. He put his arm around his wife and buried his face in her fragrant hair. 'How can you be lonely; you have four boisterous young sons and an equally boisterous daughter to cope with?'

Grannia nodded slowly. 'I know, I know, but ...'

'But ...?' Dermot prompted.

'But I miss my father, my mother, my sisters ... my family,' she said defiantly, and Dermot could see the spoiled petulant look in her face, a look that reminded him suddenly of that night so many years ago now, when she had placed him under a *gaesa* to flee with her.

'Your father does not wish to see you,' he reminded her gently.

'He will see me.' She threw down the comb and turned in the low backed chair to face her husband. 'He *will* see me; I know he will.'

'How do you know?' he asked, humouring her.

'Angus told me.'

'Angus!' he roared. 'What have you been doing?'

'I asked Angus to find out if my father ...'

'You mean, you asked my foster-father to intercede with your father for you?' Dermot demanded angrily. 'You asked him to do that once before, but I still had to go crawling back to your father and Fionn for forgiveness; I lost a lot of face then, I am not about to do so again.'

Grannia stood, and the morning sunlight outlined her in gold. 'You won't have to lose face. No-one knows – only Cormac and Fionn.'

'Fionn!'

'I have asked both Fionn and my father to feast with us.'

Dermot bit back his reply and shook his head slowly. 'You shamed me once before, Grannia; you dragged me away from my friends and family, and now you're about to drag my name through the muck again ...' He breathed deeply, calming his rising anger. 'I am not about to argue with you, nor am I about to cancel your invitation. But let me tell you this ...' and his voice turned chill and deadly, 'you have overstepped yourself this time, and I hope – and pray – that you will not regret it.' He turned away, leaving Grannia standing by the window and paused by the door. Only his eyes showed the pain and betrayal he felt. 'Remember this: Fionn never forgets, never forgives.'

Cormac and Fionn were received at Kesh Corran with all due ceremony and honour and they spent much of the first day feasting and making merry. Dermot renewed many of his old friendships with the Fianna and Grannia was received by her mother and sister – who had married Fionn in her place.

It was late into the night by the time the revels drew to a

close, but although he was exhausted Dermot couldn't sleep. He was filled with a foreboding of doom and twice he started from a light doze hearing the agonised cry of a hound. The third time he sat up and would have gone out to investigate had Grannia not awoken and bade him return to bed. And what little sleep the warrior did catch in what remained of the night was troubled with strange dreams that left him cold and shivering in the chill light of dawn.

Grannia watched her husband dress. 'If you're going hunting,' she said, as he pulled on his leather jerkin, 'take the Red Spear and Morallach.'

Dermot laughed. 'I'm only going hunting; I doubt if I'll come across anything that might call for Great Fury. Not unless, of course, I'm about to be savaged by a wild quail.' He lifted the Ga-Buidhe from the wall and belted on Beagallach, and then, catching sight of Grannia's face tight with fear, he relented and added, 'I'll take Morcolle, the wolfhound.'

Grannia rose from the bed and kissed him gently. 'Be careful,' she whispered softly, 'come back to me.'

And her words raced along his spine, touching it with ice.

The morning was bright and chill with a wind whipping in from the north and west, carrying with it the tang of the broad Western Ocean. Dermot's breath plumed before him and his eyes smarted in the wind. He found Fionn and several of the Fianna in the stables at the back of the fort. The commander greeted him civilly enough and then nodded into the north and east. 'My men flushed a massive boar sometime late last night,' he said, 'we're about to go after it now.'

'I'll ride with you then,' Dermot said quietly, and added, 'I heard the cries of hounds last night ...'

'Aye ... we lost three of my best dogs. The beast is huge and cunning, but we'll have it by noon.'

Dermot rode with Fionn out through the gates of Kesh Corran, their dogs Bran and Morcolle racing on ahead, their keen senses seeking the spoor of the boar. They rode on into the morning until they came to a small hillock on

Benbulbin, a huge flat-topped mountain. They had become separated from the rest of the hunters, although they could still hear their cries echoing across the mountain side, carried on the morning air. Fionn and Dermot dismounted, tied their horses to a low stump, and continued climbing. The view from the top of Benbulbin was astounding: the entire countryside lay spread out below them like a mulicoloured tapestry, whilst behind them, the mountain sloped downwards to the sea.

Dermot was so absorbed in the view that he didn't hear the stealthy rustlings in the underbush . . . Suddenly the boar came crashing out of the undergrowth and raced towards them, its wickedly curved tusks already stained with the blood of men and beasts.

Fionn began to back away slowly.

Dermot looked at him in surprise. 'Where are you going?'

'I am under under a *gaesa* never to hunt boar,' he shouted.

The warrior swore, and then called out to the commander of the Fianna. 'Then leave me your dog, Bran; Morcolle stands no chance against the beast alone.'

Fionn smiled strangely and shook his head. 'No . . . no, I cannot leave you my dog. He . . . he has chased this animal before and barely escaped with his life. And I doubt in any case, if either he or your dog could stand against the boar.'

Dermot pulled his short sword from its sheath, suddenly remembering his wife's advice to bring Morallach. He looked over at Fionn. 'I have never known Bran to flee from anything; the dog knows no fear.'

'Be that as it may, Dermot Mac Dyna, he will not stand with you against the boar of Benbulbin.'

Dermot caught the note of triumph in the old man's voice and sudden comprehension dawned. 'You've planned this; you've led me here . . .' He looked over his shoulder at the charging boar. 'You've led me to my death.'

And the boar was upon him.

Dermot's javelin glanced off the beast's armoured hide without drawing blood. The warrior threw himself to one side as the animal thundered past. He rolled to his feet and, with both hands clasped about the hilt of Beagallach, struck it down between the boar's shoulder blades. It squealed and reared up on its two hind legs – something he had never seen a boar do before – and the sword, tangled in its long bristles, flew from his hand and shattered against a stone. The boar turned abruptly and raced back towards Dermot. It was a truly enormous animal, standing almost as tall as a horse and twice as broad. The sharp bristles on its back were as long as Dermot's fingers and its tusks were as long as his forearm. Dermot waited until the last possible moment, until he could feel the boar's stinking breath on his face, and then he launched himself forward and over the animal's back. He fell as he landed and slid in the dew damp grass. His fingers touched cold metal and he found the hilt of his shattered sword with a jagged lump of metal still remaining in it. He pushed himself to his feet and called for Morcolle – but the dog was nowhere in sight, and even Fionn had disappeared ... but his mocking laughter remained on the chill air.

The boar turned in a surprisingly short space and was upon Dermot before he knew it. He twisted desperately to one side, but too late, and the boar's razor sharp tusks ripped into his stomach and chest. He screamed and fell on grass that was suddenly sodden with his blood. The boar turned and struck again, tearing open the existing wound ... and Dermot rammed the shattered sword down the beast's gaping mouth with the last of his strength. The crazed animal convulsed and attempted to swallow the obstruction, its squeals rose in pitch and intensity, and then stopped. The boar fell dead, its life blood welling from its torn mouth and throat.

When Fionn and the hunting party returned, they found Dermot lying in a widening pool of his own blood beside the already stiffening body of the huge boar. The warrior smiled wanly, his lips reddened with blood-flecked spittle. 'So ... so you finally achieved what ... you failed to do ... all those years ago,' he whispered slowly.

Fionn stood over the fallen warrior and shook his head

sadly. 'I never meant for this to happen,' he said quietly, but although his voice and face showed pity, his eyes were bright with laughter.

'I am close to death,' Dermot whispered, 'do not lie to me now.'

'You knew the boar would kill him,' Oisin accused his father. 'With your gift of foreknowledge, you knew he would not survive this day.'

Fionn smiled and let all pretence of sorrow and pity fall away. 'Aye, I knew, and my only regret is that all the people of Banba are not here to see their hero fall and perish, slain by a wild boar.'

'You shame me,' Oisin said, turning away. And slowly, one by one, the Fianna turned away from their commander.

Fionn knelt beside Dermot. 'And so, even in death you bring me nothing but ill luck. When you fled with Grannia –'

'No,' Dermot interrupted, 'I did not flee with her; she placed me under a *gaesa* – you know that. You know also that your own son advised me not to break my oath.'

'No woman is worth a man's oath,' Fionn snapped, 'a man should be strong enough to resist a woman's charms.'

Dermot smiled grimly. 'There will come a time – and shortly too – when your own son will ride away from you on the back of a woman's horse.'

'If you think to frighten me with your prophecies, then you are sadly mistaken. Your time has come.'

'Fionn, if you allow me to die you will have compromised your honour beyond redemption.'

'What honour had I left when you stole my bride-to-be?'

'Can you not see that your own actions compromised your honour . . . you made too much of it. If you had forgiven her, you would have emerged as the victor . . .'

'I chose not to forgive her – or you.'

'Well, make up for that now,' Oisin said, coming up and standing over his father and Dermot.

'I do not think I want to.'

'I think you should,' his son said tightly, 'because if you refuse to help him now, you will lose the respect of the men.'

'Is that a threat?'

Oisin shrugged.

Fionn rose from the ground slowly, his face tight with anger. 'What would you have me do?' he asked icily.

'Aid him.'

'How?'

'Let me drink from your hands,' Dermot said weakly, 'I know that when you were granted the gift of foreknowledge, you also received the gift of healing.'

'It is not a gift I have often used,' Fionn protested.

'That is nothing to be proud of,' Oisin snapped.

Fionn looked about the flat mountain-top. 'There is no water here; I must have fresh spring water . . .'

'Beneath the bush that lies at my feet,' Dermot said, 'there is a spring. I can feel its trembling through the ground.'

Oisin grasped the bush close to its roots and pulled it up in a shower of earth. Immediately fresh spring water gurgled up and ran down the hill in a quick sparkling brook. 'There is your water.'

Fionn went slowly to the brook and caught a little of the fountaining water in his cupped hands. He straightened – and dropped the water.

'Fionn . . .?' Dermot said gently.

'Father!'

The old commander pointed to the fallen warrior. 'For years he has made me the laughing stock of all the Forts and Raths in Banba. He has become a hero, and I the villain, and now he expects me to heal him.'

'It will show your generous spirit,' Oisin snapped, kneeling beside Dermot and cradling the warrior's head in his arms.

Again Fionn stooped and lifted a little of the chill sparkling water in his hands. He walked over to Dermot and knelt by his side. He lifted his hand and brought the liquid close to his lips whilst Oisin helped him sit up . . . and as Dermot's lips touched it, Fionn opened his fingers and let the water fall onto his blood-soaked jerkin.

'Father,' Oisin said coldly, 'unless you bring Dermot the water now, I swear that two bodies will lie on this hill.'

'You will never defeat me,' Fionn said.

'Perhaps not. But you cannot afford to destroy the Fianna if you choose to fight. For when you slay me, each and every one of the knights will challenge you in turn; how long do you think you can stand against the greatest army in the history of Banba?'

But even as Fionn brought the third handful of water to Dermot's bloodstained lips, the wounded warrior shuddered once – and died.

Fionn looked at the water cupped in his hand and said softly, 'I tried.'

Oisin stood and pulled off his cloak. He straightened Dermot's limbs and then covered him with his cloak. 'No father,' he said, without looking at him, 'you did not try. You have what you always wanted: Dermot dead ... and I will never forgive you.'

He stood whilst the remainder of the hunting party slowly filed past and laid their cloaks over the still body.

'For here lies one of the noblest of the Fianna.'

'And when Grannia heard of her husband's death – and there were some that whispered murder – she wept bitterly and blamed herself. She went immediately to Benbulbin, but when she arrived there she found Angus standing over the cold body with a host of the De Danann. And the god sorrowed with her, and he took the body of Dermot with him into the Shadowland where he instilled a flicker of life into it – but only a flicker, for it was beyond his power to bring the body back to full life.

And each evening, as the amber sunlight fades across the god's gardens, he walks with Dermot amidst the groves and magical arbors.

And until the day she died, Dermot would pass through the Veil of Sleep and walk and make love to Grannia in the Land of Dreams.

And death re-united them.'

CHAPTER 3

THE RETURN OF OISIN

The young man slowly climbed the innumerable steps leading up to the tower's summit. Standing on the small stone-enclosed platform he could see the storm far out on the horizon. The sky was grey and leaden, almost indistinguishable from the sea which boiled and seethed beneath the storm's onslaught. Sheets of white and silver lightning ripped through the lowering clouds, and he could almost imagine that he could hear the crack as the heavens were torn apart by the levin bolts.

But above his head the sun shone from a flawlessly blue sky and the sea, far below at the base of the crystal walls of the palace and as far out as the irregular circle of reefs that bounded the isle, was flat and undisturbed. He looked down, and could see the gleaming towers and glittering palaces of Tir na nOg reflected in a watery mirror.

For a single moment his clear grey eyes clouded as he looked out across the enchanted sea towards the storm beyond the reefs on the horizon. And for a single moment he longed to be standing on the shores of his distant homeland, feeling the rain and salt spray on his face, the wind plucking at his hair and the pounding of the storm-maddened sea on the sands by his feet. For a single moment . . .

'You still long for home after all this time?' He turned as a shadow fell across the crystal stones. A soft small hand enfolded his, the smooth fingers gently caressing the stiffened muscles, loosening the locked joints. 'Why?' The voice was as soft and gentle as the hand, lyrical, concerned.

'It is my home,' he said simply.

'Oisin – this is your home now,' she stated flatly.

An errant gust of wind touched his face and whipped strands of his dark hair across his eyes. He looked out across the sea once again, and emotion flickered behind his eyes, and was gone.

But Niamh Golden-Hair had seen his look, had seen the pain and loss that lurked behind them. She held his hand tightly feeling the hard muscles bunch and ripple beneath the smooth skin. She rested her head against his broad chest, feeling his strong heart pound against her cheek. He had lost none of his youth, he was exactly as he had been on that fateful day when she had taken him from his father and the Fianna almost ... how long had it been now?

But then, time meant little in the Land of the Ever Young, one of the strongholds of the Faery Folk. In ten years, a hundred years, even a thousand years hence, Oisin would still be as young and as handsome as he had been on that day when he had ridden away over the waves on her foam-flecked horse to the magical isle. His skin would remain smooth and unwrinkled, no grey or silver would touch his raven locks, neither his sight nor his hearing would dim. There would be no difference in him.

Or would there?

Already, after perhaps only thirty years in the Crystal Palaces of Tir na nOg, she could see the first signs of loneliness that had begun to grow within him – a loneliness that would quickly grow to an all consuming passion that would gnaw away at him, a passion that could so easily turn to a hatred of her and what she had done to him.

'Go back then, if you must,' she whispered gently, blinking away the tears. 'Go back, spend a little time in your own land and return to me refreshed.' She sighed and bit her lip, but there was nothing else she could do; she loved him, she could do nothing to hurt or harm him.

Oisin kissed the top of her head, breathing in the delicate perfume of her golden tresses, and then he tilted up her small oval face and kissed her long and deeply. And once again, for the thousandth time, the princess of Tir na nOg longed to belong to the world of Man once more so that she might fully experience the love of Oisin. But that was impossible; everything had its price, and the price of eternal life was sterility.

The white steed pawed at the golden sands as if it were eager to be off across the waves. Oisin stood beside the horse and held Niamh in his arms. 'I will return shortly,' he promised.

But Niamh shook her head. 'I fear I will never see you again. You were born in the world of Man and you will die in that same world.' Salt tears gathered at the corners of her large green eyes. Oisin brushed them gently away and kissed her.

'No. I will return to you some day, some way.'

She watched him mount, swinging easily into the high saddle, his burnished mail glinting golden in the sunlight, the horse's coat glistening like satin. She laid her hand on his leg and looked up into his eyes. 'Remember Oisin, remember; do not dismount from the horse. It is from this world, it is part of this world and it carries a little of this world with it always. Whilst you remain astride it you remain partly in the Otherworld, and are still subject to the Shadow Realm's laws. Dismount, and you will once again belong to your old world.'

The young man smiled and shook his head. 'I will not dismount.'

'And remember,' she concluded, 'time has no hold over Tir na nOg, but it rests heavily over your homeland. Do not expect to find everything as it was.'

He nodded. 'The years will have wrought changes,' he mused, 'but surely not that many.' He laughed, the first time she had seen him laugh in a long time. 'I will not lose my way.' He bent down and kissed her tenderly on the cheek, and then he urged the horse forward, out over the waves. The horse's golden hooves struck the water, sank slightly and then bit, as if it were galloping over soft earth.

Niamh stood on the warm sands watching her lover gallop across the seas of Faery back into the world of Man, and she wept for she knew she would never see him again.

Once Oisin passed beyond the magical reef that bounded the isle he was almost back into the world of Man, but some of the magic still lingered, and he once again saw the hart pursued by the red-eared dog, and the young maiden pursued by the warrior with the golden sword. He remembered he had first seen them – how long ago? – when he had first come to the Land of the Ever Young. He had asked Niamh about them then, but she had dismissed them, saying they were but the shadows of what had been, what would be, but what never was. He watched the dark warrior pursuing the maiden; her brown steed never seemed to gain any headway, and his white steed never gained on her mount, and he wondered if they were forever doomed to chase one another across the seas, and he resolved to question Niamh upon his return.

He passed the Land of Virtues where he had rescued a young maiden from the Fomorian king, and he smiled in fond remembrance of that battle: it had lasted three days and three nights. His father, Fionn, would have been proud of him, for his opponent had been a monster, standing almost twice his height and three times his girth and with the strength of a dozen men. And his blood had been black.

He urged his horse onwards; by the gods, what would it be like to fight again, to feel the blood-lust rising ... rising ... rising? The exhilaration of battle, the heady wine of victory, the spoils, the acclaim – what more did a man want?

The barren black Cliffs of Moher rose out of the sea in a solid line stretching from horizon to horizon. The sea foamed about their base, roared and howled through the countless caves and caverns, sending foam leaping skywards. He smiled triumphantly. He was home.

But somehow the cliffs seemed smaller, less majestic than he remembered them.

The horse's gold-shod hooves struck sparks from the pebbled beach as he came ashore. Oisin stood in the saddle, easing the muscles in his thighs and buttocks – it had been a long time since he had ridden such a distance. He eagerly scanned the land before him for any sign of habitation or movement. But there was nothing, and no-one. The beach sloped gently upwards, flanked on either side by the worn cliffs, and rolled back into flat green fields crossed with irregular stone walls. His brow furrowed in puzzlement as he urged his mount up the beach and across the withered grasses towards the open fields.

When he had left Banba there had been a Fort off towards the north, but now there was nothing but a smooth mound where it had stood. A broad highway had run down along by the cliffs and dipped down towards the beach, and now there was nothing but a thick track, overgrown and disused, and it was much nearer to the cliff edge than it should have been.

The warrior loosed his sword in its sheath – clearly some evil was abroad in the land – and rode on.

Oisin rode across Banba's green fields that day of his return from the magical isle. His amazement and wonder soon turned to something akin to fear, for nothing was as he remembered it. The Duns and Raths of his friends were gone, the roads had vanished and the great Forts were no more. Even the forests seemed to have shrunk. His wife's words echoed within his head, pounding with ever increasing intensity: *'Time holds no sway over Tir na nOg ... it rests heavily over your homeland ... heavily over your homeland ... heavily ... heavily.'*

He saw no-one as he rode across country – although he sometimes thought he saw someone disappearing into the stunted bushes that lined the small and rutted tracks, but they might have been animals fleeing his approach.

And the day wore on.

About evening he rode down into Glen na Moile in the east. He cleared the trees that lined the side of the glen – and stopped in amazement. For a group of children were attempting to lift a fallen dolmen off their companions. They must have been playing about the sacred relic when it had fallen over, trapping some beneath. But as Oisin rode forward, he suddenly realised that these were no children but rather full grown men and women. But they were so small, so puny . . . hardly men at all.

They scattered at his approach, their eyes and mouths wide with fear, but he sat there unmoving until they crept from the bushes and approached him warily.

'I am Oisin,' he said slowly, 'son of Fionn, Knight of the Fianna. Tell me of my father and of the Company, and tell me what evil has fallen over this land.'

One of the men, a tiny man in a rough brown garment with a silver cross about his neck, stepped up to the warrior and spoke to him in a voice trembling with fear. 'We know nothing of Fionn and the Fianna save what is told in the legends . . .' He pointed at the dolmen. 'There are people trapped beneath, will you use your great strength to lift it off them?'

Oisin gazed down at the little man in horror. Legend? Had Fionn and the Fianna passed into legend? By all the gods, how many years had he wasted in the Land of Eternal Youth?

'And what of Oisin?' he asked hoarsely, his eyes hard and flat, gazing unseeing into the distance, knowing yet dreading the answer.

'There was one,' said the man in brown, 'a son – I think – of Fionn who was taken by a *bean-sidhe* – a fairy woman – off to the Isles of the West, and he is said to be living still.'

Oisin smiled gently, and then he rose up in the ornate saddle, spread his arms wide and shouted, 'I am Oisin, son of Fionn; I have returned from Tir na nOg!'

And only the echoes answered him.

He manoeuvred his horse over to the toppled dolmen and leaned down. His calloused hand caught the edge of the huge slab of stone, the muscles in his shoulder and arm tensed, and then he heaved. The huge slab was torn out of the soft earth and sent whirling across the field to shatter against the ground.

And in the same instant, Oisin's saddle girth snapped with the strain, and he fell to the ground. A cry of horror caught in his throat as his voice seemed to catch and rattle. His hand reached for the reins, but the white horse shied away as his hand shrivelled into a withered claw before his eyes. The horse grew . . . and grew . . . and grew until it was enormous, and then it turned and was gone.

Oisin writhed on the ground as all the years he had passed in the magical isle claimed him now. His thick raven locks turned grey, then silver and then fell from a scalp suddenly scabrous. His sight – his perfect sight that could count the individual feathers on a sparrow's wing at five hundred paces – dimmed and faded and shadows raced in and gathered about him. The noon faded to a thick twilight and his hearing – that could hear a worm moving through the earth – died to a muted roaring. His smooth skin wrinkled, cracked and hung in loose wattles from his chin, arms and legs. The weight of his armour dragged him to the ground and as he fell he could hear his suddenly brittle bones grind together and he knew that any sudden movement might shatter them completely.

A shadow moved across his dim sight and a face – no longer tiny – swam in his vision. It was the small man in the brown cloth. The silver chain and cross about his scrawny neck glinted blindingly. Oisin could barely make out his words, but they sounded reassuring and he could feel the man working on the buckles and straps that held his armour. The last words he heard before he drifted into unconsciousness were blurred and muted and he could only make out part of the sentence . . . 'take you to Saint Patrick.'

And on the magical isle, Niamh bent her head and wept as she saw the riderless horse galloping across the waves towards her.

Oisin survived for several months after his return. He and Patrick struck up a curious friendship and they often spent the long evenings arguing the Old Celtic Faith against the New Christian Religion. And in the end Patrick prevailed and Oisin, last of the Fianna, last of the Heroic Age, was baptised a follower of the Christ.

CHAPTER 4

FIRE ON THE MOUNTAIN

(A Legend of Saint Patrick)

The grey-haired warrior leaned across the young man in the long woollen robe and pointed with the charred end of a twig. 'Tara is here . . .' he scratched in the dirt, 'and Slane is here on the north bank of the Boyne.'

'So Slane is visible from Tara?' the young man asked.

'On a clear day, yes.'

'And if I can convert Tara?'

'If you can convert Tara, you can take all Eriu.' Dichu stood and dusted off his hard hands. He looked down at the young man. 'But first you must convert Laoighre – and that,' he added, 'is impossible.'

Patrick stood and rubbed his sandle-shod foot over the rough map drawn in the dirt. 'Will he listen to me?' he asked, looking up at the grizzled warrior. He was not a tall man, standing almost a head smaller than Dichu, but the older man felt dwarfed by his presence.

'He will listen to you – but you will never bring him into the New Religion. His father was Niall of the Nine Hostages, and Laoighre follows his father's ways and is firmly entrenched in the Old Faith.' Dichu pulled his dyed woollen cloak across his shoulders, shivering as a chill breeze whistled through the almost bare trees. 'However, his queen Angras might listen to your words – and she has great influence with the poets and bards. If you could convert her, and she them, then half your task would be completed.'

The small Roman nodded, his grey eyes lost in thought.

He ran his fingers through his prematurely greying hair and sighed wearily. 'And the Druids?' he asked.

Dichu turned to face the holy man. 'You will never convert the Druids. They will oppose you every step of the way. They will call upon their gods and their Powers to strike you down and if that fails then they are not above hiring men to do their work for them.'

Patrick shrugged. 'My God will protect me,' he said with absolute confidence.

'And your followers also,' Dichu waved a bare arm at the small group of men and women huddled beneath a stand of trees, 'they too will do their utmost to protect you.' He patted the knife that hung by his side significantly.

The Roman's eyes flashed in sudden anger and his high-boned, hollow-eyed face flushed. 'I will renounce the first man who uses violence in my name,' he snapped. Clouds scudded across the night sky and the hard points of starlight sparkled in his eyes. 'I have taught you of the One God, the True God, and I have read to you from the Holy Books – and you told me you understood and would follow the teachings and honour His Name. But do you not understand that He teaches peace, not violence?'

Dichu rested his heavy hands on Patrick's thin shoulders. 'Listen to me holy man. I was amongst your first converts to the New God; you built your first church in my Dun. I honour you, I honour your . . . *our* god. But you must remember Patrick that what you are teaching is totally opposed to the codes we have lived by since the time when the Ancients took Eriu from the demons. You must be patient,' he said gently, 'give us time.'

The land was dark. No lights burned in the Duns or Raths; no fires glowed in the Forts and even the shepherds' fires on the hills were extinguished.

For this was the time of waiting. It was the time sacred to the God of Fire, a time *between*. The winter had passed, the spring and summer were yet to come. All across the land the people waited for the first sign of the coming season: the

Druid fire that would rise before Tara's walls. The fire that would signify light and life, growth and heat.

But now, 433 years since the birth of the Christ, the Festival of Fire and the Christian Feast of Resurrection fell on consecutive days.

Lucetmale the Arch-Druid watched his priests carefully weave the wands of oak and green yew into the Circle of Life and place it like a crown about the smooth circular stone. The old man bent and lifted the heavy stone in his strong arms and carried it to the small platform surrounded by bundles of green and freshly-cut wood. He bowed to the four cardinal points, then turned and faced the east where the sun would shortly rise. He pushed back a lock of greying hair under the thin gold fillet that encircled his head and his dark brown eyes raked the skies for the first sign of the approaching dawn, eager to light the fire of the new season.

He half-turned as Laoighre the High King and Angras his queen came up behind him.

'It is almost time,' he said, his cracked voice breaking harshly on the still pre-dawn air.

The High King nodded, his dark eyes moving ceaselessly over the almost flat plain spread out before him. He stiffened suddenly. Angras felt his tension and laid her small hand on his arm.

'What is it?' she whispered.

Laoighre pointed and the queen gasped in amazement.

For on the north-eastern horizon a thin tendril of fire rose into the night skies!

'Blasphemy!' Lucetmale screamed, his right arm rigid and pointing. A low moan rippled through the assembly as all heads turned towards the tiny spot of fire which flared and grew, casting its yellow light far out into the night.

The Arch-Druid screamed like an animal in mortal pain. His gaunt frame shook in rage and spittle frothed his lips. He mouthed incoherently at the light burning against all tradition and law on Slane Hill.

Laoighre instructed one of the Druids to take Lucetmale away and calm him down and then he called for his warriors and chariots, and took the north road towards Slane.

Dichu wiped the sweat from his brow and moved away from the roaring fire. He coughed and spat ash and cinders from his dry throat. The old warrior was surprised to find himself trembling like a raw recruit on the morning of his first battle. But then, wasn't that what he was: a recruit in the first battle between the New Religion and the Old Faith? He squinted back into the glowing heart of the huge fire, and while a part of him still cowered in terror at what he had done, another part rejoiced and almost welcomed the coming conflict.

The small Roman joined him as he walked away from the fire. Patrick's clothes were singed by the flames and his hair and beard still smouldered. His sallow cheeks were glowing and ruddy and his white teeth glinted in the shimmering light. 'Will they come?'

Dichu smiled at the holy man's almost youthful enthusiasm. 'Oh aye, they'll come, you may rest assured of that. You have sent them a war arrow . . . ' He pointed south and west. 'And I'll wager that even now they are preparing for war in Tara.' He shook his head. 'I don't think you know what you've started.'

Patrick nodded seriously. 'Oh, I know sure enough.' He pointed back up the hill at the raging fire still being fed by his followers. 'That fire symbolises the light of the New Religion shining out into the night of ignorance that still shrouds this land.'

Dichu laughed briefly. 'But let us hope that it is not a fire that will quickly burn itself out.'

Patrick smiled. 'It is a light that will burn forever,' he stated firmly.

'I think,' Dichu said slowly, 'it is a fire that will consume us all.'

*

The rattle of the chariots echoed out into the stillness of the dawn air and the horses' hooves struck sparks from the hard packed earth. The watchers on Slane Hill heard the company approaching before they saw them through the thin mist that rose from the soft ground.

Patrick sat by the roadside toying with a blade of grass. His rough woollen cloak was damp with dew and he was shivering with the chill, but his face was impassive as he watched the war chariots draw nearer. They stopped and fell into a box formation, with the king's ornate chariot in the centre. Armoured guards darted into the bushes, wary of an ambush. Only when they were sure that it was safe did Laoighre, Angras, the Arch-Druid and Ochru, a Druid, approach.

Patrick stood before the High King. Laoighre was almost a head taller than the Roman and broader, but even he could sense the power that radiated from the small man.

'You lit the fire?' Laoighre asked quietly, his breath pluming on the damp morning air.

'I did.' Patrick's accent sounded strange to the High King's ears, harsh and guttural, and with just a trace of the north in it.

'Why?'

'There were several reasons,' the small man said softly. 'It was a dark night and I sought to bring light into it. It is the season of my God and I wished to honour Him with a Paschal Fire.' He paused and added, 'And I was cold.'

Angras laughed. 'You are bold enough,' she said loudly. 'Tell me, what are you called and why do you flaunt the ancient laws of this land?'

The Arch-Druid frowned at the queen and snapped. 'Kill the blasphemer now!'

'I am called Patrick,' the Roman said, ignoring the Arch-Druid's outburst, 'and I have been sent to this land by Germanus of Auxerre to spread the Word of Christ.'

'I have heard of this Christ,' Laoighre said, 'there was one before you . . . ' he looked towards the Druid and raised his eyebrows.

'Palladius,' he snapped.

The High King nodded. 'Aye, Palladius, but he failed to convince me with his arguments about a God that promised nothing but peace.' He shook his head. 'No, it is not a man's religion.'

Patrick smiled. 'I am the son of a Roman, Calpornius; I am descended from a race of warriors that once conquered nearly half the known world. And yet even now, the followers of Christ grow and multiply amongst my own race.'

'But your empire is in decline,' Ochru the Druid said grimly. 'The Christian faith has weakened them.' His hand slipped under his robe and touched the hard cold metal of a sacrificial knife. Slowly his lean fingers curled about the carved hilt.

'My race declines because of its excesses,' Patrick said patiently. And then his dark eyes flashed in amusement. 'Tell me Druid, when was the last time you used that knife?' He laughed at Ochru's expression and added, 'There is a thin crack in the metal where the blade meets the hilt. One solid blow and it will surely crack.'

Laoighre's hand shot out and pulled the Druid's arm from beneath his cloak. The dagger gleamed bronze in the wan morning sunlight as the High King plucked it from the Druid's tingling fingers and held it close to his eyes. He nodded slowly and then dropped the knife point first onto the hard road. The blade cracked and snapped off just below the hilt.

'What do you want holy man?' Laoighre asked quietly, his eyes still on the shattered knife. He was a warrior who followed the old ways; he believed in omens and portents, and he knew with an icy certainty that the broken blade was such.

'I only want to talk to you,' Patrick said, brushing water droplets from his cloak . . .

Ochru cried aloud in rage and launched himself at the Roman, his fingers hooked into claws, reaching for the smaller man's eyes.

And then he stopped as if he had been struck.

A sudden gust of wind howled about the small group, plucking the Druid from his feet and hurling him backwards. The wind screamed and tore at him – but left everyone else untouched – sending him rolling across the ground. There was a sickening crack – and the Druid's skull shattered against a jagged lump of stone. The wind died as suddenly as it had arisen.

There was a long silence broken only by the murmurs of fear and wonder from the warriors about the chariots. The High King nudged the still body with his foot and looked across at Patrick. 'You will attend me in Tara on the morrow,' he said and turned away, but not before the holy man had seen the queen flash him a brilliant smile and the Arch-Druid shoot him a look of venom.

Dichu laid his hand on Patrick's arm and stopped him. The warrior's hard grey eyes narrowed as he stared towards a small copse of trees that stood just off the road.

'What is it?'

Dichu shook his head. 'I thought I ... Yes.' He bent his head and spoke quietly to the holy man. 'There is someone or something in those trees.'

'How do you know?'

The warrior glanced upwards and Patrick followed his eyes. A lone black bird was winging into the west.

'That's the second bird that landed and immediately took off again from those trees. Something must have startled it.'

Patrick ran his long slim hands through his greying hair. 'What do you suggest we do?'

'Pray?'

Conn parted the bushes and peered down the road at the small group standing there, apparently deep in conversation. He could recognise the holy man and the warrior, Patrick and Dichu standing out in front. He eased his sword from its sheath and stepped back into the shadow of a tree joining the score of warriors waiting in ambush.

The spot they had chosen for the ambush was less than an hour's march from Tara's walls. The road narrowed and wound down into a little valley and was surrounded on either side by trees and bushes, and the saint's company would have to march in single file to pass through.

The bushes rustled as the warriors moved closer to the road.

Patrick led his followers off the road and tersely explained Dichu's fears. He gathered the two score men and women into a small circle and bade them bend their heads and pray. The saint raised his hands over the group and called aloud for his God, and then he prayed silently for a long while.

He could feel the power gathering about him; he could feel the strength and conviction of his faith solidify and harden into a solid force. He gathered the force into his inner being – and cast it forth.

Conn ran his thumb along the edge of his sword nervously. The holy man and his followers had disappeared into the trees and had not reappeared. He looked around at his men, seeing his own nervousness mirrored in their drawn faces.

The trees suddenly parted and Conn squinted into the sunlight trying to make out the shape that had stepped out onto the road. But the sun was in his eyes blurring his vision. The shape moved and then another stood beside it and another . . .

And then he recognised the shapes. It was a herd of deer. Patrick and his followers must have startled them, driving them out of the shelter of the trees.

The deer ran past the trees where the warriors lay in ambush. They were sleek wild-eyed beasts and they galloped by as fleet as the wind and accompanied by a strange whispering breeze.

And Conn and his warriors remained in the trees awaiting the saint and his followers.

And later generations would call the prayer the saint had composed to protect them from the ambush the Breastplate of Saint Patrick.

The road into Tara was lined with silent waiting people. Already rumours of the small Roman's powers and deeds had begun to circulate and they were curious to see the man who had defied the laws and traditions of the land, the wrath of both the High King and the Arch-Druid and lit the fire that had blazed out over the land. Many shivered as he passed, for they felt the aura of power that emanated from the small dark man and others called upon their wild and savage gods to protect them from the holy man who was bringing demons back to Eriu.

As Patrick approached the main hall, he ordered his followers to remain outside and pray for his success. Dichu protested, but Patrick was adamant; he knew this would be the Arch-Druid's last chance to strike back and slay him, and he didn't want any of his friends killed on his behalf.

Maecadre, the Great Hall of Tara, was silent. The rows of princes and nobles stood in silent ranks, their robes of richly woven cloth and highly polished and decorated armour contrasting sharply with the stark simplicity of the Druid's white robes. All heads turned towards the door and the holy man was suddenly conscious of his travel-stained and dusty robes; he grinned in embarrassment and then smoothed his features into an unreadable mask.

As he entered the great hall an old man stepped out from the crowd and saluted him gravely.

'I am Dubhthach, Chief Poet of Eriu,' he said in a deep mellow voice, 'and I bid you welcome.'

'I thank you sir for your courtesy,' Patrick replied.

'And I too welcome you,' a younger man, also wearing a poet's robes, said quietly. 'I am Fiacca.'

Patrick bowed deeply to the young man, remembering

something Dichu had said; ' *... and the word of a poet or bard is feared by both king and commoner, and in many cases their word is law. If you can convert them ...* '

Patrick walked forward and stopped a little way from the long table at the top of the room before the huge open fire. He leaned upon his tall battered walking stick and bowed to the king. 'I have come,' he said simply.

'You are welcome here,' Laoighre said.

'He is not!' The voice was cold and rasping, filled with hate and malice. Lucetmale stepped from the ranks of the Druids dressed in his ceremonial robes of white and silver and carrying a short sickle of rank. 'He has transgressed and blasphemed one of our most ancient rituals, slain one of our company with his magic – and yet you welcome him here!' The Arch-Druid spat. 'Your father would denounce you.' He pointed at the holy man. 'Your father would have tossed his carcass to the carrion crows,' he sneered.

'Druid,' Laoighre said quietly, but with a note of ice in his voice, 'take care what you say now, for you will never have a chance to take back your hastily chosen words.'

But the Druid's rage had passed beyond all the bounds of caution. 'My words are not hasty, king. They have been carefully chosen. You have shamed your father before the assembly of the princes of Eriu; he would disown you, cast you out for not upholding the faith.'

A low angry murmur ran through the crowd and whilst some looked scornfully at the king, others glared at the Arch-Druid.

'Druid,' Patrick said in his strange accent, 'your argument is with me, do not try to strike at a king who is too honourable to strike back. Why do you fear me?' he asked suddenly.

Lucetmale laughed, and his laughter climbed dangerously close to hysteria. 'You do not frighten me,' he howled, 'you are nothing, less than nothing.'

The saint smiled enigmatically. 'Then why did you don your robes of office and carry in your symbol of authority if you did not feel threatened? Is it perhaps because you think

– or even know? – that my powers are greater than yours?'

The Druid's mouth opened and closed soundlessly and spittle frothed on his lips. 'Call upon your gods,' he snarled, 'let them protect you. But behold the power of the gods that are old beyond reckoning . . . '

His left hand traced a glowing arc in the air with the golden sickle and his voice deepened as he began to chant in the ancient tongue of the Druids. Over Tara the skies abruptly darkened and heavy storm clouds rolled in from the north. Icy winds carrying swirling flakes of snow and ice moaned through the draughty hall and outside Maecadre the terrified cries of the people rose above the howling wind.

And then it began to snow. Great silent flakes fell from the leaden clouds, quickly covering the spring fields beneath a thick mantle of white. Servants attempted to build up the roaring fire, but the wind that whipped through the chill hall extinguished the flickering flames and the princes and nobles shivered in the unseasonal cold.

Patrick tapped his walking stick on the stone flags, the sharp report catching the company's attention. 'It is a fine trick – but now remove it.'

Lucetmale laughed. 'There is no way it can be removed. It is a product of the Elementals; I can call them only once in every cycle, but they will return on the morrow.'

'What!' Angras snapped. 'Are you saying that having brought this snow and ice down upon us there is no way to remove it? The people freeze and the summer crops will be ruined.'

'It is doubtful whether the summer crops would have grown in any case since this holy man,' – he spat – 'disregarded the law and lit his fire before the Holy Flame.'

Patrick raised his walking stick and immediately the hall fell silent. His cold eyes bored into the Arch-Druid's and Lucetmale felt the fear that had seethed within him, since that first thin tendril of fire had risen into the night sky, begin to harden and solidify. And he knew then with a chilling certainty that there was no possible way he could defeat this small Roman.

'Your magic is useless – it is worse than useless for it brings nothing but ill. It is like your faith: you have forgotten the side of Light and Life, and only the Dark remains. Behold the Light of the New Religion!' Patrick slowly traced the symbol of the cross in the chill air with his long stick. The end of the stick began to glow with a gentle green light which left the image of the cross burning on the air. And suddenly a warm gust of wind blew in through the open window and almost as one the assembly moved to the windows and doors and stared out over the snow covered fields. The heavy storm clouds were visibly disappearing. The sun broke through and burned from a flawlessly blue sky, but the snow, instead of melting and flooding the fields, dried into tiny white flakes which the warm breeze scattered and carried out across the sea.

The Arch-Druid then called upon the Powers of Darkness to cover the land, and abysmal night covered Tara in a thick clinging blanket. And the Arch-Druid's laughter hung mockingly on the stinking air, for the Night had wafted from the very pits of Hell and was heavy with the fetor of the damned.

But the saint's wand cut through the night with a golden-green light, sending it howling back to its infernal pit.

Lucetmale then called upon swarms of flies and directed them towards Patrick, but they refused to land upon his person and settled back upon the Arch-Druid in a filthy shroud. He then sent glowing balls of fire floating towards Patrick, but he merely touched them with his wand and they dissolved into glittering motes of dust.

And finally the Arch-Druid threw his sickle onto the ground where it shifted and writhed and assumed the form of a huge crimson-and-gold serpent which slithered swiftly towards the holy man. But Patrick stooped and gently placed his stick on the cold stones where it assumed the form of a small brown skinned serpent – which overwhelmed and destroyed the larger crimson-and-gold snake.

In the silence that followed, Patrick bent and retrieved his stick and handed Lucetmale back his sickle. Tendrils still clung to the golden semi-circle and the Arch-Druid drew back his hand with a cry of pain as the power arced from the blade to his hand. The air in the hall was rank and bitter, metallic-tasting and blue fox-fire raced along the warrior's weapons and gathered in glowing balls in the darkened corners of the room.

Patrick dropped the sickle onto the floor at Lucetmale's feet and turned to the High King. 'Is this enough?' he asked wearily.

Laoighre nodded. 'It is enough. You have shown that your gods are greater than ours ... '

He paused as the saint shook his head. 'Not gods – but God, one God only.'

'But I thought there were three gods?' the king protested.

The holy man shook his head and reached inside his tunic. He pulled out a tiny sprig of shamrock and held up the weed. 'Look; see how the three parts grow from the one stem and yet form part of the greater leaf, the three coming from the one and the one being part of the three. It can be likened to the God of Peace: the Three Who are One, and the One that is All.'

The king raised his hand. 'You have convinced me Roman – but you will never convert me; I follow the path laid down for me by my father and his father before him. But you have my oath that you shall travel this land unmolested, preaching your New Religion in peace and dignity. Let us drink on it.'

The king and queen stood as slaves carried in tall goblets of gold filled with a pale white mead. Laoighre and Angras raised their cups to their lips and drank deeply, but Patrick paused with the rim of the goblet at his lips. He frowned and breathed in the heady fumes and then he carefully made the sign of the cross over the liquid. The mead foamed briefly and then the saint drank it ...

Lucetmale's scream of triumph turned to a howl of rage when Patrick remained standing. He snatched the vessel from his hands and stared into its half-empty bowl. He raised haunted eyes and stared at the saint. 'You should be dead,' he screamed.

'My God protects me,' Patrick said.

'And mine will protect me,' the Arch-Druid shouted and drained the goblet. He coughed as the fiery liquid burned its way down his throat and into his stomach . . . and continued burning. His throat, mouth and lips seared and blackened as the acid ate through them and he screamed in agony as the fluid ate through him. His lean body convulsed and writhed on the stones as the poison, meant for Patrick, destroyed him.

'Yours is a powerful god,' Angras said quietly.

'Mine is the only God!'

CHAPTER 5

BANSHEE

The scream cut through the brittle silence of the December night like a knife. It hung trembling on the sharp air, lost and desolate – the cry of a soul in the very depths of despair.

And those who heard it knelt and prayed for themselves and their families and made the Sign of the Cross above their doors and across their windows. For it was the wail of the banshee, the cry of death.

Maeve sat up suddenly. 'What was that?' she whispered. Her mother and brother raised their heads and listened. 'It's probably the wind coming in over the marsh,' Kieran said, and edged the candle closer to his book so that its light washed the pages in yellow.

A spark cracked in the fire and Maeve jumped, her heart pounding. Her mother smiled over her knitting, 'My, but you're jumpy tonight, dear,' she said quietly, the long needles clicking softly, her eyes never leaving her daughter's face.

'I thought I heard something,' Maeve said, shaking back her long red hair, now burnished copper in the firelight, 'a cry ... or a scream.'

The clicking of the needles stopped and Nora Slattery crossed herself quickly. 'Don't say such a thing child.'

'I heard nothing,' Kieran insisted, 'but it could have been the ice settling on the roof or a branch breaking beneath the weight of snow,' he said quickly, trying to calm the fear he saw in his mother's eyes.

He stood and stretched, the candle on the table lending

his lean face deep shadows and hollows, giving it an almost skull-like appearance. He flipped the book shut with his index finger and waved his hand across the candle extinguishing the flame. The corner of the two-roomed cottage plunged into darkness. 'Well, I'm for bed ... '

And then they heard it.

It was a scream, a wail of anguish that rose and fell like the howling of a moon-struck dog. It seemed to rise above human hearing, grating along bone and nerves, setting the teeth on edge. It struck raw nerves in the listeners, plumbing deep into their unconscious, drawing forth the primeval fear of the night, the dead and the undead, and the creatures that howled in the darkness.

'Banshee!' Nora Slattery moaned and fell to her knees on the hard earthen floor and began to pray, her thin lips moving silently. Maeve, who had risen to her feet, knelt beside her mother, the blood draining from her face, leaving her freckled cheeks ghastly in the wavering firelight.

The death-wail came again, only this time it was nearer, and there seemed to be an undertone of sobbing in the heart-broken cry. It faded and was lost on the wind.

Snow slid off the roof and thumped into the drifts piled up against the walls, making them jump, and the fire hissed as stray flakes found their way down the chimney.

'It's the banshee,' Nora whispered, 'she's calling someone this night; kneel Kieran and pray for their soul.' Her eyes, when she looked up at her son, were wide with fear and glistened with unshed tears.

'It's probably just a lost dog, Mother,' Kieran said gently, although he knew that no dog could make such a sound.

'Kieran, it's the banshee,' Nora insisted.

The cry drifted across the night again; Kieran turned his head trying to catch the direction of the sound. 'It's coming from the west, from the direction of the marshes,' he said. He knelt beside his mother and sister. 'It's just a farm animal caught in the marsh,' he reassured them, 'it's probably freezing to death or slowly drowning in the bog ... there is no such thing as a banshee, *a bean chaointe*, it's only a superstition.'

'You're better educated than I ever was,' Nora said quietly, 'but you've still a lot to learn. You won't find everything in your books, my boy.'

'Perhaps not,' he agreed, 'but there is still no such creature as a banshee, a fairy woman, a portent of death. Mother, we are almost into the twentieth century and banshees and leprechauns do not exist!'

'Your father saw a leprechaun once,' she said softly.

'Aye, in the end of a bottle, no doubt,' Kieran snapped, and instantly regretted it. He leaned across to his mother and patted her shoulder. 'I'll go outside and see what it is,' he sighed.

'No!' Nora Slattery turned and caught her son's arm in both of her frail hands. 'No, you mustn't go outside, you can't.'

He shook off her hands. 'Yes mother, I can!'

She saw the hard look come into his eyes, the same look his late father used to have when he returned home from a drinking bout and began to accuse her of some terrible things. There were times like this, times when she saw that look in her son's eyes, when she would grow cold and the old fear would begin to gnaw inside her.

Kieran pulled on an extra jumper and wound his scarf about his neck and then he took the shotgun down from above the fire. He broke it open, loaded both barrels and slipped a handful of additional rounds into his jacket pocket. He paused by the door. 'Lock this after me.' He smiled briefly and pulling back the bolt, jerked open the door and slipped out into the night. Maeve waited until she was sure that he wasn't about to return and then stood and crossed to the door and slammed the bolt home. Returning to her mother's side, she knelt and prayed.

Kieran swore as he floundered into yet another deep drift and cold wet snow drifted in over his boot-tops. He was going to catch a chill, he knew it, and then his mother would have the great pleasure of telling him, 'I told you so.'

He shook his hands and breathed on his fingers, trying to restore feeling to them. If, by any chance, he had to use the shotgun, he doubted he would be able to feel the trigger never mind pull it.

He stood beside the listing gate and looked around. Behind him, almost completely obliterated in white was the cottage with the long snaking line of footprints sunk deep in the snow leading away from it. To the left lay the flat expanse of the marsh, the murk now covered beneath a mantle of white. Before him, standing barren and leafless was a little copse of trees, the bare branches stark and skeletal against the ground.

Kieran stiffened suddenly. Something had moved through the trees. Something white – whiter than the snow, if that was possible, and he had only seen the movement because it had passed before the black branches. He brought the shotgun up and across his chest, wincing as the cold metal burned his fingers, and closed the breech with a click that echoed in the absolute silence. He thumbed back the hammers and slowly crunched his way towards the trees. Something flickered at the corner of his vision and he spun, bringing the shotgun up to his shoulder – but there was nothing there.

He almost laughed aloud when he realised he was shaking – and not from the cold either. He shook his head; here he was, jumping at shadows. There was nothing out this night – and no-one but an *amadán*, and that included himself, would be crazy enough to go wandering the fields on a bitter December night with a loaded shotgun looking for banshees! He moved closer to the trees, and then almost shouted as a white mass moved before him ... and then he laughed aloud: it was only snow falling from heavily laden branches.

He was turning back when he heard the cry. And although he was cold, the sound chilled him to the marrow. It hung almost tangibly on the night air, as fragile as glass – and as sharp. The young man stood knee-deep in the cold wet snow torn between turning back to the cottage, with its warmth and human companionship or pursuing the cry which promised nothing but loneliness and despair.

He followed the cry.

It led him to the edge of the marshes and taunted him from its depths. He knew that to attempt to cross the frozen wasteland was suicidal. Even in the height of summer he would only cross the shifting marshes in broad daylight – and only then with a very good reason.

Kieran stood on the lip of the slight depression that led downwards into the marshland and tried to identify the sound. He stood, oblivious to the cold, his head cocked to one side, listening.

It was the voice of a young woman or child; but then surely a child's voice would be shriller, and that voice seemed to hold a wealth of maturity in it: it was the voice of a young woman. And then, was it a cry of despair or anger, pain or fear? He listened again as the wailing drifted out from the marsh: it was a cry of absolute despair and sorrow. He squinted out across the marsh; did something move there or did his eyes deceive him? With this white lunar landscape it was hard to say, but he thought he had seen something – was it grey or white? – drift through the low snow-covered bushes. He was almost tempted to set out across the marsh in search of the sound. It was strange, but he felt as if he should know what cried out in such despair. He should know! He ground the butt of the shotgun into the rock-hard earth in frustration – and then he suddenly realised that it was loaded and the barrels were pointing at his head! He laughed self-consciously and, trying to ignore the hammering of his heart and the icy sweat that chilled on his brow, broke open the gun and pulled the cartridges out with numb fingers. With a last lingering look out across the frozen waste, he turned back and set out for home.

'The banshee cries for certain families,' Nora Slattery said to her daughter.

'But will it cry again tonight?' Maeve asked.

'I don't know,' Nora said, 'it usually haunts a certain family or clan until a death occurs. But whether it forewarns a death or brings death is something we will never know.'

'What are they like Mother?' Kieran asked, turning from his book.

Nora shrugged. 'No-one knows. Very few people have actually seen them and lived. Oh, legend says that they are sometimes old hags, lost souls condemned to wander between this life and the next as heralds of death. And then again, they are sometimes said to be beautiful, for banshee means *bean-sidhe*, a fairy woman, and fairy women are supposed to be either very ugly or frighteningly beautiful.' The old woman shook her head slowly and added a sod of turf to the fire. 'But they are only supposed to follow either families of the "O's" or "Mac's", or else families that have distinguished themselves in Ireland's history, and they rarely come to ordinary folk – unless there is a terrible death in store for them ... She turned to her son. 'And was it the wind you heard last night?' she asked, her voice heavy with sarcasm, 'or are you now prepared to accept our superstitious beliefs?'

Kieran shook his head. 'Oh, well it certainly wasn't the wind, but it wasn't a banshee either. I still think it was an animal trapped in the marsh.'

'You'll catch your death,' his mother said sharply, 'wandering about at that hour.'

'Aye, perhaps,' Kieran said, and then he raised his hand. 'Listen ... !'

The cry was closer now, closer and sharper. It was the sound of a young woman sobbing and then wailing aloud, her keening rising and falling in something akin to a melody.

Nora screamed and fell to her knees, pulling her rosary from her apron pocket; Maeve fell to her knees beside her mother and prayed also, tears springing to her eyes – although she could not have said why. But Kieran, moving like one possessed, shrugged on his worn coat and wound his woollen scarf about his neck. He slipped his thin hands into a worn pair of gloves, tucked the shotgun under his arm and went out into the night.

And the chill blast that whipped in through the open door was like the wind from the grave.

Kieran followed the ebb and flow of sound across the fields out towards the marsh. Tonight he would trace that cry to its source – even if he had to cross the marsh to do so. The metal of the shotgun felt warm in his gloved hands, the metal so cold that it burned, but he welcomed the throbbing pain, for it helped to blow away the cobwebs that had smothered his brain all day, making him dull and stupid.

He found himself crying, and his tears were for the woman who was weeping; he cried for her anguish. If only he could share the pain, if only he could understand it, then perhaps he could help, perhaps he could ease her pain. If ... if ... if ...

She was waiting for him by the low wall which bounded the fields from the road. A young woman, her grey garments covered in snow, ice glittering in her hair and eyes. She was terrifyingly beautiful. Her face was small and oval, her eyes huge and slightly slanted and her lips were peeled back from unnaturally long teeth. She raised her arm and beckoned to him. Kieran stopped, confused, shaking his head. Slowly, very slowly, he raised the shotgun and sighted along the length of the barrels, but the pain, the terrible pain and loss in the young woman's eyes stopped him, and he felt his own tears freeze on his face. He let the gun fall into the snow and slowly approached her.

He felt the warmth as he approached. A gradual warmth that spread upwards from his feet and engulfed him in its heat. He was warm, so warm. His fingers were slick with sweat as they fumbled with his glove and pulled the scarf from about his throat. The woman opened both arms and her eyes blazed with sudden fire ... and the heat was all about him, engulfing him, unbearable, unendurable. He closed his eyes, feeling it sear his face, burn into his outstretched hands, strip the skin from his bones, eat into his brain, burning ... burning ... burning ...

*

Sergeant Lochran touched the brim of his helmet in salute and spoke quietly to the hollow-eyed woman. 'The doctor said he must have fallen and perhaps struck his head and lain there unconscious. He was very badly frost-bitten ... the cold, the cold took him, ma'am.'

The old woman turned her glassy stare on the uncomfortable policeman. 'No,' she whispered in a thin thread of a voice, 'it wasn't the cold and frostbite that took my Kieran. Not the cold.' And then her voice rose to a shriek. 'The banshee took him! The banshee!'

The sergeant shook his head and turned away. Aye, he had heard the rumours, and he had heard the strange wailing in the night, but banshees indeed! Wasn't it curious though the way young Slattery's skin had been stripped from him in great charred lumps? Almost as if he had been burned.

Almost.

CHAPTER 6

CREATURES OF THE WERE: THE WOLVES

Andrew Connelly groaned wearily as he sank up to his ankle in thick marsh water. He pulled his foot free and attempted to shake off the clinging mud. The old man swore as he glanced up at the darkening skies: it was almost sunset and he was still no nearer to finding those damned cows than he had been earlier that morning. He leaned on his stick and attempted to catch his breath; he was no longer as young as he used to be and he was too old to go tramping the hills and marshes.

And by God, he could use a drink!

He straightened his thin frame and pressed the calloused palms of his hands to his aching back, groaning aloud as the muscles protested. His sharp grey eyes squinted towards the sinking sun, gauging its distance to the horizon: he had at most an hour or so of daylight left. He shrugged; well there was little he could do, he would look beyond the next hill – and then those blasted animals could go hang!

The sun was close to the horizon by the time Andrew crested the low hill. He was breathing heavily and his heart was pounding in his chest. He drew a soiled handkerchief from his pocket and wiped the beads of cold sweat that had gathered on his lined forehead. He shivered as a cold gust of wind blew in off the Atlantic, bringing with it the fresh promise of rain.

Andrew shaded his eyes from the sun's crimson light and stared down into the valley below him. Dusk had already gathered in the hollow and only the very tips of the trees were still touched with light. He shook his head and squeezed his eyes shut: there were tiny red and yellow spots swimming lazily behind his closed eyelids, a sure sign that he had already overtaxed himself and further exertion might bring on an attack.

The old man suddenly breathed deeply, turning his head to catch an elusive odour that had drifted past. He breathed in again and this time he was sure: he could smell smoke on the twilight air. He squinted down into the valley, his sharp eyes seeking any sign of human habitation – but there was nothing ... well, almost nothing. There was a low weed-covered mound beneath a small stand of trees which might once have been a cottage, but now? He blinked: a thin white wisp of smoke climbed upwards, winding through the branches until it reached the red and gold touched tips of the trees and was shredded by the wind.

He prodded the slope with his stick and began the slow and laborious walk down into the hollow.

And behind him the tall grasses parted and cold, black eyes regarded him hungrily.

Andrew had almost reached the cottage – he could see that it was a cottage now, although it was almost lost beneath a covering of weeds and earth, making it seem as if it had been built into the ground or grown from the soil – when a door opened. An old, old man stood in the opening beckoning to him.

Andrew stopped suddenly, his heart beginning to pound painfully again. 'Good evening to you,' he called from where he stood.

The old man nodded pleasantly and spoke in a surprisingly strong and vibrant voice. 'A good even to you. Are you lost?' He spoke slowly, carefully and his voice was almost accentless. 'We can offer you a little food if you hunger and something to assuage your thirst.'

Andrew shivered – there was something about the old man that chilled him to the marrow, but he did seem pleasant and the very thought of food had set his stomach rumbling and his mouth felt dry and gritty. He nodded and approached the old man slowly, his joints beginning to stiffen now. 'I'll thank you kindly for that,' he said carefully, 'I've wandered most of the day in search of a pair of cows that didn't come in for milking this morning and I'm fair exhausted.'

The old man nodded sympathetically. 'You look tired,' he said and then held out his hand. 'James Squire.'

Andrew introduced himself and took the proffered hand and felt it hold his in a surprisingly strong grip for so frail a man. Squire stood nearly a head taller than Andrew – who wasn't small by any means – and he was as thin as a lath. The flesh clung to his body, outlining the muscles and bones beneath, and his head was almost skull-like in appearance with large dark eyes sunk deep into the flesh. His mouth was a thin lipless slit and when he smiled he revealed abnormally long yellowed teeth. His hair was nearly gone and clung in mangy tufts to his scabrous scalp.

He stood aside and allowed Andrew to enter before him, and as the door closed, cutting out the last remnants of the dying sun, the vague stirrings of unease he had previously felt congealed into a hard knot of fear that nestled in the pit of his stomach and gathered behind his throat.

'My wife Morgaine.' James Squire introduced the haggard old woman with skin like ancient parchment, dead and dry, her face a mask out of which her eyes sparkled intently. She pointed a long bony finger at Andrew. 'Who is this?' Her voice was like cracked leather.

'He is a traveller,' her husband said slowly, as if speaking to a child or simpleton. 'He is lost and he hungers. Bring him food and drink.' There was an unmistakable note of command in his voice. He indicated a place by the small fire, suggesting that Andrew should warm himself, for it was growing chill and the hovel was damp and cold and the streaked walls ran with moisture.

Andrew sat by the fire, feeling the heat soak into his face and outstretched hands. He looked about curiously; the large main room of the cottage was filthy, with piles of wood and straw gathered in the darkened corners. Rank water pooled on the hard-packed earthen floor which was rutted and scored. Andrew wrinkled his nose in disgust: the room stank and he wondered if they slept with their animals under the same roof.

Squire returned with a dusty bottle and two chipped cups. He handed Andrew one of the cups filled with an almost clear liquid. He breathed in the fumes, his eyes watering as they stung. He caught the old man looking at him, smiled and swallowed the liquid in one go. He knew what it was even as it burned its way down his throat and enflamed his stomach: poteen. Properly made, it was one of the most potent liquors known to man, but if it had spoiled in any way ... He shuddered and wiped his hand across his streaming eyes.

James Squire smiled, his long yellow teeth glistening wetly in the firelight. 'Brewed it myself,' he said quietly.

Andrew nodded dumbly, finding his throat and mouth still numb from the effects of the poteen. He could feel it in the pit of his stomach, spreading its warmth through his system.

'I dare say you have never tasted anything like it,' Squire said proudly.

Andrew nodded and coughed and when he spoke his voice was barely above a whisper. 'There's no denying that.'

'We will eat soon,' his host said – and then he paused, his head cocked to one side, listening.

'What is it?' Andrew asked, but the old man waved him to silence.

And then he heard it: a low soul-destroying howling that echoed down from the hills. It came again and again, coming nearer, growing in intensity. 'What is it?' he whispered. It sounded like the baying of dogs ... it sounded like the crying of the damned ... it sounded like the howling of wolves – but that of course, was impossible.

'It is the wolves,' Squire said slowly. He carefully refilled Andrew's cup and then went and stood by the door, his hand upon the latch. Connelly watched in growing alarm; just what had he got himself into? Squire was joined by his hideous wife and together they waited on either side of the door, a strange smile playing about their lips, their eyes glassy.

He almost screamed aloud when something scratched at the door. He rose, about to beg Squire not to open the door, when Morgaine turned and looked at him, her teeth bared ... and the look in her eyes chilled him to the marrow: for they were filled with a terrible hunger.

Squire opened the door and a huge grey wolf loped in. It stood almost waist high to the old man and the muscles in its back and calves rippled smoothly beneath its silken fur. It turned its huge head and regarded Andrew through yellow eyes and its cavernous mouth opened, exposing long, glistening yellow teeth.

Andrew felt his heart beginning to pound forcefully and his breath shorten, beginning to come now in harsh gasps. He moved away from the creature, towards the fire, seeking a weapon, anything to use against the wolf. He had left his walking stick down beside his chair, if he could reach that...

And then the creature growled deep in its throat and the sound froze him in his tracks.

The grey wolf raised its head and howled and somewhere outside an answering cry drifted down across the valley. The grey wolf padded across the room, making no sound on the earthen floor, pushed open the door to the cottage's only other room and disappeared inside.

Andrew stooped as his foot touched the heavy walking stick and his questing fingers brushed the smooth wood. He clutched it in both hands, holding it across his chest and was about to move towards the door and if necessary, strike both Squire and his wife and flee, when another wolf stood in the doorway.

The beast was, if anything, even bigger than the first, a great black-maned wolf who regarded Andrew balefully for what seemed like an eternity before turning and disappearing into the other room.

Andrew gasped as an agonising pain shot through his chest and down into his arm. He could feel his heart pounding strongly as if seeking to burst through his chest. His breathing was shallow and harsh; black spots danced before his eyes in intricate patterns before finally coming together in a solid black tide that rose up and overwhelmed him ...

The face was that of a young man ... or a woman ... or both. Andrew Connelly groaned and opened his eyes fully, attempting to focus on the face – or faces? – looming above him. A strong hand held his shoulders and lifted him forward whilst the chipped cup which he had drunk from earlier was pressed to his lips. He moaned and pulled his head away, but someone spoke softly and insistently to him, 'Drink, it is but water.'

The liquid was ice cold and tart and the shock of it made him gasp. He sat up carefully. He was lying on the ground where he had fallen – had he fallen or had Squire caught and held him as he fell? He seemed to recall ...

There was a folded cloth beneath his head and a filthy rug had been thrown over his legs. Squire and his wife hovered in the background speaking in low tones, as if angrily debating a point. And beside Andrew knelt a young man and woman. He had to blink and look again when he saw them, for they were almost identical in every respect, except that the man – although he could not have been above one-and-twenty years – was totally grey and his twin sister was raven. Their eyes were huge and seemingly bottomless, but they regarded him kindly, and the only feature that marred their looks were their overlong teeth.

The young man helped Andrew to his feet. 'You are somewhat recovered?' he asked, his voice totally accentless and with the same slow deliberation of his father. Connelly nodded dumbly. He looked from the boy to the girl and then over to the door leading to the other room. The wolves ... where were the wolves? And then he suddenly realised the significance of the boy's grey hair and the girl's night-black tresses.

The girl touched his arm and he flinched and pulled away. 'You have no need to fear us,' she said quietly.

The boy nodded to his sister and they both moved away

from the terrified man. 'You must try and remain calm,' he said quietly, 'lest you bring on another attack.'

Andrew nodded and attempted to regulate his ragged breathing and calm the pounding of his heart. Another attack would kill him.

'Who are you?' he asked, his voice surprisingly calm.

'I am Morgan,' said the young man, 'and this is my sister Morgaine.'

'And the wolves?' Connelly asked quietly.

'We are the wolves.'

Andrew nodded slowly, accepting it as one would accept a dream. He felt light-headed and dizzy and the twins' faces floated in and out of focus with every breath he took.

'We know you,' Morgan said slowly, his voice echoing within Andrew's pounding skull.

'We have met before,' Morgaine said, her eyes looming huge before his befogged vision.

Andrew shook his head, the effort almost exhausting him. 'No ... ' he whispered.

'Yes,' she persisted, 'many years ago ... '

'Do you recall aiding a young dog trapped in a bog ... ?' Morgan asked, his voice and sallow face beginning to fragment into wispy tendrils that scattered like wind-blown smoke.

And Andrew remembered.

It had been late summer with the day darkling towards twilight. The quiet of the evening had been shattered by the piteous howling of a dog and Andrew, returning home from the market, had cut across the fields towards the sound. He had found the animal sinking in an area of marshy ground, but strangely enough, it was not the trapped animal that was howling but another standing at the edge of the bog. Andrew had approached the dogs cautiously. They were a strange breed: large-boned, small headed, one grey, one black. He leaned in over the marsh and hauled the grey dog out by the scruff of its neck. It neither whimpered nor snapped and the black animal had stood silently by whilst he had freed her companion. And before they had run off the black bitch had licked his hand fleetingly.

'I remember,' he said slowly.

'And now we would repay that service,' Morgaine said.

'There is nothing . . . ' he whispered.

'You have lost your animals – two cows, nearly a quarter of your herd.'

'We will return them,' her brother added.

'I do not need . . . ' he began.

'You need rest,' Squire said. 'Rest.'

Andrew Connelly awoke with the sun on his face. He sat up with a start and then sneezed as wisps of straw fell out of his hair. He realised with a jolt that he was lying in his own barn.

He found the cows waiting outside the wooden shed, standing patiently in the damp morning air. They were not his own animals – in fact, they were like nothing he had ever seen before: they were large-bodied, long-horned cows, but with tiny eyes. And as he found out later that day, their milk yield was phenomenal. Andrew guessed that they were a gift from the werewolves and always ensured that a little offering of food was left on the window-ledge every evening. It was always gone by morning, but he never attempted to watch the takers. And strangely enough, when his neighbours were troubled with foxes and hares later on that year, Andrew's livestock was unscathed.

When he died two years later, the cows disappeared and for many weeks after his death the local people heard the mournful howling of dogs coming from the direction of the graveyard.

CHAPTER 7

CREATURES OF THE WERE: THE HARE

Cathal shivered in the chill pre-dawn air, his breath pluming whitely before his face. He stamped his feet on the hard ground and attempted to restore circulation to his numbed toes, but with little success. He had been standing up against a newly made haystack for most of the night and now he was cold – bitterly cold – angry and just a little bit frightened.

The young man glanced up at the heavens, where a full moon was still riding high even though the sky to the east was paling towards dawn. The stars still glittered as sharply as before, but now they seemed a little more distant and somehow smaller as if the dawn and the coming sunlight shrivelled them into tiny specks. He had watched them wheel across the heavens through the night and he felt a curious sense of loss as they disappeared one by one, taking the magic of the night with them.

He blinked, abruptly realising that it was possible to dream standing up and apparently wide awake, and shook his head; he had nodded off. A tiny sound – loud in the twilight silence – caught his attention and he shifted his grip on the heavy shotgun, his numb fingers curling about the trigger, his thumb resting on the hammers. He pressed in closer to the damp straw and parted a tuft, peering out across the field now glittering with frost. He could see his few cows standing huddled together in the far corner of the field beneath the bare branches of an old chestnut. One moved, her smooth hide scraping against the worn bark of the tree with the dry rasping sound that had alerted him. Cathal slowly released his breath and eased back the hammers on the heavy gun; there was no-one coming to steal his milk – yet! But this morning, he told himself grimly, he would get them, and then ... he patted the shotgun's polished stock.

He had first realised that someone was stealing his milk almost two weeks ago when, for no apparent reason, his cows began to go dry. His father had examined the cattle and pronounced them sound and his bride's father – eager to assist his new son-in-law – had travelled the fourteen miles down from Clonmel to see the animals and he was also of the opinion that they were healthy beasts.

But they continued to give no milk.

When Cathal took them in and kept them in the sheds overnight they gave milk first thing in the morning, but if they were left out in the fields, they were dry.

The evidence was unmistakable: someone was milking the cows in the mornings before Cathal.

Cathal started awake. The sky had brightened perceptibly in the east; it would soon be time for him to milk the animals. A disturbance rippled through the cows and they slowly ambled out from under the shade of the tree – all except one which remained, stifflegged, wide-eyed and shivering slightly. Cathal squinted into the twilight; he could see no-one near the beast, there was noth ... A flicker of movement about the cow's udder caught his attention. There was something there!

Bending almost double, he darted across the field and began to creep along the side of the rough stone wall that separated his land from the road. As he neared the animal, he could hear sucking and lapping sounds, much as a babe makes at its mother's breast. He dropped flat in the high grass that bordered the wall and – ignoring the icy dampness that soaked through his already sodden clothes – began to worm his way towards the cow.

And then he saw it.

It was a hare. A large grey hare sitting beneath the cow on its hind legs and pulling at the milk-swollen teat. Thick yellow milk dribbled from the hare's tiny mouth and ran down its matted chest, pooling at its broad feet. Cathal eased the shotgun forward along the ground and sighted the creature in the centre of both barrels, and then he waited. If he fired now he would disembowel the cow. And so he waited, grinding his teeth in frustration, while the hare drank the animal dry. Several times he was on the verge of pulling the trigger, but the thought of the cost of the cow made him stop and think again.

Then the hare, with an almost human sigh of contentment, hopped away from the empty cow. It paused in the centre of the field and began to groom the droplets of milk from its fur. Cathal fired. The heavy shotgun roared and the blast tore up a sod of earth just in front of the creature. It squealed with fright, leapt straight up into the air, and then it was off, bounding towards the gate. Cathal fired again and the pellets tore into the wooden gate, shattering the bottom bar. The hare twisted and fell heavily, but then it was up and out of the gate. Cathal swore, broke open the gun and, leaving the smouldering cartridges on the hard earth, he reloaded with almost numb fingers. He raced across the field and vaulted the gate, but the hare was gone. Swearing, he bent and examined the damage to the gate, and it was then he saw the blood: tiny reddish-brown spots that clung tackily to his fingertips. He grinned, his teeth a dull grey in the wan morning light and set off down the road following the spoor.

The tracks kept to the edge of the road, leading down into the village and this was strange, for usually these shy creatures avoided the places of man. But the quickly drying blood led down the main street, up past the church and down a lane. The young man grew alarmed – he knew this lane, knew it well. And he knew – somehow he knew – where the tracks would end. His heart was hammering wildly as he stopped before a low whitewashed door. He knocked hesitantly, but received no answer. He knocked again and then pushed the door open with the barrel of the gun.

She was sitting before a low fire, dressed only in her shift, washing blood from a shallow wound along the inside of her leg. She didn't even turn as she heard the door open, but said quietly: 'Come over here, Cathal and look what you've done to me.'

'Why, Aine,' he asked coldly, 'why?'

'Because you went and married that little slut,' she snapped. 'You loved me – you told me you did.'

'That was a long time ago,' the young man said gently.

'You remind me of my late husband,' she said, wincing as she pressed grit from the wound, 'he had a short memory also.'

'Aine,' he said slowly, 'surely you never imagined ... ?'

She turned and looked at him, her large grey eyes hard and accusing. 'What was I supposed to believe? I had just lost my husband, I needed comfort and you were there when I needed you. I never forced you to visit me; I know they may call me a witch in the village, but you came to me of your own free will. And you used me,' she said, her voice cold and deadly.

He leaned over and touched the hare's shrivelled foot hanging on a leather thong about her neck. 'What is this?'

'It is a good luck charm.' Her eyes challenged his, almost daring him to question her further.

'Do you deny that you have taken the form of a hare and suckled my cows dry?' he asked, his temper rising.

Aine's grey eyes flashed in amusement. 'Oh no, I'll not deny it. But no matter what these townspeople think of me, I think they will find that a little too hard to swallow – and just try proving it!' She stood, and the slanting rays of the morning sun touched her thin shift with blinding light, moulding the shadows to the contours of her body. 'And don't think I'll stop, Cathal Mac Thomas; I'll continue until I have ruined you, left you a broken man.' She smiled, a hard cruel smile that only touched her lips.

'I'll spread the word about the town . . . ' he blustered.

'And you'll be laughed at,' she said silkily. 'The people here no longer cling to the old beliefs. There is nothing you can do.' She turned away and bent to the fire, ignoring him.

Cathal brought the shotgun up slowly and, holding it at waist level, pulled back both hammers. Aine spun round at the sharp sound and something like fear flashed through her eyes. And then she laughed. 'You don't have the courage to do it . . . '

'But it's all I can do,' Cathal whispered. 'It's the only thing I can do.'

The noise of the shotgun blasts was incredible within the confines of the room, but the walls were thick and the cottage was situated a little apart from the other dwellings. There was no-one waiting for him when he left the bloody room, there were no shouts or cries and the only sound on the early morning air was the gentle twittering of a solitary bird.

Some time later on that morning, his wife asked him whether or not he had discovered who was draining their cows and he replied with a curiously glassy smile, 'Only a hare my love, only a hare.'

CHAPTER 8

THE FAIRY MIDWIFE

The child was early. The first spasms struck Roisin suddenly, the abrupt pain doubling her up. She gasped in shock and surprise; the child wasn't due for another three weeks. The young woman staggered as another contraction rippled through her, sending her reeling back against the heavy wooden table. Crockery slid across its polished surface and shattered on the hard earthen floor . . . but the noise was lost as the storm, which had threatened since early afternoon, broke overhead.

A long flash of lightning turned the twilight into noon and thunder rumbled down the valley almost immediately afterwards. The heavens opened, the rain sluicing down in an unbroken sheet. Roisin pushed away from the table as water began to pour in through the open window and sweep across the floor. A sudden gust of wind threw open the door, smashing it back against the stone wall, chips of wood stinging her face and hands. The young woman whimpered with fear as the door tore itself loose from her grasp, slammed back into its frame and tore loose from one of its hinges.

Roisin convulsed as a series of short contractions tore through her, leaving her pain-racked and gasping. She felt real fear then; fear not only for herself, but for the child also. If she were to give birth now, without any preparations or help and alone, then she would surely die.

Lightning flared again, a long jagged streak that came to earth in one of the lower fields, striking an already much charred oak.

Roisin straightened painfully and attempted to push the

window closed. Gusts of chill wind buffeted the glass and an icy rain, laced with chips of hail, hissed and rattled against the side of the cottage. The window flapped in the wind, struck the wall once and then shattered, sending jagged splinters of glass flying in all directions, lodging in her hair, burning her face and forehead. The rain and hail whipped in through the broken glass, soaking her blouse and skirt. She shivered with the cold and then screamed aloud as the pain lanced through her distended stomach. She fell to her hands and knees and hung her head in agony, her gorge rising. Blood dripped from her torn face, spattering on the cold, damp floor. She concentrated on breathing evenly, steadily, trying to calm her pounding heart. Thunder boomed overhead, making the very walls of the cottage vibrate, sending the dresser crashing to the floor, and her last thoughts before she slid into unconsciousness were of her husband, Mark, and their unborn child ...

Mark Farrell shivered beneath the spreading branches of a tree watching the pounding rain turn the already soft autumnal fields into quagmires. Lightning flared nearby, making him start with fright. He knew it was dangerous to stand beneath the tree, but he had no choice, he had been trapped beneath it when the storm had broken. And he had to be home: his wife was into her ninth month and he feared that the storm would frighten her.

Thunder rumbled in off the hills; he could feel it trembling on the air, coming up through the soles of his feet. Lightning cracked and the air was abruptly rank with the metallic taste of ozone. He watched a thin tendril of smoke thread its way skywards beyond the hill and guessed that the ancient shell of the oak tree had been struck once again.

Suddenly, every hair on his head rose and his bare arms itched and crackled. The odour and taste of ozone was strong now and he could feel the pressure building. He looked up into the tree ... and the lightning whoomped in blinding incandescence! The lightning bolt struck the tree directly, charring its dark weathered wood to blackened cinders. The hammerblow struck Mark in the chest, throwing him away from the tree, sending him tumbling into the muck where he lay barely breathing, wisps of smoke rising from his charred and smouldering clothes.

Roisin awoke with a start, staring up at the smoke-blackened rafters in confusion, tiny spots of colour dancing before her eyes. She was cold, and her nightmare had left her covered in an icy perspiration. The last vestiges of that nightmare now drifted into the shadows of her mind leaving only fragmented images in their wake: the storm, the lightning painting the room in harsh white light, slivers of sparkling glass flying into her face; the face.

The face!

A long thin, high-boned face, stark white against the night-blackness of her long hair. The face of a young woman who had stared at Roisin through slitted grey-green eyes . . .

She closed her eyes and shook her head, attempting to dismiss the images, but when she opened her eyes the face – the face in her dream – swam back into her sight. The thin lips smiled, pulling back over a row of gleaming white teeth.

'Aaah, you are awake?'

Roisin sat bolt upright, the sudden effort making her head swim. It was no dream. But . . . she was in her own bed, dressed in her best white cotton chemise, her skin freshly washed and tingling, her hair unbound and brushed. There was a peculiar odour in the room; the metallic harshness of blood mingled with the damp freshness of hot water and . . . there was another odour, a scent of wild herbs and raw earth.

And then she realised: she was no longer heavy with her child!

The stranger leaned over and placed a cloth-wrapped bundle in Roisin's arms. The child screamed, its tiny face blotchy, screwed up in anger and fear. The young mother brushed away a tendril of blonde hair and kissed her child's forehead. Tears stung her eyes as she looked up at the stranger. 'Thank you,' she whispered.

The stranger smiled coldly. 'Do not thank me yet,' she said, in a curiously flat and exotic accent.

'Who are you?' Roisin asked.

The hard-eyed young woman smoothed the blankets and turned away. Her voice was hard and contemptuous. 'I am Maresch.'

'But, thank you – you have saved my life and the life of my child.' She looked up from the screaming babe. 'Are you a midwife?'

Maresch glanced over her shoulder at Roisin. 'I have had some experience,' she snapped.

The young woman was a little put off by Maresch's surly attitude, but persisted. 'Have you any children yourself?' she asked quietly.

The stranger rounded on her with blazing eyes. She stared through the young mother for long minutes before turning away and when she spoke her voice was cold and distant. 'No, I have no children.' She turned back to the fire and began to add more turf. The wet sods hissed and gave off a rank smoke which drifted about the room in a gritty haze. Roisin felt her eyes watering and she covered her child's eyes with a corner of the blanket. 'Could you open the door please?' she asked. 'It's very hot and the smoke ...'

The young woman turned and stared at her. In the dimness only her eyes were visible and they blazed with an unearthly emerald fire. 'The window has shattered and the door is still open ...' her voice was sharp, cutting through the haze of exhaustion which had suddenly claimed Roisin. She wiped the palm of her hand across her watering eyes and looked towards the door. It was indeed open, hanging crookedly to one side, but strangely, the smoke and fumes seemed to stay in the room and did not stream out into the evening air.

Maresch stepped closer to the young woman. She looked down at the small bundle clutched to Roisin's breast and held out her hand, the long thin nails catching the firelight and running red. 'Give me the child,' she said. 'It hungers, it needs feeding.'

Roisin shook her head slowly. 'No,' she whispered, 'I can feed the babe myself.' She raised her hand slowly, painfully, and attempted to undo the tiny buttons down the front of her chemise. Sweat beaded her brow and her arms trembled with the effort. Her fingers seemed thick and numb and she struggled futilely with the buttons. The haze in the room thickened before her eyes, biting at her throat, coating her mouth and lips with grit. She attempted to swallow, but found that her throat wouldn't work. 'Water,' she whispered.

Maresch leaned over the bed and stared down into her wide eyes. 'The babe; give me the babe. You must give me the babe of your own free will,' she insisted.

'Water,' Roisin begged, 'give me some water.'

'The babe,' the young woman hissed coldly, 'I will feed your child.' She pointed a crimson-tipped nail in the child's face. 'Like you, it thirsts.'

Roisin nodded, a barely perceptible movement of her head and tried to lift the small bundle in her arms. Maresch leaned over and snatched the child from its mother. Her eyes blazed and her smile was triumphant. She held the babe aloft, as if in offering, and then she lowered it and unpinned the neck of her curious dress. A flap of cloth fell away, exposing her smooth flawless breast. She pressed the child to it, stroking its cheek to make it open its mouth . . . and the last sounds Roisin heard before she drifted off into unconsciousness were of her child eagerly pulling on the stranger's breast.

When Mark staggered in some hours later he found the cottage a shambles. A window gone, the door half-torn from its hinges, the dresser lying broken on the hard floor beside piles of shattered crockery. Water pooled along the floor and the air was thick and heavy with turf smoke. Strangely enough, his wife was lying in their bed, sleeping peacefully in the gown she had worn on their wedding night. But what terrified Mark was the fact that she was no longer pregnant and there was no sign of the child.

*

The old woman sat in front of the fire sipping raw poteen from a cracked cup and watching the young couple sitting across from her. The only light in the cottage came from the fire and the flames only highlighted their feverish eyes and deepened the shadows in the hollows under their eyes. The old woman shivered as the chill night wind whipped in through the boarded-up window and rattled the crooked door in its frame.

Mark shivered as the cold air traced the length of his backbone and he could feel Roisin trembling beside him. He leaned over and patted her hand, trying to calm her fears as best he could, but knowing that the loss he could see in her eyes was mirrored in his face. He reached for the bottle and handed it to the old woman.

'Nano Hayes,' he said shakily, 'you are our last hope.'

The wise woman smiled, her lined face dissolving into a mass of wrinkles in which her hard eyes glittered like stones. 'Ah sure, you have nothing to worry about,' she said, her voice surprisingly mild and youthful for such an old woman.

'But can you get our child back?' Roisin asked quietly.

Nano Hayes emptied the contents of the bottle into her cup and set the bottle down on the grate beside the fire. She stared thoughtfully into the almost clear liquid and when she looked up there was a strange expression in her eyes, one almost of pity. She nodded, her grey hair dancing with flecks of silver and gold. 'I can bring your child back – but are you sure you want the babe returned?' she added softly, looking at them both in turn. She raised her gnarled hand to still their protests and continued. 'Your babe has suckled the fairy woman, she has tasted the food of Faery, and she is therefore bound to the Otherworld.'

'My child was a girl?' Roisin cried.

'You did not know?' Nano Hayes asked. 'No, but of course you wouldn't have. Aye, she was a girl; a fine lass who would have grown tall like her father, but with her mother's light colouring.'

'How do you know our child was a girl?' Mark asked, holding his wife tightly.

The wise woman smiled enigmatically. 'Oh, I know, I know,' she said quietly. She sipped the raw spirit from her cup, grimacing as it burned its way down her throat and fired her tired blood. 'To continue,' she coughed, 'if I bring back your child, a part of her will forever remain in the Realm of Faery, she will be forever drawn to it, she will never feel at home in this world. And of course, there is no guarantee that the elven folk will not send an *iarlaisi*, a changeling, in her place ...'

'I'll know my own child!' Roisin said emphatically.

The wise woman laughed. 'Perhaps. But there would always be that little doubt that the child you were rearing was not your own. Every time it cried aloud in the night, you would start awake, wondering whether a *bean sidhe*, a fairy woman, would come and take her. Every time she started screaming as children often do, you would wonder if this were one of the signs of a changeling. You would be watching her constantly, wondering, waiting, waiting ...' The old woman drank deeply, but her eyes never left the young couple.

The young man had come to her earlier that afternoon, sent there by the local parish priest. He was distraught, and his story of a storm, being struck by lightning and his wife's child being taken by a strange, cold woman with eyes of fire might have sounded like the ravings of a drunk or madman to any other listener. But not to Nano Hayes. She was a wise woman, a *mna allthacha*, aware of the country lore, learned about the various herbs and poultices that could be made from the seemingly innocent roadside weeds, one familiar with the ways of the *gentry*, the fairies. She was old; she could remember nearly sixty hot summers and an equal number of bad winters, and there were, she assured people, quite a few that she didn't bother remembering because they weren't worth remembering! But her knowledge, her lore, was traceable back almost to the dawn of time, back to when Banba had led the Caesir, the band of warrior women from the Isle of Meroe in the placid waters of the Nile, to

Ireland's wooded shore. And although many of the younger townspeople looked upon her with disdain, scorning her charms and advice, the older people still came to her when their cows wouldn't drop their calves or the hens stopped laying, or when they had a complaint the local doctor couldn't cure.

She had calmed the young man and, over a cup of tea, listened to his story, questioning him again and again about the storm and especially about the description of the young woman, Maresch.

When he had finished, she had leaned back on the hard wooden chair, her clawed hands clutching the scarred wooden table. 'Your child,' she said at last, her voice so low that Mark had to lean forward to hear it, 'has been taken by the fairies. The storm was brewed by them to keep you away from the cottage. Maresch was a fairy woman, a *bean sidhe*.'

'You must get our child back,' Mark had insisted and Nano Hayes had nodded silently and, gathering a collection of herbs and grasses and some curious knives together with a score of thin glass phials, had ridden with Mark out to the lonely cottage on the side of the pony and trap.

'Why did she take my child?' Roisin asked suddenly.

The old woman's head snapped up; the poteen was making her drowsy. She shrugged. 'I don't really know. No-one knows why the fairy folk take human children. Perhaps Maresch has just lost her own child – and that is a possibility since she was able to suckle your babe. And then again, perhaps she is unable to bear a child – many of the *sidhe* are barren, they are a dying race.'

'I don't care about the elven folk,' Mark snapped. 'I want my little girl back; I will not allow her to live in some Otherworld.'

The old woman laughed. 'That is excellent. Keep that anger, feed it, let it grow inside you and then go out and shout it at the foot of the fairy fort. If the fairies take your threats seriously, then they might just return your child to you.' She paused and then added, 'And then again, they may not; they are a curious folk,' she said wistfully, 'neither humans nor gods, feared by the former and without the latter.'

'I want my little girl back,' Roisin said suddenly, a ragged edge of hysteria coming into her voice.

'As you wish.' The old woman stood slowly, her stiff joints cracking as she stretched. 'I'll pass the night with you if I may. And in the morn, before the sunrise, we'll try and find your little girl. To your beds now, and be prepared for an early start.'

In the still pre-dawn silence the three figures moved quietly along the path and cut across the fields towards the low mound rising out of the earth like a great sea-creature basking in the waves. They sank slightly in the soft earth, the heavy bundles of withes and twigs tied to their backs slowing them down. The old woman walked in the lead, her hard eyes darting to and fro seeking any sign of the other folk who might still be abroad at this late hour, but the approach to the mound was clear and nothing moved except the wind in the grass.

Nano Hayes still carried the black-handled knife with which she had cut the fresh green branches from the trees lining their route. The grey light of dawn ran along the metal dulling the silver, making it glint like iron, catching the runes incised into the almost flat razor-sharp blade. She paused at a gap in the hedge that bounded the field in which the fairy fort rose. Her experienced eyes read the signs, seeking any disturbance in the side of the mound or on the dew-covered grass. But nothing was amiss: the Fairy Host had not ridden forth that night.

The old woman, followed by Mark and Roisin, walked across the field to the low, grass-covered mound. She paced around it, moving clockwise, her gnarled hands brushing at the grass, probing the soft soil. She encircled the mound once, twice and by the third time she was beginning to get desperate: the sky in the east had lightened to pink and salmon. Sunrise was fast approaching.

The sunrise had flamed the eastern horizon but the huge crimson orb had not yet risen by the time Nano Hayes discovered the concealed entrance to the fort. She called Mark over and instructed him to lay his bundle of sticks in the shape of a cross on the spot.

'But it looks no different from the rest of the ground, I can see no entrance,' he protested.

She patted his cheek and chuckled. 'You're not supposed to, you fool. They don't like visitors and they don't put out welcoming mats.'

The wise woman had then circumscribed the mound with a line of sticks placed end to end and had built small bundles at the four cardinal points. She then handed Mark a small bottle of oil and told him to dampen down the sticks, paying particular attention to the four small mounds. And, with a similar bottle of oil, she carefully traced the sign of the cross on the twigs above the entrance.

Then they waited.

Mark stood beside his wife. He could feel her heart pounding against his arm and although the morning was still chill, she was covered with a fine sheen of sweat. He could feel the tension building up inside him, gathering in a hard knot in the pit of his stomach, pounding in his temples. He stared into the east, watching the sky slowly brighten and run with long streaks of liquid colour. And then the slanting rays of the morning sun lanced over the mountains and burnished the tops of the tallest trees with pale gold. It touched the very tip of the fairy mound with a tiny spot of colour – and Nano Hayes struck fire from a flint and set the wooden cross alight.

The flames leaped along the length of the oil-soaked wood, the green bark and sap-laden branches sputtering and hissing, giving off dense clouds of smoke. The fire burned the sign of the cross into the dew-damp earth and then danced outwards around the mound, leaping like a wild creature, consuming all it touched. The lines of wood around the base of the hill sparked and crisped and the mounds at the four cardinal points blazed furiously and then died down to little more than glowing cinders which smouldered intermittently. Thick grey smoke began to drift across the field towards Nano Hayes and the young couple, rolling and tumbling like tangles of wind-blown weed. The fresh morning air was now fouled with the bitter stench of freshly burned wood and boiled sap.

Roisin coughed and buried her face in her husband's arms and he felt his eyes watering as the smoke bit and stung. He looked across at the old woman, but she seemed unaffected by the billowing smoke. She was leaning slightly forward, her hard eyes shining, her head tilted to one side as if she were listening. Once she nodded and Mark could have sworn that he had heard something moving through the grass at the foot of the mound ... but the smoke was too thick and it might just have been the burned wood crackling.

And then he suddenly realised that there was far too much smoke for the small amount of wood they had burned!

Nano Hayes spoke in her curiously youthful voice. But the words did not come easily to her, for her throat struggled to shape a language that was never meant to be spoken by man. It was higher, thinner, sweeter than the speech of man. It vaguely resembled Irish, but a far, far older version of the language Mark spoke; in fact, it was closer in texture and sound to the speech the priests used during the Mass. But it was not Latin.

The old woman's tone changed; it was now demanding, angry. Something moved within the twisting wreaths of smoke – a tall attenuated figure – and was gone. Nano Hayes cried aloud, raised her hands high and seemed to be invoking a god or gods. Slowly, she brought her hands down, palms upwards, her fingers slightly cupped. She crossed her wrists before her face and slowly turned her hands so that the palms now faced the mound. A sharp metallic clang echoed across the field, followed by a slow booming and Mark thought he could make out an oblong area of blackness through the smoke. A light flashed blindingly, like the sun off polished metal and horse's hooves struck sparks from a stone before him. He held his wife tightly to his chest, his eyes widening in horror as a huge shadow loomed up before him ... a shape that might have been a horse and rider.

Nano Hayes dropped her hands to her side and pulled the black-hafted knife from her belt. She sketched a sign in the air before the shadow figure which had now reared up before her and the symbol etched itself into the smoky air in thin lines of silver-white fire. The shadow reared up, terrifyingly huge, monstrously shaped, and retreated back into the shifting smoke, its scream almost too high to register on human ears. Nano Hayes dropped to her knees and plunged the knife deeply into the earth. In the wan morning light she no longer looked like an old country woman slowly killing herself on raw poteen, but rather a creature out of Ireland's misty past, a sorceress with the power of the gods, a warrior-maid about to go into battle. Her face seemed younger, her body thinner, taller, her hair thicker and her eyes ... her eyes wide and compelling.

The silver-bladed knife sliced through the soft earth in a long rectangle. Mark breathed in the fresh odour of wet earth and it suddenly jolted him back to reality. He blinked and blinked again. The warrior-maid no longer stood before him, just an old, wrinkled wise woman, desperately calling upon a power that was never meant to be used by a person of this era, for it was the magic of an earlier age. He could see the dancing blue-white nimbus around her hands and hair, could feel it crackling along the ground, writhing like serpents. It reminded him of lightning, but it was a different power; whereas the lightning had been a raw elemental force, this was a stronger, harsher power – and it was under control. But whether it was controlled by Nano Hayes or the *sidhe*, he could not tell.

The old woman lifted the sod of earth high as if in offering, turning to the four cardinal points in turn, calling aloud in the strange musical tongue. She turned back to the fairy fort and stepped forward. Immediately, the smoke retreated, flowing inwards as if sucked. It clung briefly to her and for a moment it looked as if she were slowly drifting apart as the grey tendrils broke away from her clothes and hair and flowed on into the mound. She took another step forward, another, another ...

The mound loomed out of the retreating fog like an island out of the mists and for a moment Mark thought he saw a huge gaping hole in the side of the fort, illuminated from within with tiny points of glittering light – but then it was gone, leaving only a shimmering imprint on his retina. But faint, faint in the distance and retreating downwards, he imagined he could hear the sound of a horse's hooves striking on stone.

Nano Hayes stepped up to the crisped shape of a cross over the blackened grass. She placed the sod of earth over the centre of the cross and stepped back. She turned and smiled at Mark and Roisin. 'Look,' she said, her voice strained and raw and her eyes weary.

Roisin broke away from her husband and ran past the old woman to the mound, her cry of delight hanging on the reeking air like the sound of a startled bird. She stood, picked something up and turned to her husband, her tears leaving long trails down her smudged face. She held a bundle in her arms. Mark walked across to his wife, doubt immediately forming. He paused by the old woman and searched her red-rimmed eyes. 'Is that our child?' he asked quietly.

Nano Hayes nodded. 'It is the child of your loins, the child of your wife's womb ... but it will never be your child.'

The years passed and the babe grew into a lovely young girl. They had named her Brigid, after Mark's mother, and although he loved his daughter dearly, there was always that little doubt that still niggled. Roisin bore him another daughter some years after the first, but she herself died giving birth, and Mark was forced to bring up the two girls himself.

The small family seemed forever dogged by ill-luck and it was whispered that they had been cursed by the fairies. Mark fell under the hooves of a horse soon after his wife's death and walked afterwards with a limp – and it was that which drove him to drink. His younger daughter, although a beautiful child, was blind in one eye and prone to sickness. And tragedy struck again some eighteen years after Brigid's birth when she was found dead one cold November morning at the foot of the fairy fort . . .*

**see: 'Into the Shadowland . . .' Irish Folk and Fairy Tales volume one.*

CHAPTER 9

THE HAMMER MAN

Frazer brought his gun up as the birds broke from the low scrub and fired off both barrels. One of the long-tailed grouse fluttered and fell spiralling to the wet ground and he could see the dogs splash through the shallows towards the bird. He broke open the gun and let the smoking cartridges fall to the ground, his gloved hands fumbling in his belt for fresh rounds even though he knew it was almost too late in the day for any more shooting. The light was fading fast and low storm clouds, which had been gathering all afternoon, were now massed above the lowering bulk of the Mourne Mountains and the wind from the north was chill and damp. He left the gun open, tucked it under his arm and sloshed through the soggy ground towards his host, Sir Malcome Fitzgerald. He heard a single report of a shotgun down by the trees, followed by a ripple of gunfire as the birds rose again. Another smattering of shots disturbed the late evening and then he heard shouting: the shoot was finished. It had been a good day though; he had bagged a score – perhaps more – of grouse and perhaps a dozen duck.

Sir Malcome Fitzgerald turned as the tall Englishman in tweeds clambered over a fallen tree-trunk and strode across the field towards him. The old warrior noted the younger man's military stride and bearing with approval: it was a damned pity there were not a few more young men like him in the forces now. He handed his gleaming gun to his servant and smiled as Frazer joined him. 'Good shooting John; you caught a couple of tricky ones there.'

John Frazer pushed back his deerstalker with the back of his hand and carefully eased the cartridges from his Purdy shotgun and slipped them back into his belt. 'I missed a couple of easy ones also,' he said quietly, 'and you bagged a couple I never even saw.' He smiled, his teeth startlingly white against the dark tan of his skin.

Sir Malcome laughed. 'Now that, I just don't believe. I think you let a few by deliberately so that an old soldier like myself could try his hand.'

Frazer shook his head. 'Oh, I doubt if I would do that.' He tilted his head as a bracket of shots echoed into the evening air.

The older man shook his head, took off his cap and mopped his bald head with a large white handkerchief. 'Damned fools,' he grunted, 'I doubt if they can even see anything in this light.' He nodded at the lowering clouds. 'We had better be getting back,' he said, 'I know the signs, there is going to be a downpour soon.' He took his walking stick from his servant and marched briskly across the field towards the road.

'Must remind you of India,' he said pleasantly, 'come evening, come rain.'

John shook his head and laughed. 'There is nothing here that even remotely resembles India,' he said, 'the sounds, the colours, the freshness of the rain, the scents on the wind, they are all unique, unlike India where everything is stale, heavy with sweat and heat.' He nodded at the lush fields which bordered the road. 'I can see why you chose to settle here; I might do so myself in a couple of years' time.'

'Take it from me, my boy, don't be in any rush to settle down. Make the most of your youth – see the world whilst you're still young and fit. And remember, when you get to my age, you begin to slow down,' he patted his rotund stomach, 'and you begin to regret all the things you should have done.'

'Do the locals give you any trouble?' Frazer asked, his sharp eyes catching the glint of metal as the other shooters marched across the lower fields towards the road.

'Not me, no. I've always treated the local people with all due courtesy and they respect me for it. Further south though . . .' he shrugged. 'Well, there are two sides to every story and I'm not about to go picking sides. It's true that some landlords are overly harsh, but it's also true that some local groups retaliate with equal harshness and brutality. Aah,' the old warrior waved and increased his pace, 'here are the others; let's go look at the day's bag.'

John Frazer stood at his bedroom window watching the full moon paint the wet ground with silver, listening to the water drip from the eaves and trickle down the gutters. It was almost two o'clock in the morning and the house was silent, the tired shooters already abed and the servants just retired. He struck a match and applied it to his pipe, the amber light touching his lean features with shadow, burnishing his blond hair in bronze. He puffed contentedly, leaning against the window frame allowing his tired body to relax, letting his mind wander out over the storm-drenched fields. He breathed deeply, inhaling the pungent odours of tobacco mingled with the damp freshness of the night.

It had been a good day and a good start to his leave. He had arrived in Dublin some two days earlier on leave from India; he had friends in the city and intended passing some time with them before going on to London. However, he had met Sir Malcome Fitzgerald, an old friend of his father's and he and his wife had invited him up to their country estate, away from the busy bustle of Dublin's social scene for a week of fishing and shooting. He found the countryside relaxing and, contrary to what he had heard, the people were friendly, unlike the native Dubliners who were surly and aggressive.

The Fitzgerald estate stood in the shadow of the Mourne Mountains, set in almost a hundred acres of lush grassland, woodland and marshes and it had the reputation for some of the finest fishing and shooting in all Ireland.

John pulled on his pipe, the bowl glowing warmly in the palm of his hand. He relished the silence of the night; there were no tropical birds or insects, beasts or humans crying and mewling outside his window in the stifling darkness;

there was no need to sleep beneath a net or else one would wake up in the morning with a mottled blood-flecked skin. And there was no need to sleep with a loaded revolver beneath the pillow or a naked sabre under the bed. He sighed, absorbing the calmness, the peacefulness of the Irish countryside. And whilst he stood by the window, staring out into the moonlit night, the pipe in his hand slowly went out and the tendrils of fragrant smoke died ...

John jerked awake suddenly. He realised that he had fallen asleep standing up, a trick he had learned during his patrols on the wild north Indian border. He twitched uneasily, all his instincts tingling: something had awoken him. He squinted out into the night looking for any unnatural shape or shadow on the light-dappled ground, his ears alert to any unusual sound and his nose seeking strange odours. But nothing moved in the grounds below his window and the air was sweet and clean with just the trace of his tobacco lingering. And the night was silent ... or was it?

He tilted his head to one side, listening. He thought he had heard a ringing ... but that might have been within his head. The young soldier shook his head and massaged his ears – and then he heard it again, and he knew what he was hearing was not inside his head. It was a sharp metallic ringing, as of metal on metal, distinct and musical. He closed his eyes and tried to trace the direction of the sound with his hearing alone. It was ... there!

His clear eyes snapped open and he found himself looking towards the dark, silver-tipped bulk of the Mourne Mountains. He stood by the window for almost an hour listening to the short musical notes tingling on the damp night air. At one stage he went to his bags and brought out his folding telescope and attempted to scan the slopes of the mountains, but the moonlight – even though it was quite brilliant – was too weak for his purposes, and he could see only blurs.

But the sound intrigued him. It awoke echoes deep within him, there was something about it ... something which called ... and called ... and called.

Frazer awoke with first light the following morn. He ate a hurried breakfast alone in the kitchen – much to the servant's discomfiture – and, leaving his apologies for Sir Malcome, set out across the fields towards the mountains, his kitbag on his back, a shotgun tucked under his arm and a loaded revolver in his belt.

As he tramped down the winding country road he puzzled over the conversation he had had with the cook – a small Irishwoman with tiny eyes lost in a huge round face that seemed continually creased in a smile. He had asked her whether there was any industry in the mountains, a quarry or foundry perhaps. She had looked at him strangely and then slowly shook her head.

'Ah sure, there's nothing this side of the Mournes except rock.'

'I heard something last night,' he said, sipping the scalding tea, his eyes never leaving her face. The old cook had stiffened and a mask had come down behind her eyes.

'And what sort of a sound would that have been now,' she had asked casually.

'Sharp and metallic,' he had said quietly, 'do you know of it?'

'Only what the auld folk tell me,' she had said and sat down in the chair facing him. 'And if you're thinking of following it, well then I wouldn't sir, for 'tis the Hammer Man, and many's the one that has followed that sound into the mountains and never been seen again.'

Frazer noted that she was wringing her apron in her strong hands and there had been a note almost of fear in her voice.

'Tell me about the Hammer Man?' he had asked quietly, stirring his tea.

The old cook had shaken her head. 'I know nothing sir, only that it's not safe to go climbing in the mountains. *They* are often to be found in the rocky places.'

'Who are *they*?' he had asked, although he already had some idea. In India he had heard tales of the creatures that lived in the mountains or the secret valleys. 'Demons? Devils?'

'The dark ones of the *sidhe*, sir, the dark fairies.'

He had nodded seriously. He had heard similar tales and had travelled far enough to know that there was still a lot that modern science could not explain. In India he had met with an Irish priest who had told him tales of the Dark Continent and the Far Orient that were hard to believe and he would have discounted except that the priest himself truly believed them.

The cook had impulsively reached out and held his hand. 'Don't go sir, don't heed the call of the Hammer Man.'

Frazer had gently extracted his hands and smiled at the old woman. 'Perhaps not then.'

She had returned his smile and then stood uncertainly. 'I used to have a son like you sir, and he used to humour me also, but when he was set in his mind then there was nothing that would shift him. Go then if you must. I'll pray for you.'

'Well I'll thank you for that,' he had said quietly, and then stood and left the kitchen. He didn't see the old woman wiping the tears from her eyes.

The day was warm and dry and his long measured stride covered the ground easily. By noon he was more than half-way to the foothills and he broke his march for a rough and ready lunch on the banks of a lake curiously entitled Silent Valley. By mid-afternoon he was climbing steadily. He scanned the rock face above him with his telescope occasionally, but could see no sign of habitation or even caves that might prove to be the source of the sound – although he guessed he must be close to where it had originated from. He searched the rock face and through the foothills for most of the afternoon seeking any clue – but there was nothing.

Then, as the light began to fade and the shadows lengthen, and he was beginning to contemplate returning, he heard the sound. It struck him like a bullet and rooted him to the spot. It *was* the sharp metallic sound of metal on metal, a steady, almost heart-like beat. It echoed and bounced off the rocks, reverberating, trembling . . . calling.

John Frazer turned and followed the sound of the Hammer Man up into the mountains.

The sound called yet lulled him and he followed it through the evening twilight and on into the night. A part of him knew that what he was doing was foolhardy; in India he had seen men follow voices only they could hear and fall to their deaths, or chase the marsh lights out into the bogs and sink in the mire. But this was different. This was real. It was not a figment of his imagination, neither a delusion nor a dream. Someone was hammering metal above him and he was determined to find them.

The moon slipped out from behind the clouds and spilled its silver-white light across the mountain face and the tiny figure that struggled up the worn and almost non-existent track. But Frazer recognised that he was following a pathway of some sort and he would follow it to the end. He had left his kitbag behind him on the rough track and now only carried the shotgun and pistol – and although the weapons were heavy, he welcomed their comforting weight.

He had been climbing for nearly two hours when the sound stopped.

He had been hearing it for most of the evening and on into the night and it took a few moments for it to sink in that it was gone. Echoes still belled within his head and his pulse now pounded to the same beat. With the sound gone he felt a sense of loss.

He looked around; far below him – he hadn't realised he had climbed so high! – the foothills disappeared into the moon-touched night, whilst above him the mountain still reared up into the purple, star-studded skies. However, the track he had been following led into a cleft in the mountain-side before him and from within the moonlight spilled blindingly on something. Frazer approached the crack in the rocks cautiously. The cleft itself was in shadow and the only sound was the persistent dripping of water and as he moved to one side the brilliant light disappeared. He stood by the entrance for almost five minutes listening and then, satisfied that there was no-one waiting within, he broke open the shotgun and loaded it. Frazer squeezed through the crack and found it suddenly opened out into a smooth pathway that led on downwards. On either side, the dark walls of the cliff rose upwards, whilst overhead the thin purple thread of sky was almost blotted out. Smooth stones rolled beneath his boots, the cliff walls were slimed and damp and he guessed that water had once cut through this crack in the mountain. He occasionally caught sight of the brilliance that had blinded him before, but it wasn't until he had forced his way out of the cleft that he saw the lake.

It was surprisingly large for a mountain-top lake. It stretched as far as he could see, but it was difficult to determine where the lake ended and the land began, for its still surface was dappled with ebon shadows and silver light, and the night hung heavily over the little valley.

A single musical note suddenly rang out from the depths of the shadowed valley. Frazer fell to his knees and thumbed the hammers back on the shotgun. He knelt in the mouth of the cleft, in the shade of a wild gorse and listened. He could still hear ringing, but this time he wasn't sure whether it was within his head or whether there was an actual sound.

A definite bell-like tone rang out again and in the shadows by the lake something flashed briefly and was gone. The silver point of light burned its way across Frazer's retina and even when he blinked he could still make out the vibrating spark. Silence fell again.

He rose cautiously and began to make his way towards the lake. Low clouds scudded in from the west, blotting out the moonlight, leaving him in total darkness – without the moon the night was absolute. In the darkness he splashed into the shallows – and froze, his senses flaring. He crouched in the cold water and listened. And then he suddenly realised that there was no sound: no night-birds called, no insects rustled, nothing moved in the earth or through the bushes. He felt the icy chill of fear along the back of his neck and his heart began to pound in his chest.

The shattering sound broke from almost in front of him, sending the young Englishman reeling backwards. The solid, bitter-sweet cadence was taken up again and the night was rent by the sound of metal ringing on metal.

Frazer pushed himself to his feet and peered through the bushes. For a moment he could see nothing and then the edge of the sinking moon cut loose from a heavy cloud, spilling liquid silver across the lake – and the small figure that stood on its banks. It was a man of medium stature, but muscular with incredibly broad shoulders which somehow made him seem smaller than he actually was. His long hair – silver-white in the light – fell across his shoulders and was held back from his forehead by a thin fillet of metal. His only clothing was a short leather kilt and Frazer could see the muscles in his arms and shoulders bunch and ripple as he lifted the heavy hammer and brought it down on the flat piece of metal he was shaping. He worked solidly, his muscular body covered with a fine sheen of silvered sweat and he seemed unaware of the chill breeze that had sprung up and now whispered through the tree-tops.

The young man looked up suddenly, his dark eyes mirror-bright and glassy in the moonlight. The hammer paused in mid-air and Frazer felt the sudden build-up of tension, an almost tangible force that sent ripples of fear along his spine. He brought his gun up and sighted the young man between both barrels. The hammer came down and pointed – straight towards the bushes! The Hammer Man spoke, the language guttural and rapidly interrogative. The question was repeated more urgently and now the figure took a step nearer the bushes. In his right hand he held the heavy hammer and in his left the long length of beaten metal he had been working, flat and slightly pointed at one end, resembling a sword blade.

Frazer stood, the gun pointing at the young man's chest. His heart was pounding and he felt terribly afraid even though he was facing a naked man armed only with a hammer.

The Hammer Man spoke again, this time in a different language, one that seemed vaguely familiar to the Englishman. Frazer shook his head. 'I do not understand you,' he said slowly and distinctly in English and then he repeated it in French and Hindustani.

The young man stepped closer and Frazer brought the gun up to his shoulder, his fingers tightening on the trigger. The Hammer Man stopped.

'There is no need to fear him, Mister Frazer.'

The Englishman spun around at the sound of the strangely echoing voice and in that moment the Hammer Man stepped in and struck the gun away with his hammer. The shock numbed Frazer's arm and shoulder and the gun discharged with a sound that echoed over the mountains like thunder. He fell to his knees, throwing himself to one side, his right hand groping frantically for his pistol, but the young man followed him down and laid the sharp point of his crude sword against his cheek.

'Do not resist, Mister Frazer.' The voice was high and thin, trembling on the air like a distant echo. 'Togha will not harm you.'

John turned towards the sound of the voice – and found himself looking up at one of the most beautiful women he had ever seen.

She stood, framed in the moonlight under the silver-tipped leaves of an ancient oak and although she was not tall, she exuded a presence, an aura, of absolute power and confidence. She stepped out from the shade of the tree and her long, low-cut gown flashed and scintillated in the light, almost the same shade as her white-gold hair. She smiled, white teeth showing through thin red lips, but her eyes remained hard. And when she spoke again, Frazer realised that she did so without using her lips.

'Why have you come here?'

He sat up, nursing his numbed arm. 'I followed the sound,' he said slowly.

'But surely you were warned not to,' she said, and he realised that her voice had the same slightly ringing tone similar to that of metal on metal.

'I was curious,' he said, slowly rising to his feet. 'The sound called me.' He was conscious of the young man standing behind him, the sword still resting on his shoulder with the point against his cheek. He could feel the roughness of the metal against his skin and whilst the blade had not yet been honed, the point was quite sharp.

'Who are you?' he asked the woman.

She smiled and stepped closer to him, her delicate perfume engulfing him, making his senses tingle. 'I am Delgrade,' she said, her voice echoing in his head, 'queen of the Partholonians, once of Scythia.'*

'Scythia?' he said dumbly, 'but ...'

'Do not tell me it is gone and do not think me mad. I was once the wife of Partholon, who led his people to this land three hundred years after the Great Flood cleansed this world of all life!'

Frazer forced a laugh, but a slow, cold terror was gradually taking hold of him. 'But that would make you ... thousands of years old.'

'Would it?' she said wistfully. 'I do not measure time as you do. But yes, I am old ... and weary.' She smiled up at him and her hard blue eyes were like polished stones.

Frazer breathed deeply, trying to calm the terror that threatened to send him screaming out into the glassy waters of the lake. 'What happened to the rest of your people?' he asked.

'We were of their race, but they were not our people!' she snapped, her voice crashing through the innermost recesses of his mind like the sound of the sea on a rocky shore. 'They cast us out, they renounced us ...' And then she screamed and Frazer cringed with the sound. 'But they are dead now and we remain! The plague took them, the plague that grew from my husband's body. We could see the fires burning in the south, sending up thick black smoke by day and brightening the night with the flames of the pyres and often the wind would carry the stink of roasting flesh ...' Her voice was harsh and broken now and her eyes danced with madness. The Englishman stepped back away from her until he felt the pressure of the blade begin to cut against his cheek.

'Why do you remain?' he asked, playing for time, trying to keep this wild madwoman talking.

see 'The Dawn' – Chapter 1 Irish Folk and Fairy Tales – volume II.

Delgrade stepped away from him, turned and stared out over the lake. 'We remain,' she said, her voice now nothing more than a wind-carried whisper that trickled through his brain, 'because we are the children of the gods, and like our fathers, we are both immortal and vulnerable.'

'Vulnerable; how?' he wondered. 'I thought the gods were invincible.'

'The gods need the worship of men to survive, they feed off that worship, like the harpies off the souls of men or the vampire from the blood of virgins. We remain here because time has no meaning in this valley; here it is still the dawn of the world, within this valley our gods still live; here we are nurtured and protected. Were we to venture beyond the valley we would surely die – or else our minds would crack beneath the strangeness of the new world that has arisen. ...' Her voice faded and drifted off into fragments and Frazer knew that she was weeping silently.

'And the Hammer Man ... Togha?'

She glanced over her shoulder, her eyes silver discs in the moonlight. 'He was my lover once – a whim, a brief whim, but it was because of him I was cast out of the Partholonian camp – and it is because of him that I still survive today. I owe him much: my disgrace and my life.'

'Why does he hammer metal?'

'He was – is – a smith; it is all he knows and there is nothing else for him to do.'

'And you?' John asked, 'what do you do?'

Delgrade laughed aloud and the Englishman could hear the bitterness, the sadness, the loneliness in her voice. 'You could say that this valley is my garden, I tend it,' she said. And then her voice cracked and took on a new note. 'And like all good gardeners, I must weed it out.'

Frazer felt the fear congeal along his spine and settle into his stomach.

'Togha's work often brings people to me; oh, not so many as before of course, but enough.' She turned and faced him, her eyes blazing with a cold inner fire. Her tongue darted out and wet her lips and he was suddenly reminded of a snake about to strike. 'You see,' she continued, 'no-one must know of us. They would come to look and stare and their very presence would contaminate and eventually slay us. Even you, with your woven clothes, your weapon of steel and fire, your boots of leather, your device that measures time, even you have brought a little of your time into our valley, even you have aged us a little, even now, you are killing us!'

'But you cannot remain this way for ever,' Frazer said quickly, 'this is a small country, you will be found sooner or later. The world will find you.'

'But there is a time coming when the world will return to its former beauty, a time when the machines and artifacts of man will no longer dominate, a time when the old gods will arise again, a time when we can go forth into the world. A time of killing!' She stopped suddenly, her breathing harsh and ragged and then she spoke quite casually to Togha in their own tongue, but her meaning was clear.

Frazer kicked backwards with his foot, felt it connect with the young man's shin and threw himself forward. The crude sword whistled over his head, parting his hair. Frazer rolled as he fell, his right hand tugging the pistol from its holster. He jerked aside, almost losing his grip on the pistol, as the sword flashed out of the night and spun by his side, embedding itself into the soft earth. Frazer fired. His first shot went wild, but both Togha and Delgrade fell to the ground and melted into the night. He fired twice into a clump of bushes where he had last seen Togha, heard the first shot ricochet off stone and then the gasp of pain as the second shot struck home. He began to ease his way backwards, intending to make for the cleft in the cliffs. Something cracked behind him and he rolled over and fired instinctively. Both shots took Togha high in the chest spinning him around, sending him crashing back into the undergrowth.

A sudden lance of pain ripped through him, squeezing his head in a vice. He dropped the gun and held his pounding head in both hands attempting to relieve the pain. He was aware that it was intensifying, threatening to rip his skull apart. Through pain-filled eyes he saw Delgrade approaching slowly. Crimson bursts of agony rippled across his bulging eyes, blinding him and when he could see again, Delgrade was kneeling by Togha, cradling his head in her arms.

And for a fraction the pain disappeared. The Englishman rocked backwards with the cessation of the pain and his hand touched the cold metal of his pistol. And suddenly Delgrade was upon him, Togha's hammer clutched in both hands. Frazer tried to roll aside and fire at the same time. The hammer came down and he heard his shoulder bones crack with sickening pain. His hooked fingers tore into the soft earth as he waited for the killing blow to descend.

But it never came.

When Frazer awoke some hours later, the morning sun was striking fire from the easternmost peaks of the valley. The air was damp and chill, but he was bathed in a burning fever. He tried to move, but black waves of pain rose up and threatened to overwhelm him. He wondered why the madwoman hadn't killed him. Some time later, when he did manage to move without blacking out, he discovered the small body of Delgrade, queen of the Partholonians, lying in the long grass, stiffening in the crisp morning air, a small hole beneath her breast, Togha's hammer still clutched in her long-nailed fingers.

'Here! He's here!' A lantern was held above his head and a pale face, framed by the distant stars, peered down at him. And then Sir Malcome's broad face swam into view. The old soldier knelt down beside him, his eyes wide with concern and his face tight with worry. 'My God man, what happened to you.'

Frazer coughed and spat blood, images of his nightmarish descent down the mountain still flashing behind his eyes. He had had plenty of time to think of his answer. He coughed again and swallowed a little of the brandy from the flask Sir Malcome pressed to his lips. 'I was climbing,' he whispered and attempted a smile, 'I fell.'

CHAPTER 10

THE LOVERS' REWARD ... I

They lay in the long lush grass, feeling the gentle breeze caress their naked bodies with silken fingers and dry the sweat of their lovemaking. It was late afternoon and the sun was beginning to sink down behind the trees, throwing long shadows across the little pool and the tumbled stones that encircled it, calling forth the mystery of the place. In the distance a bell began to toll.

'Peter ... ?' She ran gentle fingers down the side of his throat and ruffled the hair on his chest. He stirred lazily, opening his eyes slightly, his lips curving in a slight smile.

'Mmme?'

'It's late,' she whispered, 'I must go. No!' She pulled away from him as he reached for her again. 'I must go; Donal will be home soon.' She leaned over and kissed him swiftly, her full breasts brushing his chest, and then she stood, the slanting rays of the sinking sun touching her smooth skin in shades of crimson and bronze.

Peter Casside lay back and watched her dress, admiring the way she moved, the ripple of muscles across her back and along the length of her thighs, the pout of her breasts. She caught him looking and smiled gently. 'Tell me,' she said, almost absently, 'has Michael been asking any more questions?'

Peter rose on his elbows and stared across the quiet waters of the little pool. 'I think my brother is jealous of you ... me ... us,' he said and shrugged. 'He even warned me to stay away from you – said you were dangerous.' Peter looked up and smiled wickedly, 'Oh, and I could have told him just how dangerous!'

He pushed himself to his feet and pulled the young long-haired woman to him. He could feel his body responding to her nearness, feel the tingle of her fingertips as she traced his backbone. 'Sorcha,' he said quietly, 'what did you do to frighten him? There was a time when he wouldn't allow a word to be said against you ...'

She pressed her nails into his back and nestled against his chest. 'I did nothing – except choose you,' she added.

'But you married MacIntee,' he reminded her.

Sorcha pulled away from the young man and allowed a hard note to creep into her voice. 'I told you before; Donal is a very rich man. When he dies which, with his heart, should be very soon now, all that will be mine ...' She stepped closer to him and breathed gently, '... ours!'

Peter shook his head and turned away, looking for his clothes in the long grass. 'It's been almost two years Sorcha, and he is still as strong as ever.' He found his trousers and stepped into them. 'He sickens me: he is an animal, a gross pig, and the very thought of him ... and you ...'

Sorcha laughed quietly. 'You fool; didn't you know that he's been impotent since the first night of our wedding?' She continued mockingly. 'Mother gave me a little recipe which ensures that he is as potent as a gelding.' Her eyes locked with his and her full lips curled back from startlingly white teeth. 'Why do you think I need you so much, eh?' She pulled her shawl about her shoulders and, without a backward glance, followed the winding path around the pool that led down towards the village.

Peter Casside stood and watched her go, his damp shirt clutched in his large hands. A cloud obscured the sun and a shadow raced down the path after her and wrapped her in its embrace. He was suddenly conscious that it was very cold.

'And what then ...?' Michael Casside leaned back on the hard wooden chair and brought his paper and pencil around so that the wavering firelight could send dancing fingers of light across the page.

The old woman sitting across from him was almost lost in the shadows and only the pale oval of her face and her glittering eyes were visible. She shifted on the stool and spat into the fire. 'And so the Tuatha De Danann retreated into the hidden places, the shadowed isles, the deep barrows, for their time was past and the Age of Man had come ...' her hoarse voice faded to a rough whisper.

'Do they live there still?' Michael scribbled rapidly and looked up from the page, pencil poised.

The old woman laughed, a rough bark more animal-like than human. 'Oh, there are some that claim they do. They say the elven folk live apart from man except on those occasions when they sally forth in search of a wife or child. I have never seen one of the Shining Ones myself,' she added, 'but I have witnessed some of their servants, the creatures men call the *leprechaun* and the *Fir Dearg*.'

'Then they exist,' Michael insisted.

'Oh, they exist. They are not as you would imagine them – they are mis-shapen and ugly – but aye, they exist ...' The old woman broke off as the door opened and a stray gust of wind sent smoke and cinders wheeling about the small dark room. 'Who is it?' she called querulously.

'It's me, mother.' Sorcha dropped a bundle of wood by the door, crossed the room and kissed her mother. She gasped in surprise when she saw Michael and forced a smile to her lips. It was eerily frightening how alike Peter and Michael were; they were identical twins and the only way she could tell them apart was by the colour of their eyes, for whilst Peter's were dark, almost black in certain lights, Michael's eyes were colourless, mere alabaster ovals with just the faintest, faintest trace of pupil. But he was not blind.

Michael nodded stiffly. 'Sorcha,' he said quietly. 'How are you, how's Donal?' he added maliciously.

'I am very well and my husband also,' she said, stiffly formal. Then she added with a thin smile, 'How's that brother of yours?'

'Well, thank you.'

'Is he working?'

'He keeps busy.' Michael stood and nodded to the old woman. 'It's late now, I must be going – I'll see you tomorrow.'

Mother Cleirigh cackled. 'Tomorrow then ... and bring something with you; it's thirsty work all this talking.'

'I'll bring something.' Michael Casside promised.

Sorcha waited until she heard the sharp ringing sound of his footsteps on the path before turning to her mother. 'He is dangerous.'

The old woman stood and, leaning on her walking stick, hobbled over to the window to watch the tall thin figure disappear down the long winding road towards the town. 'We need him,' she said softly, 'the affinity between him and his brother is very strong.' She glanced over her shoulder. 'And what of Peter?'

The young woman smiled broadly. 'He's mine – he will do anything I tell him.'

Mother Cleirigh nodded. 'We are now nearly into October; I think it's time to remove Donal MacIntee – your loving husband.'

'Good; when?'

The old woman returned to the fire and eased herself onto the stool. 'Soon, soon. There remain some herbs to be gathered. On Samhain Eve then. And Sorcha,' she added, 'use Peter; it will be the ultimate test of his devotion to you.'

'And what of Michael?'

'As long as I can keep him here and supplied with titbits of folklore and legend, he is perfectly happy.'

Sorcha still looked undecided. 'Does he suspect?'

'About you and his brother? I think so. But as long as you and Peter remain discreet, he will say nothing.'

'We will,' Sorcha assured her mother.

'Good. Will you be seeing him tomorrow?'

'Of course. His appetite is insatiable,' she smiled.

'Start working on him tomorrow then, but gently, gently. You have nearly a month to bring him around to our way of thinking.'

Sorcha grinned. 'I know what to do.'

Her mother glanced across at her. 'I'm sure you do,' she said sharply. 'I'm sure you do.'

The candle had almost burned down to a stub by the time Michael pushed back the chair and rubbed his aching eyes. It was the small hours of the morning and he had spent several hours transcribing the material old Mother Cleirigh had given him. He patted the small bundle of paper covered with his neat precise hand, experiencing a sense of satisfaction. He picked up a blank sheet of paper and dipped his pen in the thick black ink. In the centre of the page he wrote: *'The Tale of Nuada Silver Hand'*, and under that *'The Tuatha De Danann'*. He placed the page on top of the bundle and stood up, rubbing his stiffened back and neck.

Glancing outside, he was startled to see how high the moon was, and he suddenly realised that Peter wasn't home yet. He smiled self-consciously. Peter was almost a grown man now; he wasn't a child that needed constant looking after. Undoubtedly, he was out drinking with some of his friends or ...

He shrugged. Well, it was none of his business. He pushed open the door of the cottage and stepped out into the night, breathing in the chill air. The wind was blowing in from the sea, carrying with it the heavy tang of salt and he could see the silver thread of the Atlantic far in the distance. He leaned back against the door jamb and allowed the tension to seep from his body.

Strange images flashed before his fatigued eyes, images born of the tales old Mother Cleirigh had told him through the long afternoon. He saw the Tuatha De Danann as they once must have been: godlike creatures, proud and commanding. He saw their heroes and heroines sally forth to do battle with the demons from the north, saw them return triumphant. He saw their king Nuada, his silver hand fashioned by Goibniu the Smith and fitted by the magic of Diancecht the Physician, leading his forces out against the Fomorians in the Last Battle of Mag Turiad. He saw the king's head shorn from his body by Balor, the one-eyed king of the demons, saw it tumble bloodily through the air ... but when it rolled to a stop, Michael found himself looking at the severed head of his brother.

He jerked back to reality with a startled gasp. He was soaked in a chill sweat that was already drying on his body, making his teeth chatter and sending shivers down along his spine. With a last glance down the deserted path into the village, he turned and entered the cottage.

When he awoke in the morning he found Peter's bed empty and although the sheets had been disturbed there was little evidence that his brother had slept in it. He pressed his hand against the straw mattress, but it was cold and dry.

He made a leisurely breakfast whilst re-reading his notes from the night before and then he moved about the small two-roomed cottage, generally tidying and cleaning up. His mother, who was spending a few days with her sister in Cork, would be arriving home sometime later that day. He moved stiffly, slowly working the exhaustion from his bones. He had slept badly the night before and his dreams had been troubled by the image of his brother's severed head. However, a new element had been added: above the head a huge crow had flapped – one of the Morrigan's creatures, the Goddess of Death ... – and the crow had Sorcha's face.

It was almost noon when he made his way down through the town towards the Cleirighs. Summer had come and drifted into autumn, but the summer weather lingered and the air was still warm and balmy, and although some withered leaves whispered along the ground, many of the trees were still in leaf. He breathed deeply, savouring the almost spring-like air; there was a name for this type of weather, Indian something ... some of the townspeople said that it forewarned a harsh winter – and an equal number said it promised a mild winter! So much for weather lore.

He bought a bottle of cheap whiskey in the local pub and

stuck it in his pocket beside his notebook and pencils. He walked down the main street and out of the town, past the cross-roads – reputed to be haunted – and cut across the fields towards the mean cottage tucked away behind a thin copse of spindly trees.

The old woman was bending over the fire when he entered, stirring a large fire-blackened cauldron. Michael smiled slightly; she looks like an old witch, he thought as he breathed in the sharp, but not unpleasant odour emanating from the pot.

'What are you cooking?' he asked suddenly.

Old Mother Cleirigh screamed and spun about, her long ladle raised threateningly. The young man stepped back from her, the look on her lined face chilling him to the bone.

For in that instant, he had glimpsed raw power and hate burning in her eyes, such that he thought was impossible in a human being.

And then she relaxed and the light died from her eyes. She looked at the ladle in her hand and chuckled self-consciously.

'Now look what you've gone and done – you've frightened the life out of me.' Shaking her head, she turned back to the fire and resumed stirring the pot.

Michael composed himself and repeated the question.

The old woman cackled. 'I'm brewing a little something for Sorcha – or rather, for her man.'

Michael felt an icy chill touch his heart. 'What is it?' he wondered aloud.

'Oh, a little something to help him . . .' She paused and saw his look of incomprehension and continued. 'The man's impotent!' she snapped. 'And what use is that sort of man to a woman, eh? Well I'll cure him.'

Michael bent over the pot and breathed in the thick vapour. 'What's in it?'

'What does it smell like?' Mother Cleirigh asked.

'Liquor of some sort.'

'It's brandy,' she said, 'with orange peel, wormwood, snakeroot, cochineal, saffron and gentian root added.'

'Will it work?'

'Of course; provided it is prepared properly, it never fails.'

Michael stepped back from the pot, rubbing his watering eyes. 'Where did you learn all this?' he asked.

'My mother instructed me, as her mother instructed her; the charms and cures are part of our heritage going back generations.'

'Do you know any more?' he asked, pulling his notebook and pencil from his pocket.

'There is a cure for every disease, a herb for every ill. They grew from the body of Miach, son of Diancecht, sorcerer-physician to Nuada of the Silver Hand ...' She glanced over her shoulder at him. 'Do you know the tale?'

'Of Nuada, yes, but not of Miach and the herbs.' He reached into his pocket and passed the bottle of whiskey over to her. 'Here; drink and tell me.'

The old woman knocked the top off the bottle by tapping it against the stone mantel and then poured the clear and deceptively innocent-looking liquid into a dirty cup. She sipped the fiery liquor and gasped and, as she continued stirring she began to speak in a sing-song fashion, and strangely, her voice lost its aged harshness and dry cackle and became smooth and rounded, her phrases polished and well modulated ...

'Now some time after Diancecht had fitted the silver hand to Nuada's arm, the physician's son came to the king and told him that he could fashion a hand that would far surpass the creation of metal and silver wire that the king wore.

But the king was wary of the youth and questioned him further. 'Tell me,' he said, 'what you have done that your father cannot do.'

And Miach replied. 'There was a young man I knew who had lost his eye in a hurling match and had been forced to wear a patch to cover the gaping hole in his face. So I took the eye of a cat and fixed it in place of the lost eye and breathed life into it and henceforth that man could see from that eye.'

'And what he does not tell you,' said Diancecht, coming up behind his son, 'is that the young man never had a night's peace again and was eventually driven insane. For, although my son had taken the eye from the cat, he had not taken the cat from the eye. It still retained its hunting instinct and at dead of night it would always snap open at the sound of the scurry of a mouse or the rustle of the wind through the long grass. It would follow the passage of a flight of birds more readily than the flight of an arrow.'

'But I had given him what you could not: sight,' said his son.

And Nuada remained silent until at length, he said, 'But if it were possible to have a hand of flesh and blood again . . .'

'It is impossible,' Diancecht protested, 'and if you remove the silver hand I have fitted you with, then it will be impossible to replace it again.'

'Trust in me,' Miach said, 'I can replace your hand.'

'Then I want nothing to do with this,' the physician said and turned on his heel and walked out.

And Nuada leaned forward and grasped the young man's jaw in his metal fingers and squeezed slightly. 'You are gambling with your life on this,' he said.

And so Miach took Nuada's severed hand which had been preserved in alcohol, and boiled it until every shred of flesh had dropped away and it was naught but bare bones. He then covered the bones with the blood of a virgin maid and the first seed of a young man and set it in a box wherein spiders lurked. The following day, the spiders had woven a web about the hand and the blood and seed had dried and hardened into something that resembled flesh. And then the young man had taken the hand and placed it against his breast so that his heartbeat might echo into it. This done, he coated the hardened hand with a mixture of wet ash and soot and left it to dry. A day later he brought it forth into the fresh morning air and washed the dirt off in the dew and dried the hand in the first rays of the morning sun.

And then he joined it to the king's arm.

It was perfect in every way: the skin soft and pliant, without blemishes, the nails long and rounded and the veins thick and alive, pulsating and throbbing. Nuada held his arm aloft, flexing and unflexing his fingers, watching the wrinkles and creases appear and the whorls and circles etch themselves into his fingertips.

'It's alive,' he cried.

But Diancecht was jealous of his son's success and, drawing his sword, struck his son across the forehead. But Miach healed the wound with his powers. Again his father struck his son and once again Miach healed the wound. And then Diancecht, grasping the sword in both hands, brought the weapon down on his son's head, almost severing the skull into two parts. And this wound Miach could not cure and he died.

And when they laid him in the earth a strange thing happened. For out of the barren ground, 365 herbs and healing plants grew, one for each joint and sinew of his body and each one with the power to cure the ills of that part of the body.

And then Aermaid, Miach's sister, carefully plucked each one and labelled it according to its nature, but Diancecht came and tore the labels from them and tossed the herbs about until they were hopelessly mixed and confused and there was no telling them apart ...'

The old woman's voice faltered and the familiar harshness crept back into it. She drank again from the cup and added, 'Oh, over the years, the druids and later the wise women, rediscovered some of the herbs and their uses, like elder for the shivers, daisy for the eyes, a gooseberry thorn for styes, the bark of an elder tree for a burn or hemlock to cause love ...' She shrugged, 'There are many such.'

'Didn't Diancecht prepare a special cauldron of herbs before the Battle of Mag Turiad?' Michael asked.

'He did; and all those who suffered wounds were bathed

in the cauldron and came out of it whole, their wounds healed.'

'Surely he could have healed Nuada's hand that way also?'

'Aaah, but the king had had his hand struck away. Had it only been wounded then it might have been healed. But whereas the cauldron could heal what was there, it could not replace what had already been lost.'

The young man scribbled frantically, the scrape of his pencil across the paper the only sound in the cottage beside the crackling of the fire. 'Are there special times for picking herbs?' he asked when he was finished.

'Herbs should be picked on Beltine Eve in the name of the New God if they are intended to be used for good and on Samhain Eve if they will be used in . . . other work. Some are best picked at the dead of night, whilst others must be plucked with the first light of dawn or at midday . . . *Sorcha*!'

Michael shifted in his seat, surprised to see the young woman standing in the doorway. The light was behind her, so he could not see the expression on her face, but he had the impression that she was angry.

'Mother!' She crossed the room in long strides, tore the bottle from her mother's hand and tossed it into the fire where it exploded in a roar of flames. She rounded on the young man. 'How dare you bring alcohol into this house.' Her voice cracked in the silence and her eyes, illuminated by the leaping flames, were chill and hard. 'I think you had better leave.'

'I don't understand . . .' Michael muttered.

'I would not expect you to,' she snapped.

Michael breathed deeply, trying to calm his rising anger. 'I meant no harm – and your mother does not seem adversely affected by the drink.'

Sorcha placed her hands on her hips and her eyes locked with his. For a moment the tension between the two was almost palpable, an almost physical entity that threatened to engulf them both. And then Michael lowered his eyes, breaking the contact that had seemed almost too intimate. Sorcha laughed maliciously and turned away.

'Drink loosens my mother's tongue,' she said, without turning around.

'But your mother has told me nothing untoward. All I'm interested in is the folklore of our country . . .'

She turned and took a step closer to him. 'And why, may I ask? What do you hope to gain by it; what use is it to you?'

'I will gain nothing by it,' he protested, surprised by the venom in her voice. 'It is interesting . . . and it should not be lost.'

'I don't believe you,' Sorcha said coldly. 'There must be another reason. Now go!'

Michael looked over her shoulder at the older woman for support of some kind, but she had turned her back on him and was slowly stirring the contents of the bubbling pot.

He nodded slowly. 'I see,' he said, not sure that he did.

'I'm sure you do.'

He stuck his pencil in his pocket and crossed to the door, conscious of the young woman's mocking gaze on his back. As he stepped out into the early afternoon, he heard a low laugh behind him and Sorcha called after him, 'Give my regards to your brother.'

All-Hallows Eve.

The time of year when the boundaries between this world and the next weaken and the dead rise and walk amongst men. A time of year hallowed back into the distant past, honoured as Samhain, the new year. A time of year hallowed by both the followers of the Christ and those who still kept faith with the older, wilder gods.

A time of power. A time of death.

When Peter opened his eyes, he found Sorcha already awake, sitting up in bed, staring at him with a strange look in her eyes. He smiled sleepily and, pushing himself closer to her, rested his head against her midriff, beneath her breasts. Her long slender fingers gently stroked his sweat-curled hair and traced the curve of his neck, sending electric tingles racing down his spine. Beneath the blankets, his free hand moved slowly up the length of her leg, fingertips circling and encircling her warm flesh. He could feel his desire rising as his heartbeat quickened. He reached for her and pulled her down across him ... and then his breath caught as he noticed the long weal that ran down her left side beneath her breasts.

He traced its length with his fingertips. 'Who did this?' he whispered.

'Who do you think,' she said bitterly.

'I didn't notice it last night; when did he do it?'

She pushed herself off him and folded her arms across her breasts, her fingers clutching her sides as if she were cold.

'Oh, it was there, you were just too busy to notice it,' she said. 'He did it yesterday morning. I angered him, so he hit me – with the edge of his belt.'

Peter felt the slow bubble of anger begin to seep through him. He sat up and examined the mark carefully. It was a long weal, nearly four inches long and about an inch wide, the skin red and angry, slightly puffed around the edges. 'Bastard! Why did he hit you for God's sake?'

Sorcha laughed bitterly. 'Why? Does he need a reason? Oh, it was because although we've been married nearly two years now, he's never been able to consummate our marriage. Oh, he's tried ...' she smiled coldly, 'but as I've already explained, one of mother's little cures ensures that he never will.' She shrugged, the movement rippling the muscles in her torso. 'But yesterday he insisted – and he tried and he failed. He just wanted someone to take his anger out on; so he took it out on me.'

'I'll kill him,' Peter swore. 'I swear it – I'll kill him.'

'Brave words,' she mocked him gently, 'but you can do nothing for me.'

His hands tightened on her forearms. 'I swear it, I will do anything for you – even if it means killing him. I will not allow him to mistreat you.'

'Will you?' she breathed.

'I will.'

Sorcha leaned over and kissed him gently and then she

pulled a small bottle from beneath the pillow. The morning shafts of sunlight caught the bottle and held it, turning the dark liquid within ochre, sparkling from tiny flecks that circled slowly within the liquid.

'What is it?' he asked.

'It is a cure for potency!' She laughed at his shocked expression and then she laid a finger across his lips and her voice turned cold and urgent. 'Now listen to me, my love, and if you truly love me, then you will do as I say. Will you listen?'

She waited until he nodded slowly and then continued. 'This night is Samhain Eve – All-Hallows Eve, one of the Four Great Sabbats of the Old Faith, and the night when the dead walk.

'Now Donal is intensely superstitious and he will spend the night securely locked indoors, drowning his fears in a bottle, starting at every little scratch and knocking in the rafters and generally trying to drink himself into a stupor by early evening.

'But what I intend to do tonight is add a little of this,' she raised the small bottle, 'to his food.'

'But why?' Peter protested, 'what good will that do?'

'It will arouse in him an intense desire and, coupled with his long abstinence, a desire that should prove overwhelming.'

'But he will take you.'

'No. He will not take me. As soon as his lust is aroused – and I will do my best to aid him in that – he will come for me ... and I will flee into the night.'

'And ...?' Peter prompted.

'And he will follow,' she said quickly. 'Now, the drug will only last a short time and soon his old fears will take over ... and all we have to do is make sure those fears claim him. All we have to do is frighten him to death!'

Peter caught his breath. Oh, he had often thought of killing the old man. He was an animal, a beast; he deserved death. But certainly nothing so clever as frightening him to death – shooting him in an "accident", pushing him into the pond or sprinkling some of the poisonous mushrooms on his food. Somehow, actually terrifying the old man to death was . . . different and to hear it spoken of in the cold light of dawn was somehow cruel . . . and terribly frightening.

'And with him dead,' Sorcha continued, 'it will be just you and me and his money. We will be rich; we can move from here, go to Dublin or London or even Paris. Just you and me. Will you do it?'

Peter stared at the small glass bottle as if mesmerised . . . for in the morning sunlight, the liquid was slowly taking on a blood-red hue, but then Sorcha tucked it back beneath the pillow and gripped both his shoulders, staring deep into his eyes.

'Will you do it for me?' she whispered gently.

He nodded slowly, the decision forming somewhere deep within him, but although he nodded, he could not dispel the idea that he was merely acting out a part and that the decision had never really been his to make in the first place.

Sorcha breathed her thanks and then gently pulled him across her body. Her legs opened in invitation as he settled between them and took his pleasure from her body.

But had he seen her a few moments later as the height of his passion swept him aloft to a shattering culmination, he would have seen such a look of disgust and triumph mingled on her face that perhaps his decision would have been different.

Donal MacIntee huddled over the fire, a plate on his knees, shovelling the food into his mouth. A bottle of whiskey stood on the floor beside him, already one-third empty. He was a short, squat man running to fat. His head seemed tiny on his wide shoulders and was totally hairless. Tiny eyes and a small mouth were almost lost beneath rolls of fat, and his face was lined with scores of broken veins.

Sorcha stood in the shadows at the other side of the room, watching her husband eat and drink, disgust and repulsion on her face. She had laced both the food and drink with the liquid 'cure' and it would start to act soon. She had slipped into the bedroom while he ate – the bedroom she had shared only a few hours earlier with Peter Casside – and when she emerged, she was dressed only in a flimsy garment of black lace. It was completely transparent, falling to just below her knees and open from her throat down to her deep navel. She had touched her temples, throat and wrists with a delicate perfume and unbound her hair, allowing it to fall down her back in a long shimmering wave.

Donal dropped the plate to the floor with a crash and, snatching the bottle from the floor, drank long and deeply, as if he sought to assuage a raging thirst. With his free hand he loosened his collar and looked around the shadowed room for his wife.

'Sorcha . . . ?' His voice was harsh and raw, both from the liquor and the hot food. Damn her, where was she?

'Yes?' The single word hung on the air for a long moment whilst Donal tried to absorb the image before his eyes. It was his wife Sorcha . . . but it couldn't be. His eyes floated down her body, lingering at her breasts with the hard nipples showing through the black lace and down to where the shadows fell across her long legs.

'You called me?' she asked quietly, her voice a husky whisper.

He stood and took a step nearer to her, suddenly conscious of the pain in his groin, the pounding of his blood in his head and his sharp breathing. He wanted her – he needed her! And tonight he would have her!

He lunged across the room, reaching for her, but she slipped to one side, eluding him. Again Donal reached for her; one of his hands brushed the long shining length of her hair and he held on and came away with a thick tuft. Sorcha squealed in pain and stumbled to the door. She waited until he was almost on top of her and then she flung the door open and fled out into the night, her long black gown floating out behind her like a huge pair of wings.

Donal paused by the door, all his old fears coming back to haunt him and then the sight of Sorcha's almost naked body racing down along the path inflamed him further and he took off in pursuit.

And as he disappeared down the path, a single figure

dressed in black and carrying a large bundle stepped out from the shadows and silently padded after him.

Sorcha paused before entering the wood and pulled her gown over her head and hung it on a low branch. She revelled in the caress of the wind across her body; felt her breasts tighten as they would when her lover touched them, felt the long muscles in her thighs and abdomen tighten. She shuddered in pleasure and then turned and fled into the wood like some elder sprite or nymph from a dim and distant legend.

Donal was breathing hard by the time he reached the wood. His heart was pounding in his chest and his temples throbbed. He leaned against the bole of a fallen tree and felt the wind dry the sweat on his face. He shivered and was abruptly conscious of the silence of the night, the only noise the whispering insinuation of sound made by the wind soughing through the branches all around him. Something flickered before his face and he almost cried aloud, his hand striking out at the object only to become entangled in something soft and clinging. With his free hand he tore the cloth from his arm and held it to his face and inhaled Sorcha's delicate perfume. The scent inflamed him and he turned and followed the path into the fastness of the wood.

And behind him, the shadowed figure knelt on the ground and unwrapped his bundle and when he arose the outline of his head was somehow different, almost unnatural. And then he set off at a loping run into the wood.

By day the wood was a place of peace and solitude; it was small and familiar, almost friendly. The trees provided shade from the sun and shelter from the wind and rain. It had once been part of the great forests that covered Ireland in the far distant past when the land had been called *Inis na bhFodhbhuidhe* – the Woody Isle. But time, the elements and man – the worst offender – had gradually eaten away the great forests, leaving only a few small, almost pathetic looking woods in their place.

And if by day the woods seemed to sleep, by night they came alive with malign memories.

Donal MacIntee raced down the rough track between the

trees, the long branches lashing at his face and hands, clutching at him with taloned fingers. He stumbled through bushes and the thorns tore through the cloth of his trousers and flayed his skin bloody. Unseen roots sent him sprawling and as he lay panting on the ground, the huge trees crept closer, towered over him, leered down, prepared to rend and destroy . . .

With a muffled sob, he pushed himself to his feet and continued on, running deeper and deeper into the forest, taunted by a mocking laughter and pursued now by someone moving through the wood.

He was almost mad with fear by the time he broke out from the forest and into a small clearing. He stopped suddenly, his heart hammering and his lungs labouring.

A low, throaty laugh came out of the shadows behind him. Donal whirled around and Sorcha stepped out into the light. Donal caught his breath and stepped backwards, out into the centre of the clearing. Here, in this wild and lonely place, on this night, with his wife standing naked before him, he was suddenly terribly frightened, even more so than he had been in the wood.

Sorcha took a step closer to her husband, the wan light from the heavens touching her skin with grey, lending her an almost ghostly appearance.

'S-S-Sorcha. . .?' His voice was hoarse, only a little above a whisper.

The young woman reached out with her left hand, the fingers splayed, palm downwards and then she slowly contracted her hand into a claw. 'I have called Him for you,' she whispered sibilantly.

'What!' Donal yelped.

'I have given you to my Master,' she whispered. 'He is coming for you!'

'Your Master?'

'My Lord Satan!' she cried aloud. 'Listen, even now he comes.' She suddenly jabbed a finger at Donal. 'And he is coming for you!'

And from the shadows behind Donal a terrifying laugh suddenly issued, low and obscene. He whirled around as the bushes trembled and shook and then something stepped out from the trees that sent Donal reeling back in absolute terror. It was a creature, taller than a man, with eyes of burning fire. And from its head rose antlered horns.

Donal turned to flee, but stumbled and fell and before he could rise a heavy clawed hand fell on his shoulder and the hideous face closed with his. *'You are mine!'*

Donal felt the pain lance through his left arm and shoulder and then blossom in his chest. His head exploded in fire as one hand tore at his breast, seeking to ease the pain, the unmerciful, unremitting pain. And he wondered, as the darkness exploded into fire, why he did not feel his heart pounding ...?

Sorcha walked across the clearing and stood above the corpse, staring down at the sightless eyes and the gaping mouth and then she turned to the antlered figure and nodded. 'You did well.'

Peter struggled with the heavy mask, pulling it from his head, drying the sweat on his face with the back of his hand. He was gasping for breath with the heat of the mask and the exertion. He ran his fingers through his sweat-dampened hair. 'Is he dead?' he asked.

Sorcha nudged the corpse with her bare foot. 'He is.'

'What do we do now?' Peter asked. Reaction was setting in and he began to shiver.

'We do nothing,' Sorcha said. 'We leave him. I'll report him missing around noon tomorrow ... he will be found sooner or later.'

'And what about us; what will we do?'

Sorcha stepped over the body and pressed herself against Peter. 'Oh, I'm sure we can think of something,' she said, feeling his body beginning to respond to her closeness. She pulled him down into the dew damp grass and with practised fingers pulled the clothes from him and there, beside the stiffening body of her husband, they made love.

November quickly gave way to December, bringing with it snow and ice. The scandal surrounding Donal MacIntee's death soon passed only to be re-inflamed almost immediately when she and Peter Casside announced their engagement and posted the banns. There was talk in the town and there were some, including the local doctor, who had seen the look of absolute terror on MacIntee's face, who believed that his death was not entirely natural.

Michael Casside kept to himself and avoided old Mother Cleirigh. He had his own suspicions about the death of Sorcha's husband and a terrible gnawing fear was growing about his brother's involvement in it. Their mother was shocked with her son's involvement with the young widow and especially so soon after the death without allowing a decent time for proper mourning.

But Peter merely laughed at his mother's disgust and his brother's fears, and ignored them both.

As the year drew quickly towards its turning, a small party of strangers, who were passing through the town were forced to stay there by the bad weather. They took shelter with several of the villagers until such time as the roads were opened again. However, they were friendly people and entered into the preparations for the coming Christmas with great enthusiasm. And Peter noticed that Sorcha also, became very involved with the preparations and seemed curiously excited at the prospect of the approaching festive season.

Michael's eyes snapped open and he lay still on the hard bed listening to the pounding of his heart, wondering what had awoken him. The sound of cloth on cloth brought him bolt upright ...

'Sssh, it's only me.' His twin moved closer to his bed. He leaned over, his face a pale oval in the darkness. 'I've got to go out,' he whispered.

'But mother ...'

'Mother is inside, snoring drunk, she'll never know.'

'But Peter, for God's sake, it's Christmas Eve ...'

'I know ... I know ... Look, I won't be long.' He shrugged

into his coat and pulled on a pair of woollen gloves. He gently eased open the frost encrusted window, allowing a chill blast to sweep through the room and then pulled himself up onto the sill and slipped out into the night. Wearily, Michael climbed from his warm bed and quickly closed the window, the cold metal stinging his fingers. He rubbed a circle on the glass and squinted out into the night, but there was no sign of his brother.

Peter hurried down the road, head down, hands tucked deep into his pockets. He walked by the side of the road on the stiffened grass, the only sound in the night the slight crunching of his footsteps.

Sorcha was waiting for him at the crossroads. She was enveloped in a long hooded cloak and her features were lost in the cowl's shadows. She started almost perceptibly as Peter crept up behind her and as she reached out to embrace him, he was surprised to find her arms were bare. She drew his head down close to hers and breathed gently into his ear. 'Follow me; tonight I need you so badly . . .' She ran a long-nailed hand down the side of his face and traced the contours of his lips. 'Tonight,' she whispered, 'I will make you mine – forever.'

Sorcha led him into the wood – the same wood they had led her husband into a few weeks ago. Beneath the trees the ground was hard but unmarked by ice and the tiny brook that wound its way amongst the trees still trickled sluggishly. Sorcha stopped by the brook, stooped and touched it with her fingers and then brought them to her lips. She gasped with the chill and then huddled closer to Peter. 'Tell me,' she whispered, 'did anyone see you leave tonight?'

He shook his head in the darkness. 'No-one, no-one except Michael that is.'

She smiled suddenly, her teeth startlingly white in the darkness. 'He is of no consequence,' she murmured, and then asked, 'Does he still talk about me?'

Peter laughed grimly. 'Oh, he does occasionally; and now he warns me about you. He says you're an evil influence and ... other things.'

She smiled slightly. 'Tell me, what does he say about me?'

Peter shrugged uncomfortably. 'He says your mother is a witch and in all probability you are also.'

'Oh, and how does he make that out?'

'He said something about the stories your mother told him, something about charms and spells.'

Sorcha nodded. 'I told my mother to keep her mouth shut!'

Peter stopped suddenly. 'But ... it's not true is it: you're not a witch!'

The young woman laughed and in that desolate place, at that time of night, her laughter was hideous and obscene. 'You fool!' she said, her voice hard and chill. 'Of course I am a witch, as my mother was before me and her mother before her. I was dedicated to our Lord and Master whilst still in the womb.'

Peter dropped her arm and stepped back away from her, fear and confusion flickering across his face. 'But ...'

'But that shouldn't bother you now, should it? All you wanted was me ...' She suddenly opened the cloak, revealing her nakedness beneath. 'All you wanted was this!' she spat contemptuously.

Peter took a step backwards and would have turned and fled had Sorcha not called out in a hollow, commanding voice. 'Stay!'

His muscles abruptly locked and he was unable to move. He broke out in a cold sweat as shadows moved on either side of him and from the trees a small group of cowled and cloaked figures emerged. Sorcha gestured to him. 'He is ours!'

'A twin?' The voice was that of a man, and the accent was strange, definitely not from the town.

'They are almost identical,' Sorcha said, a deferential note creeping into her voice.

'You have done well; and the other?'

Sorcha smiled grimly. 'He will be mine,' she promised.

'We must have him.' There was a hint of a threat in the man's voice.

'We will,' Sorcha snapped, 'but first let us take this one.' She tapped Peter lightly on his shoulder, sending pain lancing down his body.

'Come!' she commanded in the same hollow, slightly echoing voice she had used before.

Obediently Peter turned and, surrounded by the cloaked figures, followed Sorcha into the depths of the wood.

And although it was warm beneath the blankets, Michael Casside shivered, tossed and turned, his dreams uneasy.

Peter immediately recognised the clearing into which Sorcha led them: it was where they had trapped and terrified Donal to death. Like some dumb animal, he was led to the centre of the clearing to where a huge slab of stone had been recently cleaned of its lichens and mosses. Tiny crystals sparkled in the rock in the wan light and the stone itself seemed too regular to be natural.

Sorcha turned and smiled coldly at Peter and a long black-hafted knife glittered in her hand as she raised it. Her eyes held his as she approached and he almost vomited as she slashed at him with the knife. A thin thread of fire blossomed across his chest and his coat and shirt hung in long tatters. Again and again Sorcha slashed at him, the razor sharp blade lacerating his flesh as it cut away his clothing. Soon, he stood naked, his clothes in an untidy bundle about his feet, hot blood trickling in thin lines from scores of cuts on his chest and arms. Sorcha laughed and wiped the blood from the knife on the edge of her cloak and then stood back as two of the hooded figures caught him by the arms and legs and laid him across the stone slab. Curiously enough, the stone was not as chill as he expected and it was as warm as if it had baked in the afternoon sun.

Peter felt absolute terror engulf him; his mind screamed aloud and he attempted to pray, but his gods seemed so very distant on that cold December night and he felt so alone.

Michael came awake suddenly. He glanced over at his brother's bed, but it was empty. Silence pervaded the cottage and he could tell from the position of the stars through the window that the night was far advanced. He settled himself back; the uneasiness that had troubled him earlier had returned, but now it was something more, for now it was something approaching fear.

The figures had shed their long cloaks and now moved widdershins about the naked figure lying on the slab. And although they too were naked, they seemed unaffected by the December chill. Peter strained to make out their features, but from his horizontal position it was almost impossible. No-one looked familiar . . . and then he suddenly realised that these were the strangers who had been 'forced' to stop over in the town by the harsh weather.

They were chanting aloud in a strange tongue, a language that sounded not unlike Irish, but a far older version of the language. And although he could not understand their words, even he knew they were calling someone . . . or something. He squirmed on the stone, but the invisible bonds that held him were immovable, unbreakable.

Suddenly a figure loomed up out of the night and stood over him. It was Sorcha, her breasts heaving as if she were in the throes of passion. There was something wild and free about her, something primeval. And then the realisation struck home, perhaps fully for the first time; she was a witch and she was about to sacrifice him to her pagan gods!

To his amazement, she leaned over and kissed him, and he found then that he could speak once again. 'Why Sorcha, for God's sake, why?'

'Whose gods?' she murmured softly, almost intimately. 'Yours or mine - and remember, mine are far older, far stronger. They were ancient when your Christ was butchered on a tree; they were strong then and time has only made them stronger, whilst your faith is still growing.' She ran her fingertips down the length of his body, from collar-bone to groin and then down again, tracing a long V ón his flesh. 'Your faith may have driven us underground, but as your own church should know, a faith is at its strongest when it is being persecuted.'

'What are you going to do with me?' Peter asked calmly.

'We are going to sacrifice you to our Master,' she said simply.

'Is your god so weak that he needs the sacrifice of men to sustain him?'

Sorcha laughed gently. 'You sound like your brother,' she said, almost absently. 'But no, our Master does not need the sacrifice – but we do. You see,' she said slowly, 'twins are linked in a very special way, there is a bond between them, an unbreakable bond. And although they are complete in themselves, yet they are like two parts of the one person.'

'What are you trying to say?' Peter snapped.

'Oh, gently, gently,' Sorcha chided. 'What I am trying to say,' she whispered, climbing astride Peter, 'is that we are going to sacrifice you at a critical moment, thus ensuring that your powers, your abilities – undeveloped as yet – will be passed on to your brother. We will give him part of your soul as it were; we will make him something more than a man – and I will control that man!'

'Never!'

'Oh yes,' she whispered, 'oh yes.' She slid her body down his, arousing and exciting him against his will, for although he felt revulsion, his body betrayed him and responded to hers.

The feeling of oppression had become stronger and Michael Casside shivered in a cold sweat. There was a terrible feeling of foreboding within him . . . and there was nothing he could do about it.

Sorcha clinically observed Peter's reaction. When he

became too excited, she drew back and allowed his excitement to lessen, for the timing must be right, and it would be soon, for the dawn was almost upon them.

The small clearing was now enveloped in a glowing nimbus of raw power; it cracked and sparked like summer lightning, writhed along the cold hard ground like a serpent. The tiny crystals in the stone glowed with a blue fire bathing both Sorcha's and Peter's bodies in a ghastly hue. The stone was now warm, almost repuslively so, for it resembled human flesh.

And as the first rays of the Christmas morning sun broke over the trees and touched the stone with golden fire, Sorcha brought Peter to a shattering climax – and plunged her dagger into his labouring heart!

Michael awoke screaming.

He felt as if something had been torn from within him. There was a void, a terrible aching void ... and then something seeped into that void, something which trembled and shivered like a new-born babe. It was both strange and familiar; it was and at the same time was not, his brother. But it *was* part of him.

Michael knew then what Sorcha had done to his brother. She had slain him in a mid-winter sacrifice and now the power that had been his brother's, his essence, his soul, had passed on to him. And soon, he knew, she would come for him.

But she would never get him. He would flee now, hide away where they would never find him. And in that instant he swore an oath; an oath to cleanse Ireland from the scourge of witchcraft.

And in that moment, Morand the Witchfinder was born.

CHAPTER 11

THE BLACK BOOK . . . II

'Burn it. Burn all of it!' Tom Kennedy spat into the hay rick and turned away in disgust. He walked the length of the field, pausing at each rick in turn and at each one breathing in the heavy sweet odour of mouldering hay. He turned as he reached the low stone wall that bounded his fields and watched his men systematically torch the ricks, sending plumes of grey-white smoke curling up into the early morning sky. He shut his eyes to the destruction and shook his head; unless he bought expensive feed for his cattle during the winter, they - and his family - would go hungry.

'Tom . . . Tom, get over here.' He turned and ran across the field to where his foreman was stamping out the flames that licked hungrily about the base of a small stack.

'What is it Pat?'

The wizened old man pointed silently into the rick with his pitchfork.

Tom Kennedy stared into the heart of the haystack, covering his nose and mouth with the sleeve of his coat. The stench was revolting - and it was not just the odour of burning wet straw. It was stronger, nauseous and cloying. His eyes watered and he drew back shaking his head. 'What is it?'

The old man prodded the stack with his pitchfork, dislodging a sizeable amount of hay, revealing the interior. Tom took a step forward and swore. 'Jesus preserve us; what is it?'

'It's a side of meat,' Pat Coonan said, 'and I dare say you'll find a couple of eggs in there also, aye, and in each and every one of the spoiled ricks.'

Why?' Tom prodded the mouldering, maggot-infested slab of meat with his stick, knocking it to the ground.

'Why? Well to ruin the stored hay of course. I told you before this lad, someone doesn't like you and they're doing their damnedest to ruin you.'

Tom shook his head stubbornly. 'I don't believe it,' he said.

Pat Coonan looked up at the young man standing before him, the early morning light bringing out the grey streaks in his black hair, although he was no more than eight-and-twenty, and softening the hard lines of his cheekbones and jaw. He was the spit of his father - and as stubborn.

'Now listen to me,' he snapped. He held up a gnarled hand and began ticking off points. 'Your wells have gone dry and if they haven't gone dry then they have been poisoned. The cows have slung their calves - there's not one that has carried her calf full term this season. No hen has laid a fresh egg for a month and we had to destroy the abominations the sow birthed. And now, someone has gone and ruined a year's growth - and ensured that you'll either starve this winter or enter the new year without a penny to your name!' He laughed and spat at Tom's feet. 'And you tell me no-one has done this to you!'

The younger man suddenly slashed at the hay rick with his stick, sending tufts flying into the still air, where it hung momentarily and then drifted down in silent wisps. 'What in God's name am I to do then?' he demanded. 'Who is going to believe that someone has put a curse on me . . . is trying to destroy me?'

The old man shifted some dry straw onto a smouldering patch of grass and watched it smoke and suddenly burst into flame. With the end of his pitchfork he hoisted the burning grass onto the piled straw and watched the flames rapidly regain their hold over the rick. 'Oh, there's plenty would believe you,' he said quietly. 'Some already have,' he added. He looked up and caught the spark of anger in Tom Kennedy's eyes and raised his hand placatingly. 'Now before you get all hot and bothered, I've only done it for your own good.'

'Done what?' Kennedy snapped.

'I've spoken with some of the old folk, people who have some experience with this ... sort of thing, and I've also spoken with Father Horgan ... '

'And when they were finished laughing what did they say – beside the fact that my foreman has gone just a little out of his head?'

Pat Coonan ignored the jibe and continued quietly. 'Oh, there was no laughing I can assure you; they believed what I told them and treated it very seriously indeed.' He paused and prodded the burning rick with his pitchfork, sending sparks spiralling upwards. 'And they advised me to find the Witchfinder!'

Ireland never experienced the witch hunts that plagued England and the continent, and there was never a witchfinder to equal the status of Matthew Hopkins who carried on his reign of terror through the length and breadth of England during the 1640's. There were however, certain people, mainly clerics or those wise in the ways of the country people and the country lore, who took it upon themselves to seek out those who practised the darker side of witchcraft, and foremost amongst them was the priest men called Father Morand, the Witchfinder.

Father Michael Morand strode down the length of the field past the still smouldering hayricks. Tom Kennedy hurried to keep up with the priest's long-legged gait.

'We checked all the ricks Father and it was as Pat said, there was rotten meat and eggs buried in every one of them.'

The tall dark-haired priest nodded impassively as he reached the loose stone wall at the south end of the field. The sun reflected off his eyes, turning them into mirrors, the effect sending shivers along Tom's spine, for the priest's eyes were the most frightening he had ever seen. They were colourless, but with the texture of frozen water and they never seemed to look at a person, but rather through them to a point beyond.

And if the truth were known, Father Michael Morand terrified Tom Kennedy.

'Your foreman said you had been experiencing other ... difficulties,' the priest said softly.

'Coincidence only, Father,' Tom said in embarrassment.

'Tell me,' Father Morand commanded.

'I'm sure you have already been told,' Tom snapped and walked away from the priest.

'Indeed, I have.' The priest's voice drifted across the still morning air, 'But I want you to tell me. Now come back!' The tone of command stopped the younger man in his tracks and he turned, almost unconsciously, and walked back to the priest.

Father Morand placed his hand on Tom's shoulder and spoke in a quieter, gentler tone. 'I'm only trying to help you; if you resist me, you are only aiding those who are trying to destroy you.'

'Father,' Tom said, almost desperately, 'I have no enemies; no-one has any cause to hate me.'

'Ah, but my son, someone has cause enough - aye, and reason enough - to use the Dark Lore to ruin you.' He stretched to his full height and with his stick pointed out across Kennedy's fields. 'Tell me; who owns the lands that border on yours?'

'I own the land as far as the stream.' He pointed south. 'Beyond that it belongs to my brother Seamus.'

'Is your holding greater than his?'

'Considerably. There is also a great difference in age between us - around ten years or so.'

'That would make him about eighteen,' the priest said.

'It would.'

'Is he married?'

Tom laughed. 'Oh no, he lives with our mother. He is very devoted to her - and she to him. I can't see him marrying whilst she still lives.'

Father Morand nodded and then pointed across to the west. 'And over there?'

'The land beyond the road has been held by the Dilane

family for generations – although when Paddy Dilane dies it will have to pass into other hands,' he added.

'There are no children?'

'None.'

Father Morand turned and squinted into the morning sun. 'And here, how far does your land extend?'

'Well most of the land this far east is infertile. I'm treating it of course and allowing it to lie fallow. In a couple of years ... ' he shrugged, 'well it might yield something then.' He pointed to a small copse of trees beside a broken down wall. 'The wall marks the boundary of my land. Beyond that it's more or less common ground.' He spun around and pointed back across the fields towards the north. 'My lands end just behind the white-washed house.'

The tall priest turned slowly and surveyed the land that bordered Kennedy's fields and then his strange colourless eyes fell on the younger man. 'Go home Tom,' he said gently, 'try and get some rest.'

'What will you do?'

The priest smiled curiously. 'I will do nothing,' he said quietly.

Father Horgan lowered his voice and spoke quietly to the tall priest standing by his side. 'You're attracting a lot of attention.'

Michael Morand nodded courteously to a small group of gossiping women who were staring openly in his direction. 'I know,' he said softly, 'I always do.'

'It doesn't seem to bother you,' the older priest remarked.

'No, not now. It did at the beginning; it was one of the many reasons I changed my name.'

'Morand is not your true name then?' Father Horgan said in surprise.

'It is not the name I was baptised with,' he said slowly, 'but Morand was the name of my own choosing – I've grown used to it.'

The two clerics turned off the main street and down a

winding lane that led to the side entrance of the church.

'Was there any official announcement made of my visit?' Father Morand asked.

Father Horgan pulled a long key from a pocket in his sleeve and laughed roughly. 'There was not! We wouldn't like it whispered about that the Witchfinder had come . . . although,' he added ruefully, 'I dare say most of the town already know, or if they do not, then they will by nightfall.'

Father Morand nodded as he entered the gloom of the church. 'Good.'

'You want that?' the older priest said in surprise.

'I have a certain reputation,' Michael said quietly, lowering his voice to a whisper in this place of worship, 'it is a reputation I must admit to have fostered somewhat. Those who dabble in . . . the Elder Faith and the Dark Lore and . . . other beliefs, have cause to fear me. Often that same fear will cause them to make a mistake or attempt to complete a task before its appointed time. All I need is that tiny slip.'

'Is that what you're looking for now?'

Father Morand's colourless eyes took on the pale gold of the candles' glow. 'That is what I am waiting for,' he said quietly.

And beyond the town, in a decaying, weather-beaten cottage, two figures sat in the foul-smelling silence and listened to the first spatters of rain hiss off the mildewed straw on the roof.

'The Witchfinder is in town.'

'He does not frighten me.'

'Then you are a fool.' There was a pause and a rat squeaked in a corner and then the voice continued. 'We must hurry, we must finish it tonight.'

'It is too soon.'

'We have no choice.'

The storm had lessened somewhat by the time Father Morand reached the Kennedy house perched on the rise above the road. Although it was not yet seven o'clock, it was already dark. Low clouds, heavy with rain, rolled languorously across the heavens, propelled by an icy wind.

Father Morand rapped on the heavy wooden door with the iron ferrule of his stout walking stick. The door was opened almost immediately by Pat Coonan, Tom's foreman. He stepped back from the door with a gasp and brought up a long-barrelled shotgun and levelled it at the priest's chest.

Michael Morand chuckled. 'It would surely be embarrassing if you were to shoot me now,' he said gently.

The foreman stepped back and, with his free hand, reached for the candle burning on a small side table in the hall. He lifted it above his head, shedding its wan light onto the priest's hard features. He sighed and lowered the shotgun. 'It's yourself, Father.' He laughed shakily. 'You put the heart crossways in me,' he admitted, and added, 'when I opened the door and saw you standing there, I thought you were the Devil himself.'

'What has happened Pat?' the priest said urgently, stepping into the hallway.

The foreman closed the door and shot the bolts, and then led the way down the short hall and into the main room. It was large, taking up almost the entire ground floor of the two-storied building, but it seemed smaller with the number of people gathered in it. All conversation stopped as Pat led the priest into the room.

'This is Father Michael Morand,' he said unnecessarily.

The group of men nodded respectfully and a low murmur ran around the room ... '*Witchfinder ...*'

The priest stepped up to the fire and stood with his back to it, soaking up the heat, letting it take the chill from his damp clothes. He looked around the room. There were almost twenty men present, most of them armed with shotguns or long-barrelled fowling pieces, some with knives or pitchforks. He was about to demand an explanation when the door opened and Tom Kennedy entered. He looked tired and drawn and there were dark circles under his eyes. He accepted a drink from a hip flask and his hand was visibly trembling as he raised it to his lips.

'How is she?' Pat Coonan asked quietly.

Tom coughed as the raw spirit burned its way down his throat, but when he looked up his fingers were still and his voice was steady. 'The doctor is still with her,' he said, 'and the midwife said she will stay the night.' He shrugged. 'She is sleeping now ... she'll be alright.'

The priest stepped away from the fire. 'I think you had better tell me what happened ... and the reason for this gathering.'

The young farmer started, noting the tall priest's presence for the first time. He smiled wearily. 'I'm glad you're here Father, truly I am.' He waved to a chair. 'Sit down please, all of you, sit down. Pat ... ' he turned to his foreman, 'some drinks for my friends.'

'What happened Tom; tell me.'

The young farmer poked the fire to a blaze and then placed a log in the centre of the flames. He sat back on a low stool, his eyes never leaving the flames licking hungrily about the dry wood.

The room grew silent as he spoke, the men drawing closer together, occasionally raising their heads to listen to the sounds of the night and the rain dripping from the trees outside the windows.

'I returned home when I left you this morning, Father. I delayed only a few minutes to talk with my brother Seamus whom I met on the road. He was heading into town and couldn't delay. As I crossed the yard however, I noticed that it was unusually quiet, and there were no hens running about. I had a look around, but couldn't find them.' He paused and breathed deeply. 'Just before I went in, I checked the barn. And I found them ... Someone ... someone had torn their heads off and then ... tied the carcasses about the rafters with their entrails ... ' He shuddered and drank deeply, allowing the liquid to sear the foul taste from his mouth.

'On the back door I found a frog crucified head downwards, and some words drawn onto the wood in the frog's blood.'

'What words?' Father Morand snapped, leaning forward in his chair.

Tom shook his head. 'I don't know; Sab ... sab-something.'

'"Saboath?"'

'Something like that. And then,' he continued, 'in the kitchen ... in the kitchen I found ...' he broke off and swallowed, and when he continued, his voice was barely above a whisper. 'I found the hens' heads sitting in the tea cups on the dresser. And I found Berni unconscious on the floor ...'

'How is she now?' the priest asked.

'She awoke briefly, but she was very distressed and the doctor gave her a powder. She is sleeping now, but her dreams must be disturbing, for she is speaking and mumbling.'

Father Morand stood. 'Is she speaking now?'

Tom Kennedy nodded.

Without a word, the priest pushed his way through the crowd and made his way up the stairs to the bedroom where Bernadette Kennedy lay in her troubled sleep.

The doctor was packing his small black bag when the priest entered. He looked up, a hand raised to prevent whomever it was from entering, but stopped when he saw the priest's collar. The midwife, a stout young woman from the next town, rose from her seat by the fire and curtsied to the tall figure in black.

Father Morand turned to the doctor. 'Will the shock have any adverse affect on the child?' he asked directly.

Doctor Johnson shook his head. 'I don't think so. The child is due this month, it should be fully grown, and there is little likelihood of any deformity forming now. However, the shock may bring the child on prematurely,' he added.

The priest walked across the room and stood by the bed, and his colourless eyes softened as he looked down at the young woman tossing and turning in her sleep. He turned to the doctor. 'Is there nothing you can do to ease her sleep?'

Johnson shrugged. 'She sleeps, I can do nothing more for

her. I have no control over her dreams.'

Father Morand nodded slightly and then leaned over the bed, listening to the rasping whispers that came from the young woman's slack mouth.

'Raum . . . Shax . . . Vine . . . Gaap . . . Andras . . . Flauros . . .'

The tall priest blanched, and with trembling fingers traced the Sign of the Cross on her fevered brow. The young woman shuddered once and then sighed. Father Morand turned to the doctor. 'She will sleep peacefully now.'

'What was she saying?' the doctor asked quietly, glancing across at the young midwife who was regarding them curiously.

The priest ran his fingers through his thick black hair and shook his head. 'She was calling upon the demons of destruction, hate and revenge,' he said slowly.

'The time approaches; is everything prepared?'

'It is.'

A shadowy figure moved across the floor of the cottage, careful not to disturb the circle drawn onto the hard floor with tiny flecks of powdered lamb's bones. 'Tonight, we will destroy the mother and unborn child - and ultimately the father!'

The night drifted on towards midnight, and the storm which had blown most of the afternoon and intermittently through the night now died down leaving a chill silence in its wake. The room was quiet, men speaking in whispers, drinking carefully or tending to their weapons. They had come of their own accord when they heard of the afternoon's happening, drawn together by the common country bond. Tom Kennedy was one of theirs, his family had lived in the county for generations, he was well liked and respected. And, much as they would gather together to hunt down a fox that was attacking their coops, they gathered now to do what they could to help him fight the force that was threatening his family.

The clock on the wall struck midnight, its hollow chimes

making everyone jump, but helping to break the morose spell that had fallen over the room. Pat Coonan, who was more than a little drunk, suddenly turned to the priest. 'Father, is it the witches?'

Michael Morand spoke into the deathly silence that now claimed the room. 'It is possible. There is some evidence of witchcraft,' he said carefully.

'Ah, I knew,' Pat said, 'I was in Clonmel in '94 when there was that witch burning.'

The priest nodded. 'I was there also; it was a shocking affair,' he said.

'What happened?' one of the men asked.

Father Morand poked the fire and tossed a length of wood onto it. 'It must have been around March 1894 or thereabouts, when I was called in to investigate what was later called the Clonmel Burning.'

'Did they ever hang that madman, Father?' Pat Coonan asked suddenly.

'They did not; they gave him twenty years hard labour.'

'It was no more than he deserved,' the foreman said.

'Yes,' the priest continued, 'it was in March '94 when I was asked to assist an Inspector Wansborough in the investigation of a brutal murder which had taken place in Ballyvadlea, which is some ways to the north of Clonmel, between Cloneen and Mullinahone.

'A young woman, Brigid Cleary, had disappeared, and her husband, Michael, her father Patrick Boland, along with an aunt, cousins and a local herb-doctor, stood accused of her murder. But what made this affair unusual - and the reason I was called in - was the fact that Michael Cleary claimed that his wife had been taken by the fairies and a changeling, who was also a witch, had replaced her.

'Michael Cleary, with the aid of his relatives, forced Brigid to drink potions prepared by Denis Ganey, the herb-doctor, and when these did not have the desired effect of driving out the changeling's assumed form, one of the group, her cousin, John Dunne, suggested that they hold her over a fire, so that the flames - which she was accustomed to in hell - might shake off her form.

'They tortured her in this fashion for several hours, and then calmly retired for the evening.

'In the morning however, Michael Cleary went completely beserk, and after repeatedly burning his wife with a red-hot piece of metal, emptied the contents of an oil lamp over her and set her alight.

'But this time there was a witness - a neighbour, a Mrs Burke, who had called upon Brigid Cleary, and was a horrified witness to the morning's events. She alerted the police ... ' the priest's voice trailed off and he drank quickly from a glass of water. 'I found the body several days later with my ... craft. She had been buried in a shallow grave just a little ways from her home.' He shuddered and breathed deeply. 'Her injuries were terrible; her legs were but charred stumps, and the skin of her back and abdomen was burnt almost beyond recognition, and her left hand was but a withered claw.

'Michael Cleary was insane of course, and the others ... well, some were definitely evil and took some delight in the poor woman's sufferings, but the rest I would say truly believed in what they were doing.

'But they confused the fairy and the witch-lore; they believed Brigid was a changeling who was also a witch ... ' Father Morand shook his head, 'and that of course, is impossible.'

'And was the woman of the *sidhe*, Father?' someone asked in a hushed voice.

The priest shook his head. 'I doubt it, although her husband claimed that she was some two inches taller than his wife, and that he had seen her astride a smoke-grey horse riding out of Kylegranagh, a local fairy fort. However,' Michael Morand added, 'while I was in town, I discovered that Michael Cleary's mother has something of a reputation for being wise in the ways of the fairies and that she would often go to the fairy fort.' The priest drank again. 'Undoubtedly, the son knew of these rumours, and perhaps his own fear that his wife might do the same drove him over the brink of madness.'

'And I thought such things were long since past,' Tom

Kennedy murmured, almost to himself.

The priest smiled. 'Unfortunately not. I know for example that you Tom, spent some time both in Cork and Dublin, away from the land and the elements; you have forgotten your country lore - otherwise, you would have called me in much sooner.'

'But witchcraft, Father!' the young man protested.

'Yes my son, witchcraft. Whilst there is good, there must also be evil: one cannot exist without the other. And there will always be those who are attracted to the mystique that surrounds witch-lore, they are attracted to the power and secrecy that clings to the occult. For such people, its lure is unbreakable.'

'But does it work?' Tom asked.

The priest nodded grimly. 'It works, because they believe that it works.'

The storm which had died down briefly, now blew up again, venting its fury in a maelstrom of destruction about the house. Gale force winds ripped the leaded tiles from the roof and sent them winging into the night like obscene birds. The rending and tearing brought the group in the sitting-room to their feet, and then Morand, followed closely by Tom Kennedy went out into the hall and up the stairs, taking them two at a time. They burst into the bedroom to find the doctor lying on the floor beneath a pile of shattered tiles, an angry cut welling blood from the side of his face, and the midwife cowering in a corner. Father Morand pointed to the sleeping woman, and screamed above the howling of the storm that was now tearing in through the open roof. Even though Tom couldn't hear him, his meaning was clear. As Tom bundled his wife up in the blankets, the priest pulled the shivering midwife from the corner. She struggled and struck at him, seeing only a tall figure in black that reached for her with long talons. Her hooked fingers caught his face and one long nail caught and tore the skin of his face, just below his eye. The priest grunted, and then struck the girl a glancing blow on the point of her chin. Her eyes rolled in her head and she slumped unconscious. With surprising ease, the tall priest caught the heavy girl in his arms and ran for the door. He dragged the doctor to his feet and pushed him out onto the landing and slammed the door shut just as the chimney, which had been swaying wildly in the wind, tore free and came crashing down through the roof into the bedroom below.

The priest tucked the unconscious woman under one arm, and hauled the stunned doctor to his feet, and then, pushing Tom in front of him, headed for the stairs. They were half-way down, when they met Pat Coonan coming up fast. He swore briefly at the sight of the priest holding the two still bodies and Tom carrying his still sleeping wife.

'What's happening?' he shouted above the howling of the wind.

'Witch-storm!' Morand shouted.

The storm howled around the house, ripping shutters from the windows, tearing up fences and rails. The barns and outbuildings were battered into matchwood; all standing crops were flattened and the fields turned into muddy quagmires.

In the sitting-room, the assembled men were numbed with fear, the weapons they had handled so confidently earlier that evening, now useless against the outraged forces of nature.

As Father Morand, Tom Kennedy and Pat Coonan pushed their way into the room with their charges, the fire in the grate suddenly blazed azure and emerald and then exploded in a shower of flaming cinders and sparks. The men scattered, stamping on the scores of tiny fires that started in the room. The priest ducked as a lump of wood came through the window and shattered on the wall above his head. He handed the groaning midwife to Pat and then walked to the centre of the room. He stretched to his full height and, seemingly oblivious to the storm that now whipped in through the open window, crossed himself and his lips began to move in silent prayer.

The storm grew in strength and force immediately. The

room's three other windows shattered beneath an onslaught of fist-sized lumps of hail. The temperature in the room plummeted. The oil lamps shattered and the flames burned blue-green before dying. A foul odour pervaded the room, an odour of rotten meat and burned flesh, of putrefying fish and ozone.

Tom Kennedy gagged and covered his wife's mouth and nose ... and then he felt the child kicking. Bernadette moaned and her face spasmed in pain. Tom felt the muscles in her back ripple and flow, and he could feel the sudden increase in her heartbeat. A small cry escaped her lips, and then she cried aloud in pain. She was going into labour.

The priest bowed his head and crossed himself once again. And then he raised his hands high and, with splayed fingers began to gather the force of the storm to him, reeling it in as an angler a catch ... He could feel the abrupt upsurge of power as the force was concentrated about his body, could see the writhing blue nimbus gathering about his head, could hear the sharp crackling along his body. Tendrils of fire ran along his pointing fingers and gathered in small pulsating blue globes about his nails. Tiny silver and black dust motes danced about his head, twisting and turning like flies, suddenly flaring into incandescent spots of white-hot heat that threatened to blind the priest.

Every hair on his head rose and crackled with the raw power that now encircled his body. His head became a ball of livid metallic colours as the forces sparked from his hair, and Tom Kennedy watched in horror as the colour was slowly leeched from the priest's hair, leaving it silver-white.

Father Morand began to cry aloud in a strange language, the words seeming to echo slightly in the room. He then turned to the four cardinal points and spoke in a different tongue - and suddenly the electrical tension in the room increased, forcing everyone onto the floor or up against the walls leaving the Witchfinder the only one standing. And then he faced the East and cried aloud in what everyone recognised as a variant of English.

'And we abjure and abhor thee, and command thee depart in the Name of the Living God and of the True One, of the

Three that are One, and the One that is All. I command thee depart in the All-Powerful Names of the Most High God: On, Alpha and Omega, Eloy, Eloym, Ya, Saday, Lux, Mugiens, Rex, Salus, Adonay, Emmanuel, Messias!

'I command and compel thee depart with all thy infernal legions by the Names which are Unutterable save by the sigils, V, C, and X, and by the Names which are Holy: Jehova, Sol, Agla, Riffasoris, Oriston, Ophitne, Phaton, Ipretu, Ogia, Speraton, Imagon, Amul, Penaton, Soter, Tetragrammaton, Eloy, Premoton, Sitmon, Perigaron, Irataton, Plegaton, On, Perchiram, Tiros, Rubiphaton, Simulaton, Perpi, Klarimun, Tremendum, Meray!

'By the Names of Power, I command thee depart: Gali, Enga, El, Habdanum, Ingodum, Obu, Englabis ... DEPART!'

The priest brought his hands together. A blue-green light abruptly detonated in blinding incandescence which seared the flesh and blinded. A demonic howling filled the room, and then a voice, like that of brittle glass, spoke, '*You can never defeat me priest; whilst your god remains, so do I!*'

And then ... nothing.

The silence was almost as terrifying as the howling. It hung, heavy and cloying over the shattered room and the numbed figures. Michael Morand had a momentary vision of floating above the house, looking down at the devastation that had turned the building and the fields around it into an almost circular spot of utter destruction. And then he was falling, plunging down and down, through the shattered wood of the stripped roof and the destroyed bedroom, and into the sitting-room, where one lone figure still stood in the centre of the room, surrounded by the destruction and the cowering bodies.

The priest shuddered as he felt the presence of his dead brother sink back into quiescence, and with the withdrawal of his occult and spiritual strength, he slumped, exhaustion washing over him in a long grey tide, and he fell to the floor unconscious.

*

'He has defeated us!'

'But we have called the Master forth – He will demand payment!'

'Then let us ensure that it is not us He takes.' A pause, and a small naked figure broke the circle with a word, and crossed over the thin white lines on the damp floor. An aged hand reached for a large red bound book and pulled it from its shelf above the fire. 'We must try again – and this time we must not fail.'

Father Morand awoke to the sound of a child's cry. The plaintive wail brought him bolt upright, and then he staggered as blackness washed over him and set his head spinning. He sat on the edge of the couch, feeling the morning sun warm on his face, before pushing himself to his feet with a groan. The door opened and Pat Coonan entered. His old face looked even more lined and exhausted and his eyes were red-rimmed and hollow. He forced a smile when he saw the priest on his feet.

'It's good to see you up, Father. For a while there . . . ' he let the sentence hang.

The priest patted him on the shoulder. 'Thank you,' he said simply, and then he smiled wanly. 'If I look half as bad as I feel, then I need a good strong drink.'

The foreman laughed slyly. 'Father,' he said, pulling out a hip flash, 'if I looked half as bad as you, then I'd need a drink.'

'Join me?' The priest lifted the metal flask and swallowed some of the raw liquor. He coughed and handed the flask back to the foreman.

'My pleasure!' Pat drained the remainder of the flask in one long swallow.

'And now,' the priest's expression turned serious, 'the mother . . . ?'

The foreman grinned. 'The mother and child are doing fine.' He smiled at the priest's expression.

'And Tom?'

'Shaken, but otherwise all right. He's outside now, having

a look at the damage.' The foreman shook his head in amazement. 'I was here – and even I don't believe it.' His voice changed, taking on a more serious note. 'We're ruined, you know?'

Father Morand nodded slowly. 'I know that. And you know it's not finished yet.'

'Aaah, I thought that,' the foreman grimaced in disgust.

'However, there might be something I can do about that,' Father Morand said. 'I might be able to stop them.'

'You specialise in miracles also?' Pat asked.

'Only sometimes.'

Father Michael Morand spent the remainder of the day in the church, searching through the old parish records, reading through the diaries of past parish priests. He was unsure what he was looking for, he was merely following an instinct he had followed many times before, instincts which had never failed him.

And towards evening, as the golden light of afternoon faded from the dim attic through which he had crawled unearthing the records, he found it. In the dim light, he couldn't even read the title of the dusty manuscript, but he knew, he *knew*, that this was what he sought.

He dusted off his hands and, tucking the manuscript into his shirt, climbed down from the attic and lit a candle. In the wavering light the thick paper turned parchment yellow and the ink inscription on the first page seemed to fade before his eyes. '*A Historie of ye Local Churches and ye Holie Places of Worshippe.*' The date at the bottom of the page was faded, but Father Morand thought he could make out the numerals, one, seven, one, one ... 1711. It was written in a scrawling hand that tended to diminish almost into illegibility as it neared the right hand margin of the page. The priest took the manuscript downstairs, cut across the church and out the side door, and slipped into the parochial house he was sharing with Father Horgan. He sat down by the log fire that blazed in the grate and began to read.

He was still reading some hours later when Father Horgan came back after saying evening mass and all his attempts at conversation were rewarded by monosyllables. The parish priest retired around midnight, but Father Morand remained deep in the manuscript until early morning when he suddenly found the answer.

He knew how to discover the identity of the witches who were attacking Tom Kennedy and his family. For he knew the location of one of the infamous Black Books.

The character of Saint Mochta's Abbey changed as evening drew on. It was something to do with the way the light seemed to retreat from the aged stones, making it one with the gathering night. By day, it was a place of worship, sacred to the teachings of Christ and his followers, but by night it re-assumed the mystery and majesty it had held as one of the Old Places, places that had been sanctified to gods that were old before the New God walked this world.

Tom Kennedy winced as the tall priest let the heavy brass knocker fall to the metal stud set into the dark aged wood of the huge double doors. The sharp metallic sound hung on the still night air like a clarion call, sending birds in the forest below the Abbey wheeling and cawing into the sky.

The priest stepped out of the shadow of the door and looked down the winding road, noting the almost obscured signs of defensive earthworks. From the low hill, the Abbey commanded a view of the four roads that met beyond the forest at Dead Man's Crossroads, where the locals, with a certain degree of morbid humour, maintained the gallows that gave the spot its grisly name. Father Morand breathed deeply, savouring the slightly scented fresh night air, and he could almost imagine himself dressed in skins and leathers with torcs and rings of gold or bronze about his forearms, guarding the hill-fort in some ancient time of legend. He smiled fondly at the image, and then the shuffled sound of footsteps brought him back to the present.

The huge door opened silently, revealing a yawning cavernous interior. A shadow moved across the opening and a small figure stepped out into the night. The balding monk bowed slowly and addressed the pair in Irish.

'Good evening brothers; how may I be of assistance?' He spoke slowly and in a voice barely above a whisper.

Father Morand greeted him in Irish and then switched to rapid Latin. The monk listened intently, his round face expressionless, his eyes flat and unemotional. He nodded once when Father Morand had finished and then stepped aside and allowed the priest and the young man to enter before him. The old monk then leaned against the door and slowly pushed it closed, until it shut with a curiously final hollow booming. The Witchfinder clutched the young man's arm above the elbow, making him jump, and whispered quietly in his ear. 'Follow me; say nothing unless you are spoken to.'

Tom nodded, and thought bitterly that there was little else he could do.

The monk led them down through high-ceilinged corridors, with huge vaulted windows, stark and plain, but with a simple beauty in their austerity. They saw movement in the distance, shadowed figures intent on their own private tasks, and once a door opened and a cowled monk stepped out into the hallway. He stopped when he saw the young man and the priest, bowed slightly and crossed himself, remaining in the doorway until they had passed.

The hall was badly lit, only smouldering torches set into verdigris-stained holders, set high on the smoke-stained walls brightened the gloom, the wan pools of light only serving to make the corridors seem darker.

The monk eventually led them down a side corridor and out into a small enclosed garden surrounding a miniature pool, where he bowed and left them without a word. Father Morand waited until the monk's shuffled steps had faded, then looked at Tom and silently pointed to a stone bench that ran along one wall. The priest walked around the pool, admiring the sudden flashes of gold and bronze that danced within its night-blackened waters. He breathed in the heavy bitter-sweet odours of the herb garden, briefly recalling his youth and the herbs that used to shed their comforting scents beneath his window at night.

'There are many ways to God, are there not?'

Father Morand turned at the voice, and found himself looking into the broad smiling features of a bulky man clad in the simple brown sackcloth of the monks. The priest nodded. 'God is found in many places,' he agreed. 'You are the Abbot?'

'I am. Diglach, I am called in this holy place.' He spoke in calmly measured tones, his voice smooth and cultured. He gestured. 'Tell me; what do you see? We do not have many visitors here and it is always interesting to have the opinions of outsiders,' he explained.

'I see a place of great beauty, of peace and calm. A place where nature has been fashioned for the greater glory of God.'

The Abbot smiled. 'For the glory of God,' he repeated, shaking his head. 'It is an Eastern idea,' he said, 'to set aside a garden, a place to feel God's hand touch the earth, and to be one with Him again. Stone walls are not enough.'

'Has the idea found favour with the brothers?' the priest asked curiously.

'We have always been workers of the soil,' Diglach said quietly. 'Our Order has cultivated seeds and crops, trees and shrubs since the time of the Norsemen. And whilst such natural things all possess a certain beauty, they are still functional. The brothers find it comforting to come here and meditate amidst that which is grown for beauty's sake.'

Father Morand nodded silently.

'But you must excuse me,' the Abbot said, 'I fear I tend to ramble on about my garden; I will do penance for my sin of pride.' He shook his head sorrowfully and crossed himself.

The priest couldn't resist a smile at the huge man's woeful expression. 'It is something to be proud of,' he remarked, looking around at the carefully tended shrubs and ornamental bushes.

Diglach smiled. 'Well perhaps it is at that. And now Father,' he said, his small eyes darting across to Tom Kennedy and back to the priest. 'How may I help you?'

Michael Morand glanced over at the young man sitting on

the cold stone bench and then looked back to the Abbot. Diglach caught his look and deliberately turned away, nodding with a barely perceptible movement of his head. The priest dusted off his hands and moved away into the shadows, followed by the huge Abbot, leaving Tom Kennedy alone with his troubled thoughts.

It was almost an hour later when Father Morand returned with the Abbot. Diglach looked troubled and there was a slight sheen of sweat on his bald head. The priest's face was set in grim lines, and his eyes were hard and pitiless. He gently roused the younger man, who had dozed briefly and, without a word or a backward glance at the Abbot, led him back into the echoing halls of the monastery.

Tom Kennedy struggled to clear his muzzy head of the ragged remnants of his dream. He had been standing in the middle of his sitting-room whilst everything around him slowly melted into a sticky putrefying mass. As he watched the walls ran like liquid and disappeared and he could make out two figures through the gaping holes. Their faces had been in shadow, but there had been something terribly familiar about them ...

The priest stopped before an arched doorway. The door had not been opened in a long time, and a delicate tracery of silver cobwebs clung to the door and lintel. Michael Morand gently brushed aside the spiderweb and left the tattered strands against the wall. He took a rusted key from a bent nail above the door. In the light of a distant torch the key glittered blood red and screamed like a soul in torment as it turned in the lock. The door cracked and groaned as it opened before swinging silently inwards. Father Morand paused before entering the windowless room and, taking the stub of a candle from a ledge just inside the door, handed it to Tom. 'Light it,' he commanded.

And the young farmer was not surprised to find his fingers trembling and his palm wet with perspiration as he held the wick to the wavering flame of the torch in the corridor.

*

The room was dark and chill, the flickering candlelight sending monstrous shadows scuttling into the corners. It was almost completely circular, but where there had once been a window was now only a wall. Along one wall stood a low wooden chest and in the centre of the room stood a high reading desk - and there was nothing else.

Father Morand took the candle from Tom and knelt by the chest. He ran his fingers along the heavy dark wood which gleamed wetly in the wan light. A section of the wood clicked and the lid cracked open. The priest crossed himself before opening the chest and then he stood and looked down into the interior.

Tom Kennedy edged forward and looked around the priest. The chest was lined in white silk, which gleamed as whitely as if it had been freshly washed, and it was empty except for a large cloth-wrapped bundle. The priest pointed. 'Pick it up - but carefully.'

The young man bent and lifted out the bundle, clutching it to his chest. It was surprisingly heavy, and it was wrapped in a thick, parchment-like cloth which made it difficult to hold. He carried it over to the reading stand and put it down, looking to the priest for instructions.

'Untie the ribbon.'

Tom unpicked the wide black ribbon that bound the bundle and let it fall to one side.

'Now, unwrap the ... covering.'

The thick cloth cracked and snapped as he carefully eased it away from what was revealed as a book. Tiny flakes of white material fell in a powdered snow to the dusty floor, and even when it had been removed, the heavy cloth still retained the impression of the book.

The young man drew back slightly when the volume was finally uncovered. It must, he thought, be almost ten inches thick, and it was bound in a thick black leather which gleamed with purple highlights. The wan candlelight ran like oil from its tooled surface, lingering briefly on the metal rims and clasps that held the book. Tom reached out and traced the design of a five-pointed star etched deeply into the leather, and then he drew his hand away with a gasp.

The leather felt warm, almost like ... human flesh.

Father Morand intoned briefly in Latin, and then he turned to the young man. 'Undo the clasps carefully and allow the book to fall open.'

'But it's lying flat and it's too thick,' Tom protested.

'Do it!'

The young man carefully unhooked the two clasps and let them fall back onto the wooden reading desk. There was no possible way a book that size would - could - fall open of its own accord.

An icy wind rippled through the room, making the two men shiver and sending dust motes circling into the dry air. The heavy black binding flapped like a stranded fish and then fell back, striking the wood of the reading desk with a solid thump. The thick white pages fluttered in the wind, whispering sibilantly together.

And as suddenly as it had started, the ghost-wind died, leaving an almost echoing silence in its wake. The Witchfinder pointed to the book. Tom Kennedy looked at the pages in confusion.

They were blank.

The priest abruptly gripped his arm and pulled it taut, forcing it out over the blank pages, twisting the hand until his palm faced upwards. The younger man struggled, but the priest's grip was unbreakable. Father Morand shifted his hold, bringing Tom up onto his toes as his elbow threatened to crack. With his free hand, the priest took the small silver crucifix from around his neck and with the sharpened edge, cut a small cross into Tom's index finger. The young man gasped in pain and surprise, but the priest ignored him. Father Morand squeezed blood from the tiny cut and then turned the hand downwards so that the blood dripped onto the virgin sheets. The crimson spots spattered and then haloed, like ink on blotting paper, until there were four red circles on the page in the shape of a cross. The priest then released Tom's arm and closed the book.

The young man stumbled away from the priest, rubbing his aching elbow. 'Are you mad?' he screamed.

And Father Morand's eyes caught and held his. The

priest's strangely colourless eyes swirled with colour which rapidly changed until they took on a predominantly amber hue. The priest held out his hand. 'Come!'

As if in a trance, Tom Kennedy returned to the reading desk and the Black Book.

'Place your right hand upon the book and repeat after me . . . '

The young man placed his hand on the flesh-warm cover, feeling the arcane design etch itself into the palm of his hand, and repeated the priest's formula.

'In the Name of God the Father and of His Son Who is of the One, and of the Spirit Who is of the One, I call upon Ye now in the cause of Truth and Righteousness, to show unto me my malefactor. I ask this in the Name of the Three Who are One and the One Who is All. Amen.'

Tom staggered as he finished repeating the prayer and the priest caught and held him. 'Easy now,' he whispered gently, 'we are almost done.'

'Father . . . ?' He raised a trembling hand to his forehead and looked around with a blank confused stare.

Father Morand placed his hand on the young man's head and, calling upon his strength, poured it out. The farmer shuddered and then immediately straightened. His eyes had cleared and the tremor had left his hands. 'What remains to be done, Father?' he asked calmly.

'Perhaps the hardest part of all,' the priest said wearily. 'When you open the book, you will find . . . something. A name, a face . . . or perhaps just a hint of the identity of whomever wishes you evil. But as soon as you see and understand what is on the page, you will cry out in a loud voice, "*In Name of the God Who is One and the One that is All, I cast thee forth from this world, never to work thine evil again.*" And then you will sprinkle the page with holy water.' The priest held up a small crystal vial. 'But Tom,' he added solemnly, 'you must act immediately when you open the book, if you delay it will mean your death . . . or worse. For you will have forged a link with the witch and yourself, and whereas they will have been drawn here and will therefore be confused, you will have the advantage – but only for a moment. On your life you must not delay – no matter who you see!' The urgency in the priest's voice was unmistakable and the young man thought he could detect a hint of fear in his colourless eyes. He nodded quickly and took the bottle of blessed water from the priest's hands and then, breathing deeply, prepared to open the Black Book.

He felt the raw power surge through his fingertips and up through his hands and into his arm as soon as he touched the cover. The thick black binding was warmer now, and seemed to writhe beneath his fingers, and it felt like sweat-slickened skin. The air in the small chamber was heavy and rank with the taste and odour of something resembling ozone mingled with a scent of wild herbs. The atmosphere was oppressive and ... waiting.

With the fingers of his right hand he pushed the cork from the small bottle and held it over the book, ready to use. And then he opened it.

The pages sparked and cracked as he opened them, leaving sharp gleaming after-images imprinted on his retina. The pages seemed to flicker and what had once been blank was now misted over with script and characters in a score of tongues. And almost of its own accord the book fell open to the page tinged with red. It took Tom Kennedy a few seconds to interpret the red design on the page. The blood had run and twisted, forming a design that at first glance seemed abstract, but on closer examination ...

He blinked ... and the image seemed to leap off the page and sear itself into his brain.

It was the image of his mother!

He stared in horror at the crimson picture, slowly shaking his head. 'No ... no ... no...' From a great distance he heard the priest shouting at him to act now ... now ... *now* ... And then the lines on the page twisted and the image opened its eyes and its thin lips moved in a grim parody of a smile. Tom Kennedy screamed – and dashed the page with the blessed water. He could hear a voice inside his head, a cold mocking voice, the voice of his mother. It was laughing at him, a chilling evil laugh – that abruptly changed to a hideous scream as the holy water struck the page. '*In ... In the N-Name of the God ...'* he intoned in a shaking voice.

The image on the page mouthed silently and the aged face contorted and grimaced in rage or fear or agony, or perhaps all three. Where the water had struck, the crimson mark began to run down the page, leaving a dark brown scorch mark in the paper.

'*... cast thee forth from this world never to work thine evil again.*'

The fireball ripped through the tiny cottage, leaving little more than a crumbling stone husk in its wake. The roof caved in and one of the walls collapsed. Perhaps old Mrs Kennedy had been storing liquor as some of the local people thought, or maybe Seamus, that crazy son of hers, was brewing poteen.

Wasn't it curious though, the way the spell of bad luck that had hit her other son, Tom, died with her. Of course, she never liked Tom - always preferred Seamus, her pet. And wasn't it strange that they only found one body - that of a young man, presumably Seamus - in the ruin; of course, the destruction was such that it was perfectly conceivable that the old woman's body was completely destroyed.

CHAPTER 12

THE HAND ... III

The pre-dawn air was raw and the animals' breath plumed whitely as Sorcha walked out across the field towards them. Ice cracked underfoot, and she clutched the worn shawl tightly about her thin shoulders, but it was poor protection against the chill.

Sorcha ran her hands along the flanks of the two milch cows, feeling the wasted muscles beneath the cold skin. With numb fingers, she examined the udders of both animals; they were thin and shrunken and there seemed little likelihood of milk from either. Nevertheless, she set her pail down beneath the smaller of the two cows and, with expert hands, grasped the teats and squeezed a few pitiful drops of thin, yellow milk from them.

The second cow was dry.

Sorcha set the pail down on the scarred wooden table with a bang. There was barely enough milk to cover the bottom of the container. She tugged the woollen scarf from her head and flung it onto the room's only chair as she crossed to the smoking fire. With a short length of metal, she coaxed the fire to a blaze and then fed it with lumps of wet turf. She sat back on her heels absorbing the heat, allowing it to soak into her chill bones. The wavering flames painted her lined face in warm bronze, gilding it with the appearance of youth, hiding the years, and turning her eyes to points of amber light. She ran a broken-nailed hand through her greying hair and massaged the muscles at the base of her neck.

Sorcha eased herself to her feet and crossed to the table. She poured the contents of the pail into a chipped cup, and then tasted it with her finger. She grimaced with the taste; it was thin and bitter, with a hint of musk about it. She glanced out the window. There was still a little while to go before sun-up, although the sky had paled considerably to the east. But whilst the night still lingered, she could work.

Swiftly, she brushed the table clean, sweeping crumbs of stale bread onto the floor and then, crossing to a low cupboard under the window, took a small, ornately carved box and a dark folded cloth from it. Carefully, almost reverently, she spread the cloth over the table. It was of heavy, dark silk, with a curious design picked out in silver thread on it. Sorcha positioned the cloth precisely on the table, making sure that the centre of the star design was exactly in the centre of the table. She then placed the cup with the milk in the centre of the star.

Sorcha stepped back to the sink, and poured icy water from a bucket over her hands and scrubbed them thoroughly, scraping away the grime and encrusted filth. Returning to the table, she bowed thrice to each of the four Cardinal Points, and invoked the four elements of Earth, Air, Fire and Water. She then walked widdershins around the table, tossing salt over her left shoulder and murmuring an incantation in a tongue that was older than man.

Sorcha sensed the gathering forces. She felt the eerie trickle of power along her forearms, raising the hair, sending painful tingles through her fingertips. The fire in the grate - which had died to little more than glowing embers - suddenly blazed into a roaring furnace, the flames tinged with blue and green, before abruptly dying completely.

In the silence, she could hear the pounding of her heart, and her breathing was as laboured as if she had run a great distance. Mastering her trembling hands, she undid the metal catch on the dark wooden box and threw back the lid. Inside, the box was lined with crimson silk, tiny points of what might have been jewels, picking out an arcane design. Sorcha reached in and carefully withdrew a withered hand!

She held the mummified claw aloft as if in offering and swiftly kissed the palm. And then, with infinite care, she placed the hand above the cup and began to stir the milk with the stiffened forefinger. The long talon scraped along the bottom of the enamel with an almost animal-like screech.

And even as the claw continued its circular motion, the cup began to fill. The clear white liquid rose slowly, until it threatened to overflow the cup. Sorcha grinned triumphantly, and held the claw aloft once more. And what had once been a shrivelled, withered claw, was now young and fleshily-plump, resembling the hand Sorcha had hacked from her lover's corpse so many years ago. Once more she kissed it, and this time her lips lingered on the warm flesh before she replaced it in its ornate box.

She was replacing the box and cloth in the cupboard when the first rays of the morning sun turned the window molten with light.

Sorcha took the cup and, careful not to spill anything, emptied it back into the pail. The liquid hit the bottom with an almost musical drumming, which was quickly replaced by a thick viscous gurgling as the pail continued to fill ... and fill ... and fill ...

By the time the sun had risen above the trees, Sorcha had two pails full of fresh, warm milk, and the enamel cup was still not empty. The old witch ran her hand across the top of the cup and nullified the spell with a phrase, and then drained what remained with a swallow. She felt the fluid course through her, invigorating and refreshing her, and she knew she would feel neither hunger nor thirst that day.

She glanced at the window again, gauging the time from the position of the sun: it was almost time to leave for the market.

Sorcha hurried down the rutted track carrying the heavy pails on her shoulders. She walked upright, even though the heavy length of wood that held the pails bit deeply into her flesh. The early morning air was sharp and bracing, and the late November sun touched the hard, barren earth with its wan light. Sorcha's shadow danced along the track before her; a long thin wraith, with the bar of the pails across her shoulders, resembling a cross.

There was a small crowd gathered at the cross-roads, the women gossiping animatedly together, and the men sharing a pipe, leaning against the hedge. Sorcha smiled inwardly as all conversation stopped as she approached. She was fully aware of her own reputation, and at times revelled in it. It gave her a curious sense of power to know that she instilled fear into the townspeople and local farmers.

She walked through the group without a word, glancing neither left nor right, and as she walked on towards the town, she could feel the hostile stares directed towards her back and the low buzz of conversation. A sod of earth struck the ground beside her and another sailed over her head - but she also knew that they were almost afraid to hit her because of her reputation.

Dunogh was typical of many small Irish country towns; a row of low houses built along both sides of the main street, a post office, a few small family run shops and a church. The church - with its new steeple - dominated the west end of the town, and in front of it, a few small children played on the green.

Sorcha began to peddle her milk at the first house she reached. She would then work her way down one side of the street, up the other side, and then head off home.

She stuck her head in the open door and, forcing a smile to her thin lips, called out 'Hallo ... Mrs O'Brien are you in ... ?' She heard muffled footsteps approaching from the other room, and a short stout woman appeared from the shadows.

'Aaah Sorcha, it's yourself. I was just thinking of you: I need some milk for the childer ... '

The young priest sat in the back of the church, attempting to absorb the peace and calm of the ancient building. But the peace would not come and he found it difficult to pray, to concentrate on the well-polished phrases of his faith. He looked up with such despair on his thin face that the older man sitting by his side was forced to smile. He leaned over and patted the young priest's shoulder. 'Come now Father, compose yourself and tell me the full story.'

Father Fintan nodded slowly and sat back on the hard wooden pew. 'I don't know what to do,' he said quietly.

The older man clasped his hands about the hawthorn walking stick and smiled gently. 'If you knew what to do, you would not have brought the matter before your superiors, and they would not have passed the matter on to me.'

The young man looked up. 'Is it true what they say about you Father Morand?'

The old priest smiled. 'And what do they say about me?'

'They say you are an expert on the ways of the fairy folk and witches - a Witchfinder.'

Father Morand tapped the metal ferrule of his stick on the polished floor, the sudden sound echoing like gunshot. 'Aaah, but you mustn't confuse the two. The fairy folk, that is, the descendants of the Tuatha De Danann, the People of the Goddess, who once ruled this land, are not always evil. They can be capricious, and even by our standards wicked. But their wickedness is like that of a child – and it can usually be traced to a cause.' He waved a gnarled hand expansively. 'This church, for example, is built on a fairy fort. Was there any trouble during its construction?'

Father Fintan shrugged. 'It was before my time, but I could check for you ... '

'It might prove interesting.'

The young priest sat upright suddenly. 'There is something,' he said, almost apologetically.

'And that is?'

'We've recently had a new spire installed. The old one had been severely damaged during a series of thunderstorms over the past few years, and had been struck by lightning on numerous occasions. But while the new construction was going up there were several strange instances: tools missing, cement hardening too quickly, wood warping and cracking overnight . . . '

Father Morand laughed quietly. 'That's it exactly. The fairy folk at work. And I dare say,' he added, 'that once you sprinkled the work area with holy water, said a few *pater nosters* and *ave marias*, the trouble stopped?'

Father Fintan swallowed audibly. 'How did you know?'

The old priest laughed again. 'Oh, I've seen the same pattern repeated over and over.' He dismissed the subject with a wave of his hand. 'But to continue. Whilst the fairy folk are not by nature evil, witches, be they male or female, make a conscious decision to follow either the Right- or Left-Hand Paths, the Roads of Light and Darkness. But it is their own choice, made with their own free will, although,' he added ruefully, 'the Left-Hand Path is often the more attractive, with its immediate rewards and power.'

'Are there many witches in Ireland?' The young priest's voice had fallen to a whisper, and he glanced uneasily at the altar.

Father Morand shook his head. 'We are lucky in that respect. There are but four organised covens throughout the country, but they are slowly dying out and one is almost finished. Of course, there are many wise women, called witches, wise in the country-lore, conversant with the *Sidhe* folk, the fairies, and their ways. But these are not true witches.'

'Is Sorcha a witch?' Fintan asked.

Father Morand shook his head, his colourless eyes gazing into the distance. 'I do not know; I've only read a second-hand report. Tell me what you know of the woman.' He stood suddenly. 'Let us walk; I'm not as young as I used to be and I feel my bones stiffening.'

The two priests walked down the side of the church, turned and genuflected towards the altar, and then made their way out the door. Michael Morand breathed deeply, savouring the country air, whilst the young priest examined his companion covertly. It was the first time he had seen him in the full light of day. The older man had come late the previous evening and had been shown straight to bed by

Fintan's housekeeper, and in the morning he had been gone, and the young priest had found him praying on his knees at the back of the church.

Father Morand stood a head taller than the younger man, and the shock of snow white hair and colourless eyes gave him the appearance of a blind biblical prophet.

The older man repeated his question. 'Tell me what you know of this woman.'

Father Fintan muttered an apology and, tucking his hands into his wide sleeves, began. 'She is a strange woman in many respects,' he said, 'she lives alone in a tiny run-down – even by country standards – cottage on the outskirts of town. She owns two cows, a few hens and a cat . . . '

'Nothing else?' Father Morand interrupted.

'Nothing. The only name I have ever heard her called in the town is Sorcha,' he continued. 'However, I went back through the parish records and came across a marriage between a Donal MacIntee, a local farmer, and a young girl by name Sorcha Ni Cleirigh. This was back in the '40's, some sixty years ago. Now, two years later, in November 1844, there is a note of a burial of the same Donal MacIntee. In December of the same year, a record has been made of the banns being posted for a Peter Casside and Sorcha MacIntee!'

'One month later,' Morand whispered. 'How did MacIntee die?'

'It didn't say in the records, so I went to the home of the local doctor. He is the son of Doctor O'Connell, who practised in this neighbourhood around that time. And in one of his old journals, I found a note of the death.'

Father Morand rubbed the iron ferrule of his stick against his boot as he listened; he didn't need to be told any more, the story was terribly familiar. 'Go on,' he murmured.

'Apparently the husband died of a heart attack . . . at least that was the medical finding. But Doctor O'Connell had added a footnote in his own hand to the effect that, in his opinion, the man had died of fright, for there was a look of absolute terror frozen onto his face.'

The old priest nodded slowly, his hard face set in grim

lines. 'Would I be correct in thinking that he was found in a clearing in the wood?' He pointed south towards the trees.

'Yes!' Fintan looked around, startled. 'But how did you know?'

'The case is not unfamiliar to me. I was ... passing through this town about that time.' Father Morand gripped the handle of his walking stick until his knuckles showed white. The younger man drew back from his fellow priest, for the light in his colourless eyes was dreadful.

'And what of her lover?' he asked suddenly, his voice harsh and grating.

'I checked the records,' the young priest said quietly. 'She never married him, for his death is recorded on Christmas Day of that same year. Apparently, he died on Christmas night – although his burial did not take place until the end of January.'

'The Winter Solstice,' Father Morand said. He caught the young man's look of incomprehension. 'The festival of Christ-tide is not a Christian one,' he explained, 'it is an arbitrary date chosen by the Church in all its wisdom to disguise the old pagan festival.'

'It is the birth of Our Lord,' Fintan protested.

Father Morand shook his head. 'It symbolises the birth of Christ on earth; but do not think that it is an exact date. Read your Testaments man,' he snapped. 'It is a pagan feast – take my word for that, and I will wager my eternal soul that young Peter Casside was sacrificed to the Great God Pan on that date all those years ago.'

'Father!'

'The body; was it ever found?'

'Not all of it. It was washed ashore some weeks later – the fishes had been at it, it was recognised by the clothing.'

The old man tapped his stick against the stone steps. 'Aye, that would disguise the mutilation, sure enough.'

'I don't understand.'

Father Morand ignored the question. 'And just why did you contact your superiors about this woman?'

'Some of the townspeople came to me accusing her of witchcraft.'

'Indeed; and what makes them suspect her?'

Father Fintan shivered slightly in his thin coat. The whole subject was disturbing enough, without having this old man taking it so seriously. 'Apparently, she has two cows, Father. Now, according to what I have been told, her land is neither rich enough, nor does she spend enough on feed for her animals to produce either the quantity or quality of milk she sells.'

The old priest smiled suddenly, and his smile was almost as terrible as his anger.

'Have you ever heard the like?' Fintan said despairingly. 'Here we are, into the twentieth century, and people still believing in magic and witches ... ' he trailed off and coloured.

'Including old priests who believe in fairies, eh?' Father Morand smiled. 'You have a lot to learn, my son. I travelled in my youth with a friend of mine who later became a priest, a missionary. He opened my eyes to some of the evidence of the Otherworld that still lingers in Ireland. And when he went away we kept up a regular correspondence over the years. And the stories he wrote concerning the beliefs and rites of the pagan lands he was preaching in, convinced me that there is still magic abroad in this world. Oh, perhaps the word magic offends you? Call it a force then, a power. A power that may be tapped for either good or evil. Some of the great saints could touch this force and work their miracles through it, but there were others who perverted it to their own evil ends ... ' He reached out and patted the young man on the shoulder. 'You are young, wait; do not form any hard and fast judgements on such matters yet.' He looked back down the street and continued in a different tone. 'But to answer your question; then the answer is yes, I have heard of similar spells. And the belief that a witch can draw off a neighbour's milk is not uncommon across the water in Britain and Wales.'

'Do you believe it?' asked Fintan slowly.

'Perhaps.'

'That is not an answer.'

'Father, when you asked for help and guidance from your

superiors, they did not send me just because I was handy or close-by. I joined the priesthood later than most, and in my youth I had made a special study of the Otherworld, the Shadowland of Fairy and the Realm of Witchcraft. And when I took holy orders, rather than lose all that knowledge and experience, I was given the brief to seek out and study the occurrence of the Otherworld and the *Sidhe*.'

'You *are* a witchfinder!'

The old priest laughed, tears starting into his eyes. 'So I'm called, but dear me, nothing so dramatic. I am a folklorist certainly, a collector and recorder of the rapidly vanishing country lore. Occasionally, I perform an exorcism – in many cases the mere fact that the exorcism had been performed provided all the patient needs, and they are "cured". And then, in a tiny fraction of cases . . .' he smiled. 'Tell me,' he said suddenly, 'do you know what my name means?'

Father Fintan shook his head.

The old priest smiled slightly. 'Aaah, few do. It is an ancient name – an honourable one also. It was borne by the Abbot of Clogher and the Bishop of Nemdrum in the Middle Ages and later, but it goes back further, for Morand was one of the Judges of Banba and, like Solomon, his judgements were always fair and honest.' He turned and held the young priest's eyes with his hard stare. 'You see, I too am sometimes a judge,' he paused and added softly, 'a judge, a jury and sometimes . . . an executioner!'

It was mid-afternoon by the time Sorcha returned home. The sun was already beginning to sink down behind the low mountains in the west and the chill wind that had blown through the day had taken on a sharper, keener note. Low clouds gathered in the north and west, promising rain or sleet.

Sorcha kicked open the scarred wooden door and entered the dark interior of the single-roomed cottage. The fire she had kindled that morning had sunk to low embers and bathed a small circle before the fire in warm amber light, but otherwise the room was in darkness.

The old witch stopped just inside the door, her senses tingling; something was awry. Her hard eyes darted about the room, noting the dark shape of the table in the centre of the room, and the black oblong of her straw-filled bed in one corner. Everything seemed in place ... but she couldn't shake the impression that she wasn't alone in the room.

Water dripped somewhere from the roof, the sound curiously muffled in the silence, but it broke the spell that held her by the doorway. She dropped her two empty pails in the corner by the door and slowly crossed to the fire, still clutching her shoulder brace. She knelt before the grate, her questing fingers seeking the candles tucked into a niche beside the fire. Normally, she didn't use them, but tonight was different and the darkness, usually her companion, now threatened.

The wick sputtered and then flared, shedding a warm opalescent light around her, dusting her grey hair with silver and turning her skin to wax. Sorcha held the candle over her head and looked about – and screamed!

There was someone sitting at the table.

A light flared in the centre of the room and a small stub of a candle blossomed light, lending the tall figure sitting behind it a demonic cast to his features. 'Hello Sorcha.'

The witch gasped and held the wooden shoulder brace tightly in both hands. 'Who ... who are you?' she whispered.

The figure in the shadows chuckled. 'What, don't tell me you're surprised? Surely you knew I would come for you one day?'

'Who are you?' she suddenly screamed, feeling a dread chill envelop her heart.

The figure moved the candle away from his face, so that the light illuminated it more fully. He smiled regretfully. 'You do not remember me, Sorcha – although,' he added, 'I think for a moment there you confused me with ... something else. I am Father Morand,' he said suddenly.

With an almost physical effort, Sorcha composed herself. For one single moment, she had thought ... She caught the look of amusement in the old priest's eyes: he had planned it that way.

'Who are you?' she repeated, her voice chill with fury.

'I have already told you: I am Morand.'

'What are you doing in my home?' She stepped closer to the table and raised the length of wood threateningly.

'I have come for you Sorcha – as I swore I would so long ago.'

'But I've never met you before ... '

'Never?' The old priest smiled curiously. 'Never?'

Sorcha brought the shoulder brace crashing down onto the table, sending the candle toppling onto the floor. 'Get out of my house.' Her voice was hard and flat – tinged with anger and something approaching fear.

'You know me, don't you Sorcha.' Father Morand stood, a huge hulking figure in the semi-darkness. His eyes caught the spark of light from the last embers of the fire and glowed with tiny pinpoints of red light. 'You remember Peter Casside?' He caught her sudden intake of breath. 'Yes, I see that you do. He was your lover ... your sacrifice ... and my brother!'

The witch drew back suddenly. The anger and hate in the old priest's voice was almost palpable. His words struck her like a blow. 'You are Michael Casside?'

'I am Father Morand,' he said icily.

'Morand the Witchfinder!'

'Only occasionally,' he said laconically. 'A priest, a researcher, a folklorist – but yes, witch hunting is part of my profession.'

'Why have you come back?' she asked quietly.

'I've been drawn here by chance – if you believe in such a thing called chance.' He smiled grimly. 'I always swore to come back for you someday.'

'I looked for you,' she continued in that same quiet reflective tone. 'But you just disappeared. You didn't even attend your brother's funeral. You were always different, always special ... it was one of the reasons we chose you. You have a strange aura, do you know that? You would have made a fine warlock.'

'I prefer to use my powers in the cause of good,' he said wearily. 'It was not a difficult choice to make when I learned what you had done to my brother.'

'He was to be the sacrifice – you were to be my husband.'

The old priest smiled, his teeth showing white in the semi-darkness. 'I know. You needed the affinity of twins, didn't you? Sacrifice one, and send the power released through that death into the soul of the twin, and then, once the twin is kept under control, you would have access to almost unlimited occult power.'

'And it so nearly worked,' Sorcha said, her voice lost in distant memories. 'With that power, we could have called forth Our Master into this world.' And suddenly hate and anger blazed in her voice. 'And you destroyed all that!' She struck out with the heavy shoulder brace, but Father Morand turned the blow aside with his stick, and rapped her across the knuckles. She dropped the length of wood with a curse and sucked her bruised fingers.

Father Morand shook his head slowly. 'Listen to me; my faith teaches forgiveness and, although it's hard, a lot of time has passed between us, and if you're willing to forswear your witchcraft then I am prepared to forgive you.'

'And if not?'

The old priest made his way to the door and opened it. He stood, outlined against the gathering storm and shook his head slowly. 'If you do not . . . ' he murmured softly. And then he continued in a different tone. 'Well then, I shall be forced to pray for you.' He nodded briefly, turned and disappeared into the night.

Long after he was gone, Sorcha crossed to the open door and carefully closed it. She leaned back against the rough wood, feeling the boards through her thin clothing and looked around the room. Night had fallen fully and, with the heavy clouds obscuring the stars, the room was in complete darkness with only two burning embers, that reminded her of eyes, glowing in the hearth.

Feeling all her years, she went to the fire and lit one of the candles from the embers, and then she sat on the hard wooden chair, placed the candle on the table before her and gazed deep into its wavering flame.

She knew, somewhere deep inside her she knew, that

what was happening now had been ordained long ago, even before she had sacrificed Peter to the Old One on that hard cold night so long ago. She stared into the flame and watched the years roll by, rising with the thin tendril of black smoke and disappearing into the shadows. She saw herself as a young woman, drunk with the power of sacrifice, feeling the force slide through her body and engulf her. That had been a time when she could have had anything she wanted. The coven had been powerful then, for it had achieved the ultimate offering: the sacrifice of a baptised follower of the Christ to the Master.

But the power they had gained was but a fraction of the total. The force released by Peter's death passed on to his twin – and had she been able to find and keep that twin then nothing would have stood in their way of absolute power. Sorcha ground her teeth in rage; but Michael Casside had disappeared that night. She had spent years searching for him, and over those years her powers had wasted away, and the coven had broken up and gone their separate ways. And so she had returned to her native village, practically with nothing, and so poor that she was forced to draw off her neighbour's milk with a dead hand.

Until now.

For now Michael Casside had come back. She found it curiously ironic that he should have entered the priesthood, but on reflection it did not seem so strange, for the power that she would have utilised to her own ends, he now shaped in the Church's work.

She passed her hand over the candle flame, dousing it. The sweet smell of candle grease enveloped her, making her think of the church, bringing with it old, old memories of her childhood when her father used to bring her there every Sunday morning. She smiled at the thought; how could she have explained to him then that she was already one of the Old Faith; how could she have explained to him that she had been promised to the Horned God while still in her mother's womb?

She pressed her nail into the soft wax around the top of the candle; there had been a time when she had shaped with more than wax. She thought of the tiny dolls made from mud and blood, with flecks of hair or nail parings or blood woven into them, and how she had manipulated men with them. And then she wondered whether it might be possible to create a doll of the priest . . . ? But she shook her head. His faith alone would protect him.

The witch stood and went to her low pallet of straw in the corner of the room and prepared for bed. She wondered why she had never connected Michael Casside with the priest, Morand. She had known that Michael would have the power that his twin's death would have given him, and she knew that the priest had a reputation for having a frightening and powerful presence. On reflection, the connection seemed simple. But she had been looking for a frightened young man, possibly crazed with the sudden unleashing of strange powers upon him, she had never connected him with the ice-cold Witchfinder.

She unrolled her long hair and let it flow down her back. Once it had been as black as a raven's wing and as soft, but now it was streaked with long strands of grey and silver, and was hard and brittle under her fingers. She lay back on the rough pillow, feeling her heart beating in her breast. The sound was loud and strangely solemn; it seemed more like the tolling of a distant bell.

'And you spoke to her?' Father Fintan pushed aside the remains of his supper and leaned across the table.

Father Morand patted his lips with a napkin and nodded briefly.

'Does she admit her witchcraft?' the young priest pressed.

Father Morand sat back in his chair, toying absently with the silver crucifix about his neck. 'She did not deny it,' he said quietly, 'but then, she hardly could with me.'

'I don't understand, Father.'

Father Morand smiled. 'You see, my son, I knew her once, oh, many years ago, before I took Holy Orders. In fact, you might say she was one of the reasons I joined the priesthood.' He laughed suddenly. 'Who would have thought it: a witch driving a young man into the church?'

Father Fintan smiled uncertainly, unsure of the joke.

The old priest leaned over and patted his hand. 'Oh, don't look so worried – I've not lost what little sense I've left.' He leaned back in the chair and continued, his voice soft and wistful.

'But first, a confession. I lied to you when I said I was passing through this town when MacIntee and later Peter Casside died. I was born in this town, I was living here at the time.

'I first met Sorcha many years ago, when I was a young man. I was deeply interested in the fairy lore of this part of the country then, and I had been recommended to speak with Sorcha's mother, who had something of a reputation as a witch. But of course, the dividing line between witchcraft and fairy lore is very faint and in some cases almost indistinguishable.

'The old woman was very helpful, and her knowledge was phenomenal. I visited her over several years making notes from her fund of stories about the superstitions and beliefs, cures and herbs. Some of it I've never forgotten. And it was then I met her daughter, Sorcha. She was a stunning beauty, but a wild, untamed – and dangerous – beauty. I fell in love with her immediately.' Father Morand laughed. 'Oh, let me tell you, I made a fool of myself over her. At first she ignored me, but later, she did accept my advances. And then one day, my brother Peter accompanied me to the Ui Cleirighs. And suddenly everything changed.' The old man closed his eyes, and his face tightened in pain. 'You see, my brother and I were twins, he being older than me by a few minutes. In looks we were identical, the only difference being that whereas my eyes are almost colourless, his were dark, almost black.

'Sorcha took an immediate interest in Peter, and they soon became very close. But you know,' he opened his eyes and looked at the younger man, 'the more I came to know of the family, the more I came to distrust – and eventually fear – them. The old mother's lore, whilst being true in every sense of the word, was always dark and forbidding, and although she often talked of the Dark Elves and the Hidden Ones, she knew very little about the Shining Ones, the last of the De Danann, the *Sidhe*.' He shook his head slowly. 'Oh, it's so easy to say now that I should have known, and I did warn my brother, but he laughed off my fears and eventually came to believe that I was jealous of him and his involvement with Sorcha ... and who knows, perhaps I was.' He was silent then for a long time, and when he continued, there was a new note to his voice, a harder, harsher note, one of anger and rage ... one of power.

'And then it was suddenly announced that Sorcha was to be married to old MacIntee. He was rich – even by English standards – and almost twenty years her senior and, strangely Peter wasn't unusually heartbroken by the whole affair. Two years later the old man was dead, and one month after that my brother became engaged to her. A few weeks later, he was dead.' The old priest sat forward, resting his elbows on the table and cupped his face in his hands. 'And I can tell you the exact night and the precise moment he died.' He looked across at Father Fintan, and the younger priest winced at the look of anguish in the older man's eyes. 'I felt him die!'

There was silence in the small dining room after that, and the crackling of the fire seemed unusually loud. Father Fintan was the first to move, carefully unclasping his hands, which he had unconsciously squeezed together. He winced as the circulation returned. 'What happened?' he whispered hoarsely.

The old priest's eyes glazed as he gazed into a different time. 'It was Christmas night; a hard, cold, bitter night, the sky cloudless, bright with stars. I lay awake in my bed watching them wheel across the heavens, waiting for my brother to come home. He had crept out earlier that evening, gone off to see Sorcha, but now most of the night was gone and the dawn was almost upon us.

'I dozed, but even so, I began to feel his distress just as the sky was brightening; just a tingling at the base of my spine, but that quickly grew into an all-pervading panic, a soul-consuming fear. And as the first rays of the morning sun touched the eastern sky, he died. And I felt it. It was as if a part of me had been torn out, ripped asunder.' Father Morand shook his head slowly, as if in wonderment. 'I lay there helpless, sobbing like a child; I had never felt so alone in my entire life. But as I lay there, I felt the first tendrils of a strange power creep into me. It was part of my brother, a . . . a force, an inner strength if you will, and in that moment I knew what had happened to him, and I knew what I must do . . . '

'Yes . . . ?' Fintan prompted.

The old priest's eyes lit on the younger priest's. They blazed with an inner fire, and Fintan was suddenly terrified. 'I decided I would seek out and destroy witchcraft at its very roots, and I would do so with the full authority and backing of the church!'

'The church has never condoned killing,' Fintan said. 'It teaches love and kindness; it teaches forgiveness.'

'There are some who are beyond forgiveness.'

'No-one is beyond Our Lord's mercy.'

'Why should those who have renounced God's mercy and love on this earth hope to find it in the next?' Morand brought his hand down on the table, making the plates and cutlery jump. 'They have lived by a sword of their own choosing, let them die by it.'

'Your hate will destroy you, Father,' Fintan said quietly. He stood and bowed to the older man. 'I will bid you a good night; I will pray for you.'

Father Morand smiled apologetically. 'My son, you cannot tell me anything about myself that I do not already know. But I will thank you for your prayers.'

Fintan nodded. 'I will, Father.' He paused by the door, and then added impulsively. 'Perhaps it would be best if you left . . . ?'

Morand nodded. 'Perhaps it would,' he agreed. 'To-morrow then; I have a little business to finish in the morning, but afterwards I will go.'

*

Stray wisps of chill mist seeped through the door as Sorcha prepared for the ritual. The cottage was cold and damp and even the turf fire blazing in the grate did little to dispel the dampness or take the bite from the air.

Sorcha shivered in her worn clothing, but it was something more than the weather that sent icy shivers up along her spine. For some reason, she felt extremely reluctant to use the Hand this morning, and there was an almost physical revulsion at the thought of touching the withered member.

And then she looked at the pitifully few drops of almost colourless milk that barely covered the bottom of the pail, and knew that she had little choice.

'Ah, here they are now!' Martin O'Leary pushed open the door and held it whilst his two young daughters struggled in with the pails of milk clutched in each hand. 'The best there is.' O'Leary dipped a finger in one of the pails and sucked the thick white liquid from it.

Father Michael Morand nodded sharply. 'Where is it stored?'

'Here Father.' The farmer patted a series of large wooden churns. 'And they are leakproof,' he added, anticipating the priest's next question.

'But you have been losing milk?' Morand insisted.

O'Leary nodded. 'Someone has been drawing off my milk. I know the signs,' he continued. 'It happened when I was a boy and my father warned me about it.' He sniffed the cold air. 'Can you smell it?' he asked. 'Like lightning . . . '

Morand nodded. 'I know,' he said quietly, 'it has begun, and it will get stronger presently as she draws upon the spell.' He paused and looked around the shed. 'Did you do as I requested?'

'We have.' O'Leary pointed. 'We've poured the milk into one pail only, and we've had a fire burning since late last night with a poker heating in it; it should be white-hot by now.'

'Good; then all is in readiness.' Father Morand glanced

out the grime encrusted window and noted the first grey tinge of dawn lightening the eastern sky. 'Then there is nothing more for us to do but wait.'

The old witch ran her fingers across the wrinkled palm of the withered hand. She could feel the residue of power still lingering in the leathery flesh, could feel it race through her fingertips, setting her nerves afire. It was a powerful talisman, she knew – but it could have been so much more powerful. Stifling her regrets, she hurried on with the incantation.

The spell was almost complete. The cup sat in the centre of the table on the dark, heavily worked arcane cloth, like a chalice in some blasphemous offering; salt had been sprinkled and the words said. All that remained to be done was the Drawing with the Hand.

The air in the shed had grown even colder and taken on a definite metallic taste and odour, and a barely audible crackling pervaded the room.

Morand tensed and then breathed deeply. 'Soon,' he whispered, 'soon.'

Sorcha kissed the palm of the hand and then dipped the index finger into the small cup and began to stir the milk. She could feel the power growing, could feel the tenseness in the air as the hair on her arms and head rose in wavering strands. She felt the hand begin to pulse in her palm and the flesh softening and swelling. She felt her own hand grow numb as the tingling made its way up her arm, into her shoulders and down into her breasts and then on into her stomach. She felt the feeling growing, rising to engulf her.

And as she stirred, the level of the milk began to rise . . .

O'Leary swore briefly. 'Look!' He pointed into the open

churn. And before their eyes, they could see that the level of the milk was slowly but surely sinking.

Morand wrapped a thick cloth about his hand and pulled the white-hot poker from the glowing coals. With the red firelight beneath his face, he looked truly godlike ... or demonic. He called aloud in a language O'Leary didn't understand, crossed himself – and plunged the hot poker into the slowly disappearing milk!

The mummified hand exploded into flames. Sorcha screamed in agony and dropped it onto the ornate cloth, which immediately sizzled and burst into flame. She fell back nursing her badly burned hand. The flames quickly took hold of the old wooden table and ate through the dry wood, filling the cottage with thick black smoke – and the foul odour of badly burned meat as the hand was consumed.

Sorcha attempted to crawl to the door, but had to throw herself to one side as the blazing table fell to the floor, sending sparks and hot cinders around the room. One fell on her straw pallet, and a single wisp of smoke rose steadily, and then it too, burst into flames. The heat was intense, and Sorcha felt the skin on her face and bare arms sear and blister. She could barely see and her breath came in pain-wracked sobs. As she reached the smoking wooden door, the windows blew out and the ornamental plates on the dresser shattered with the heat. She burned her fingers on the metal latch as she lifted it and pushed. But the door wouldn't move – it had swollen with the heat.

The milk boiled and discoloured as Morand twisted the sizzling poker in a clockwise fashion. A thick – almost human-like – skin formed about the metal, quickly darkening until it assumed a leathery consistency. It suddenly became more and more difficult to turn the poker and the skin was becoming harder and harder, until now it even looked like leather. It assumed strange shapes and patterns, some suggestively obscene and others ... even more disturbing. And sudden a hand formed in the dark skin, a severed, long nailed claw ...

Morand shouted and attempted to withdraw the poker – but it was stuck fast, and he couldn't remove his hand! The metal grew uncomfortably warm, warmer, and then unbearably hot. The metal glowed red and then white hot. The priest screamed as the poker ate into his hand, searing and crisping the flesh, peeling it back from the bones. A thick stench of burning meat filled the shed and O'Leary, gazing in horror, gagged, before turning to run for help. Morand fell to the floor and writhed in agony, the poker still clutched between his smoking fingers.

And then in his pain, he whispered, 'I forgive her ... ' And the poker fell from his hand.

And the door snapped open.

'How is she?' Morand asked the doctor as he changed the dressing on the priest's hand.

Doctor O'Connell shook his head in amazement. 'Oh, she is much the same as you are – in fact, her wounds are almost exactly the same as yours.'

'Will I ever use it again?' Father Morand nodded at his left hand, now swathed in thick bandages.

The young doctor shook his head. 'Never, I fear.'

'Will she have the use of hers?'

Again the doctor shook his head. 'Never.'

Later, when the doctor had gone, Father Fintan came in and sat with the older priest. The young priest thought the older man looked tired and ... aged. He had lost a lot of weight in the last three days, and he was no longer the avenging biblical prophet he had first seemed.

'Sorcha's confessed,' he said quietly.

Morand nodded. 'Good; I'm glad.'

'She wants to see you.'

'When I can get up again, I'll go and see her,' the old priest promised.

'Father,' Fintan said slowly, 'what happened?'

Morand was silent for a moment and then he said softly, 'We were linked, my brother and I. It was a link that had been strengthened by my brother's death, a link that had been forged by Sorcha. I struck at her through him – or that physical part of him which still survived. It struck back at me.' He turned and looked at the younger man with his strange unwavering stare. 'I sought revenge,' he said softly, 'where I should have offered forgiveness.'

There are not many people in Ireland now who remember the Witchfinder; indeed, many will deny his existence altogether. But in some of the lonelier country towns and villages, the older folk will occasionally tell of Father Michael Morand, the Witchfinder.

IRELAND
a history
ROBERT KEE

the book of the major
BBC/RTE Television series

'A careful, well-balanced, sensitive book, the fruit of long, fascinated reflection over its subject matter; it is warmly to be recommended, not only to those who know little or nothing about Irish history, but also, and especially to those who think they know a lot about it . . . an excellent book.'
Conor Cruise O'Brien, OBSERVER.

'His achievement is to explain, lucidly and vividly, the bloodiness of the conflict . . . he is twice the man in print.' SUNDAY TIMES.

In the book of the successful, and often controversial, television series, Robert Kee examines the 'prison of Irish history', going back to its very beginnings to identify the principal groups involved in modern Ireland. He traces the emergence of each group and their links over the ages, establishing how past facts have bred present myths.

HISTORY 0 349 12081 1 £5.95